Hotel Bars and the Art of Being Conscious

August Delp

Gasworks Publishing

The characters and events portrayed in this book are fictitious. Any similarity to real persons, living or dead, is coincidental and not intended by the author.

ISBN 978-0-578-97189-6

For everyone whose path has crossed mine,
or will in the future ...

Contents

Title Page
Copyright
Dedication
Book One: Daisy 1
1 2
2 13
3 18
4 26
5 38
6 46
7 56
8 61
Book Two: Bianca 73
9 74
10 81
11 92
12 103
13 110
14 119
Book Three: The Art of Being Conscious 129
15 130
16 147
17 156

18 166
19 176
20 188
21 202
22 211
23 222
24 233
25 241
26 250
27 262
28 267
About the Author

Book One: Daisy

1

The first briny, shimmering, ice-crystal-flecked sip changed her outlook, as it always did, wiping away the weight of the day, the weight of existence. The second martini sip begged for the third, and contemplation. *Life*, thought Daisy from her perch at the end of the bar. *It continues.*

The bar was located in the Lucerne hotel in which Daisy was staying, but it also had a street door, thereby upgrading itself in Daisy's mind. Pure hotel bars were too sterile, too formulaic, catering to amateur drinkers—you could safely bet Einstein hadn't drunk there in his patent-clerk bender years. But with a street door, there was a chance the bar existed independently of the hotel—at least it tried to compete for passerby business. This bar, *Der Beschwipste Bulle*, The Tipsy Bull, featured a honeycombed mirror behind the bar with inlaid mirrors set at different angles, reflecting a hodgepodge of scenes from around the room. The tables, booths, and walls were dark cherry, as was the centuries-old-looking bar top itself. Patrons had quiet conversations. All in all, it had a nice ambiance, a worthy place for thinking and drinking on the eve of one of the last rites of passage in modern life, losing your child.

Daisy flipped through the leather-bound cocktail menu printed in German and English. It featured drinks with ingredients reflecting the hotel's aspirations: elderflower, thistle, cacao, aloe, rose, chai tea syrup. Daisy smiled, wondering what thistle tasted like.

Tomorrow Daisy would drop off her sixteen-year-old son, Tom, at a boarding school outside of Lucerne for his final two years of high school. Daisy had no fear that Tom wouldn't adapt well. His father now lived in Zurich, working as a vice president at Barclays. The school was only about a thirty-five-mile drive from his home.

Lucky, Daisy thought, *how well Tommy turned out*. A bit of a throwback, maybe, to when kids were more carefree. She knew that she was pretty much irrelevant to Tom now, a mother he loved, yes, but he was ready to leave the cocoon of childhood.

As Daisy raised her dirty martini to take a sip, a drop of condensation rolled off the bottom of the glass onto her white cotton blouse. She continued with the sip and pondered rites of passage. So very few rites of passage exist anymore. High school graduation is now only a pit stop in someone's education. College graduation might qualify, or the end of a person's formal education. Marriage, but the high divorce rate seems to disqualify it—rites of passage can't be revoked, after all. First sex, we'll allow it. Birth of a first child, certainly. A child leaving home is a rite of passage for the child. In Tom's case, leaving home came before high school graduation. Oh well, zag zig, yang yin.

The last child out of the house also qualifies as a rite of passage for the parents. The empty nest is probably the penultimate rite of passage, with only retirement remaining. Well, death, but that's just an end.

A rite of passage implies some threshold is crossed; you transition from one way of life to another. As an only child, Tom's passage from childhood to adulthood was also Daisy's passage from parenthood to whatever comes next. Death-waiting period? The slow decline? Freedom? *What does come next?*

Daisy finished her martini and signaled the bartender for another with a deft double-point hand signal, finger up to draw attention, finger swooped toward the empty glass to indicate *noch ein*.

"Another?" the bartender asked.

"*Ja*," Daisy answered. She held back from answering with the one German phrase she knew, "*jawohl, herr commandant*," from her sitcom rerun heritage.

"Could I get some thistle in it, rather than a dirty?" Daisy requested, pointing to the thistle ingredient in the cocktail menu. Her soft, friendly eyes and curvy physique tucked into fitted, dark-blue denim jeans offset her language shortcomings.

"Uh ..." the bartender, in his late twenties and with a shock of ash-blond hair pointing skyward, didn't understand Daisy's English.

"Thistle," said Daisy.

"You want the Petal Splendor?" It was the drink at which Daisy's finger pointed.

"No, just the thistle, in my martini." But then, fearing the language barrier and a drink solely of some thistle liqueur, Daisy reconsidered. "Never mind. Just same as before, dirty martini."

The bartender smiled and nodded in hopeful understanding. When he returned with a normal drink, a relieved Daisy engaged with him. "I'm at a crossroads in life. Tell me, what do you find good in life?"

She was greeted with a quizzical expression. "Good tourist sites in Lucerne?" he asked.

"No, in life. You. What is your favorite part of life?"

Settling into his bartender role, he seemed to understand. "For me?"

"Yes."

"My favorite part of life is I read a bedtime story to my girl and tuck her into bed, and then join my wife in bed."

"Okay," Daisy laughed, "now how would you answer if you were talking to a single mother about to drop off her only child at boarding school."

"Oh, I am sorry," the bartender said. "Maybe, good drinks?"

"You were telling the truth, right?"

"*Ja*," the bartender answered tentatively.

"It's all good then, nothing to apologize for," Daisy said with a wink.

Daisy drank and thought. Big picture, there are three life stages. Childhood, sexual, and the difficult to name one, postsexual. *We are not going to call it old age.* Each stage is a generation. In the first stage, the child is completely dependent on parents. Any newborn would fail to thrive without parental support throughout the stage, with the need tailing off toward the end. In the sexual stage, a person needs a lover to reproduce and so, through the procreative generational lens, is dependent on a sexual partner. In the beyond stage, though, a person doesn't really need anyone else. At that point, all you really need to do is die, and everyone dies alone. *Cheery thoughts. At least, we gain perspective*, Daisy thought.

In the sexual phase, the joys of childhood are discounted. In the child phase, the pleasures of sex are unknown. In the beyond phase, a person can appreciate both without being enslaved by either.

Daisy thought back to when she left home in 1989, freshly out of high school, heading to university in Seattle. Her parents weren't the first thing on her mind, and now she was glad that she was likely not on Tom's mind. Life goes on. She could look forward to dying alone.

Daisy noticed an attractive middle-aged man enter the street-side door and instinctively flipped her caramel-brown hair to the opposite side to increase its volume. It was unnecessary though because something in the Swiss water was enhancing the hair's natural bounce. The man wore a navy sports coat over an untucked button-up shirt and blue jeans. A half second elapsed before the recognition hit that it was Glenn, Tom's father. He waved to Daisy and she returned the wave. "Looking good, stranger," she said. "Want to buy a lonely girl a drink?"

Glenn perused the cocktail menu, settling on a Mad Hopper. "You know there's aloe in it, right?" Daisy asked. Glenn shrugged.

"It's been a while Meg," he said. "Four years? Something like that? It's good to see you."

Daisy's legal name was Margaret Turner. Her father

had wanted to call her Daisy but thought the name was too informal as a given name. In French, Marguerite is the name of the white-and-yellow oxeye daisy, leading to the somewhat incongruous nickname. Growing up, everyone called her Daisy other than her mother, who called her Meg. She was Meg at IntelliScope.com where she and Glenn worked in the late 1990s. After Tom was born and she left the workforce, she introduced herself exclusively as Daisy, occasionally spelled Dazy on bar tabs. Tom called her Mom.

"Tommy is excited to be here and spend more time with you," Daisy said. Glenn had worked in Zurich for the last eight years, during which time Tom had flown out for some summer months and holiday breaks.

"I'm excited, too," said Glenn.

"And this school—holy smokes. It should be great for Tommy," said Daisy. "Top notch academics, kids from around the world, the responsibility of being on his own."

"For the price, it should be an idyllic wonderland," replied Glenn. "But I agree, it seems like a perfect fit."

They caught up and reminisced over drinks. Daisy handed Glenn an envelope with a detailed accounting of his child support, documenting how it was spent or saved, everything appropriate and accounted for to the penny. Daisy was a part-time accountant for a restaurant group in Seattle, and her predilection for monetary precision carried over to her personal life. The child support from Glenn was maintained in a separate account, with all expenditures documented, and Tom's expenses honestly split seventy-five percent to twenty-five percent as originally agreed. Glenn tucked the envelope into his jacket's inside breast pocket without looking at it, being used to these quarterly reports from Daisy.

"I'm proud of the father you've been for the last ten years. You're a good man, Glenn. Tommy's lucky to have you as his father."

"Well, I wish I'd been there in the beginning, but glad I got it right before too long.

"What comes next for you Meg, with Tom out of the house?" Glenn asked. Daisy reflected on the question, the same one that had been popping into her head for the last few months as Tom's departure neared.

"To be determined," she answered after a pause, then let the topic drop. Pedestrians on the sidewalk outside peered into the bar, as if deciding whether to come in. Daisy stared back absently.

"What about you Glenn, what's on your horizon?" Daisy asked. "Still living the parenthood dream?"

"Yeah, Sally is nine now, so we're about nine years from empty nest."

They finished their drinks and stood up to leave.

"We had some good times back in the nineties. I value those memories," Daisy said.

"Yeah. We did."

* * *

In 1993, Daisy was hired at IntelliScope.com after graduating from the University of Washington with a double major in finance and computer engineering. She accumulated a large stash of stock options and eventually rose to Director of Product Development. Glenn, eight years older than Daisy, was Senior Vice President of

Finance. It was the go-go dot-com nineties; financing flowed freely, and valuations jumped like salmon up small-stepped fish ladders at the Ballard Locks. Both Daisy and Glenn were making good money and positioned well with options when the company went public in early 1999.

They worked together on a few projects, interacting primarily in meetings. Daisy caught him stealing glances at her breasts, tempted by fitted shirts. Once, twice, more. She welcomed it, flirting back, lingering after a meeting, hand on his shoulder to make a point, point him in the right direction. When the team achieved a milestone, she went into his office to celebrate. High five, followed by Daisy's arms raised, fists clenched, in victory/dominance, her tight shirt riding up with the motion, exposing her midriff, which didn't go unnoticed.

"We should drink to our success," Meg/Daisy said, aiming at a cocktail outing.

Glenn pulled a bottle of Johnnie Walker Black and two rocks glasses from a cabinet and poured drinks. "I'm down with that."

The game continued like that for over a year. These things take time.

Eventually, after a rare 5:00 to 6:00 p.m. meeting, the office had largely emptied out. Daisy went into Glenn's office for a drink, as had become a common occurrence at days' ends. Glenn poured two fingers of Jack Daniel's. "Two fingers, huh?" Daisy asked. "What's on your mind." Daisy drained hers in one swallow, head and glass tilted back in unison, held in a statuesque pose, the drinking Heisman. She closed the distance with Glenn while unbuttoning her blouse. "This is what I want," she said, wrapping her arms around him. She kissed him, leaned back on his desk, and pulled him onto her. Glenn did not resist, and they had sex on his desk.

It continued like that for a few months. Glenn's office had a door that locked but had frosted glass, so care had to be taken to ensure the angles of obscured view would not betray them. His office was on the 28th floor of an office tower in Seattle, overlooking the Pike Place Market, Puget Sound, and Seattle's cityscape. He stood while they made love, her legs wrapped around his body, their bodies leaning against the window. One of the windows was marked as able to be kicked out in case of emergency, so they took care to not flirt with disaster on that window—but what a way to go; they gave a flying fuck to avoid a flying fuck. Daisy would make Glenn turn so his back was against the window and Daisy could look out, presiding over the twilight city, sidewalks filled with bustling shoppers and restaurant crowds, theater and bar lights.

Glenn was married with a young child. He was more experienced than Daisy and in a higher position in the company's hierarchy, although she did not report up through him. Some observers would say there was a power imbalance and Glenn took advantage of Daisy. They would be right about the power imbalance but have the directionality wrong. Daisy got what she wanted.

Daisy became pregnant. She told Glenn the news one day over lunch, sandwiches from a corner shop brought back to his office.

"You should get an abortion," he said. "I don't want to ruin my family."

"I'm not getting an abortion," said Daisy. "I'm going

to have this child."

Eventually, after many painfully long pauses, their positions were clear. Absent an abortion, he wanted to keep it hidden that he was the father. He would support the child financially, somehow hiding that from his wife, but not have any role in raising the child. She was having the child with or without his consent or support.

"I get that it's hard for you," she said, "thinking that your life could take an off-script turn. And I don't begrudge you your storybook life, don't get me wrong, you've earned it. You're a good person—your offer of financial support demonstrates that, but you've got this one wrong. Kids are more important than spouses. It's that simple; kids are more important than spouses. You're passing up the opportunity to have a relationship with your child."

They settled on the agreement that seventy-five percent of the child's expenses would be borne by Glenn, twenty-five percent by Daisy. Everything would be on the down low. He paid her an initial sum of three-hundred-thousand dollars, part of the value of his options when IntelliScope.com had its IPO. She would maintain a thorough accounting and he would pay in the future as necessary.

"You're making a mistake, Glenn, there's no one as good as me to ride through life with." But that might just have been a parting shot. Daisy had no desire to cohabitate for the long term, much less get married.

Daisy quit her job as the pregnancy progressed. She exercised her options and sold most of the stock near the peak of the dot-com bubble in late 1999. With that money combined with what she'd saved from salary and bonuses over the years and Glenn's three hundred thousand in child support, she had over a million dollars. The late 1999 timing of her stock sales caused her to avoid most of the damage of the dot-com meltdown in 2000, but she kicked herself for not recognizing the opportunity to short the riff-raff names (like IntelliScope) rather than just minimizing losses. She was long again in the market until Bear Stearns went under in 2007. Having learned her lesson, she shorted the market for the Great Recession and turned long again soon after CNBC's Mark Haines' devilish bottom call, at 666 on the S&P 500, in March 2009. She had turned the initial one million into more than five-million dollars by 2015 when she dropped off Tom in Lucerne. Glenn had never needed to make another payment, with Tom looking to be set with a good launch pad into adulthood.

Due to her investing acumen, Daisy hadn't really needed to work as an accountant. She did it mainly to teach Tom a way of life, the value of work, but also to stay connected to the adult world.

Glenn had maintained his deception for the first four years of Tom's life, but then came clean to his wife. Glenn met with Daisy and they worked out a visitation schedule. His wife divorced him about a year later; Glenn had told Daisy it was largely unrelated to her or Tom, and she believed it. He remarried two years later and had one child with his new wife, Melinda, ten years his junior.

2

The next day at the boarding school, parents sat on bleachers in the gymnasium while the school's headmaster rambled on about this and that, academics and scholarship, fraternity and networking, opportunity and tradition. Glenn sat sandwiched between Daisy and Melinda. The students were on a tour of the school. A friend of Tom's from high school in Seattle was also attending, and they were set to be roommates. They were scouting the female prospects and sorting out the male social hierarchy, assessing likely fault lines among cliques. The tour ended at the dormitories. Classes were scheduled to start on Tuesday following the weekend of social events.

The preparatory school sprawled across eighty acres in the outskirts of Lucerne. The grounds were bisected by a stream that was just a bit too wide to jump in most spots. Half of the property was wooded, with the remainder split between hilly fields, the classroom facilities, and the dormitories. The dorms were co-ed, but with girls and boys on alternating floors. Until recently, the sexes had been segregated in different dormitory buildings altogether. Approximately six-hundred students attended, largely drawn from upper-class European and North American families, but with an increasing number of Japanese students in recent years.

"Where ya at?" Daisy texted Tom while suffering through the headmaster's continued rambling. "Luv ya."

After the presentation, the parents filtered out of the gym into the bright August sunlight and alpine air. The gym opened to a multi-purpose sports field, bordered by the woods. Tom found Daisy and gave her a bear hug. He was taller and stronger than her, with his sixteen-year-old physique providing boundless physicality. "I love you, Mom. I'll miss you."

"Ha, you have no idea kid," Daisy said. "The missing will be all by me. I love you too!"

"What will you do next in life Mom?" asked Tom.

What is it with the men of this family? Daisy thought. "I guess I'll find out soon. Whatever it is, it'll be good—a new opportunity. I'll miss you, Tommy."

A gaggle of kids called for Tom and his roommate to join them, and they headed to the wooded area. Tom gave Daisy a final hug, and that was that.

Daisy, Glenn, and his wife Melinda ate dinner back at *Der Beschwipste Bulle.* Daisy would spend one more night and fly out the next day; Glenn and Melinda planned to drive to Zurich after dinner. With Glenn in Switzerland for the last several years, Daisy had never really spoken much with Melinda—a "Hi, how are you" here and there, but that was about it. Melinda was close to Daisy's age, two years younger at forty-two. She had a petite build and tight muscle tone like that of an aging gymnast. Daisy had originally pegged her as perky but was considering reclassification to energetic.

The light from the streetlights refracted through the bar's windows to produce elongated ovals across their tabletop in the darkened bar. All three drank beer with dinner. Melinda's choice to go with beer rather than wine elevated her a notch in Daisy's estimation. Too few women embrace beer.

"So, Daisy, I've never properly thanked you. I understand you're the reason Glenn and I are together," Melinda said.

"Partially," Daisy laughed, "Yes, partially. Although I'm not really sure, I think his first marriage may have failed without me. Is true love so weak as to be torn apart by some work-wife sex?

"You two have a much different vibe, it seems to me, a much better relationship than Glenn had with Angela. But, sure, I'll take credit. I delivered him to ya." Daisy smiled and winked at Melinda and took a long drink of weak German lager.

"What's next for you, with Tom out of the house?" Melinda asked Daisy.

"Once more into the breach—everyone's been asking me that. It's a good question. I've been asking myself as well. I'm flying solo now—no commitments to anyone but myself. I'll take some time and assess. All I can really tell you at this point is that I'll die in the end.

"I'll probably quit working; I'd mainly been doing that to serve as an example for Tommy. Maybe I'll start painting again. Although that sounds so cliché, god. I know," Daisy said in an affected voice, "I'll travel. As the kids said when I was a kid, gag me with a spoon. Gag me with a pitchfork." Despite its low alcohol content, the lager had had its intended effect.

"About ten years ago, I went on a road trip with a guy who wanted to do what is good in life. I mean, he didn't know what is good, but that was his goal, find what is good and then do it. Maybe I'll do something like that, find the meaning of life."

"You went on a road trip searching for the meaning of life?" asked Glenn. "How American."

"Well, close, I went with a guy who was looking for what is good in life," Daisy answered. "He was a good guy, married, kids, career, midthirties, just wasn't enough, wasn't good enough. He was friends with my friend Miyu's husband, you might remember her Glenn."

Glenn pursed his lips, trying to recall.

"Anyway, this guy called his friend saying he needed to talk and drink, and Miyu and I came along. He needed to figure out what is good, needed to do what is good. We met at Linda's Tavern in Seattle, then ended up going on a road trip around the Northwest for a week or so."

"Isn't Linda's the last place Kurt Cobain was seen?" asked Glenn.

"I think that's right," said Daisy.

"We drove around on secondary highways, avoiding the interstates as much as possible, just resolved to find what is good. He ended up making a list and also a list of techniques. I wonder whatever happened to him."

"Where was Tom?" asked Glenn.

"He was actually with you, when you had him for two weeks in the summer.

"My point though, is maybe I need to explore this stage of life, figure out what it's all about. Maybe it provides a kind of clarity, living with no real purpose. No need to grow up, no need to raise a kid, just exist and then die, right?"

Glenn took the last swig of his beer and leaned back in his chair. He remembered the child-support accounting and pulled it from his jacket's breast pocket. "Daisy, I think you missed your calling," he said. "You should have been a hedge-fund manager. I paid you a lump sum of a three hundred thousand in the late nineties and it's now one million net of all Tom's expenses, my share of Tom's expenses, for sixteen years." He shook his head laughing.

"Yeah, I helped your punk ass," Daisy laughed. "I should charge you two and twenty annually."

Glenn and Melinda gathered their things, getting ready to leave. Glenn was driving so had had only one beer, a lowish-alcohol lager at that. Daisy hugged Glenn goodbye and then hugged Melinda as well. Melinda held the hug for an extra second. "I'm glad you're in our life," Melinda told Daisy.

Glenn and Melinda turned to leave. "Watch out Glenn," Daisy said with a slow squeeze on Melinda's hip, "maybe I'll break up your second marriage by sleeping with your wife."

3

Back home in the Wallingford district of Seattle, Daisy cleaned house dressed in a tee shirt and fraying jeans. Her house was a small two-story built in the 1920s, just north up the hill from Gasworks Park and Lake Union. The landscape had grown up and engulfed houses in the neighborhood: gargantuan rhodies, oversized maples with laughably large leaves that rained down in the fall, an occasional ivy-covered tree, yards that weren't quite unkempt but also weren't kempt, crumbling curbs lining streets wide enough for only a single car at a time. Anywhere there was a bit of dirt in the Emerald City, something grew in it, massaged by the drizzle.

The house had two upstairs bedrooms and one down. Tom's room was upstairs, and Daisy's was on the main floor. The other upstairs room was used as an office. Daisy undertook a cursory cleaning; the house wasn't too dirty to begin with. She cleaned Tom's room, finding an old candy wrapper here and soda can there. She rounded up stray laundry, washed sheets, got organized, put things in their places. But other than that, she left Tom's room as it was for when he would visit; she left the door open so that it would remain an active part of the house.

With the house in order, Daisy sank into the couch, her head on a cushioned armrest, feet up. The setting summer sun filtered through leaves and branches and through the house's front west-facing windows, making a shadow mosaic on the worn hardwood floor. Son Volt played on the Sonos. As she cleaned, Daisy had pulled a few scrapbooks from her youth out of storage, along with a box of loose mementos collected over the years; she flipped through the scrapbooks on the couch.

She closed her eyes and tried to think of books or movies that explored the meaning of life. Other than Monty Python's *The Meaning of Life*, she didn't come up with very many. So many coming-of-age stories, so so many transitions into second stage—woo hoo sex and romance and ... love. Of course, a huge universe of children's books, memorized by work-weary adults: "Goodnight moon." Far too many love stories. Perhaps the over/under on the percentage of non-children's movies and books that include a love story is seventy-five percent. *That's so stage two*, thought Daisy.

There was *The Hitchhiker's Guide to the Galaxy* trilogy with its answer that the meaning of life was forty-two, a worthy attempt at a small step forward. There was *Zen and the Art of Motorcycle Maintenance* with its Chautauquas and gumption traps, but that deteriorated into unreadability with the protagonist's deterioration into insanity. There wasn't much else of note.

It makes sense, perhaps. Twenty-somethings and thirty-somethings reminisce and tell stories about coming of age, yearning for a purity of existence and possibility. Thirty-somethings and forty-somethings reflect and tell stories about sexual love, regretting their missteps, proving they know a better way now. Aren't any forty-somethings and fifty-plusses writing stories about the meaning of life? Or does everyone remain captivated by the love theme?

The first scrapbook Daisy flipped though had pictures from her high school years, physical photographs. A homecoming picture from her junior year, how young and awkward she looked. A girls soccer team picture. Some snapshots with friends.

She sifted through the box of loose mementos. A flirtatious note from a boy she dated off and on in high school. Her high school varsity sports letter. An essay she wrote in college in a philosophy class. A poem she wrote that ran in the university newspaper arts supplement.

Thinking backward to think forward.

Daisy pulled on a gray hoodie and thought through, though didn't jot down (which was tough—going against her instincts), potential next steps: potential goals to pursue at that point, potential values, potential meanings.

I have near total freedom. Now what? I need to do something with the remaining half of my life.

Some pursuits were easy to discard, like power (*don't want it*), money (*got it*), youth (*can't get it*), and beauty (*I'm still pretty hot*). "Beauty is truth, truth beauty. That is all ye know on earth and all ye need to know." *Ya think so Keats?* thought Daisy. *I think you need more.*

Love was society's obvious choice, but one Daisy had already decided was not her primary goal. And that included love's ugly stepchildren: relationships and romance.

Religion had been abandoned in modern America for good reason, but insidiously replaced by spirituality. *I can't stand those spiritual mother fuckers*, thought Daisy. They think by renouncing religion's silly beliefs they are getting closer to truth, but then they embrace and revere a completely amorphous, non-defined, and silly spirituality.

There is a redeeming quality, though, to a lot of remaining religion in America and that is the worshipers largely ignore the doctrinal silliness and focus instead on concepts like being kind, doing good deeds, and acceptance. The church's leaders largely embrace the silliness while the congregations largely ignore it, and the leaders think they know the truth while the congregations are more tuned to reality.

Experience itself was a strong candidate; Daisy added it to her mental list. Maybe experience itself should be the goal. People tend to remember their new experiences; maybe they're simply more valuable than other things.

Entertainment popped into Daisy's head. She easily dismissed it. Entertainment can fill in the gaps, but it's only a way to pass time. Pastime, itself, is an interesting word. It's generally thought to have a positive connotation, but it should be negative—giving away a slice of your life with minimal payoff, a distraction, a forgettable dalliance.

The act of artistic creation could be a goal: music,

painting, writing. At least it shouldn't be strictly dismissed. Daisy had painted earlier in her life, a teenage pursuit that persisted through her twenties. She'd never sold any pieces, or really even tried to, but had displayed works in local galleries and coffee shops.

Solving puzzles. Doing crosswords, sudoku, those tragically sad supposed Alzheimer's-fighting brain teasers. No point. *Yeah, you solved a puzzle. You somehow exist, you somehow can think, you somehow can manipulate and interact with the world and other people, and you spent your time solving a bullshit, contrived puzzle.* Pass.

What else do we have? thought Daisy. The Son Volt playlist tapped out. R.E.M.'s greatest hits tapped in. Long, low rays from the sun still slipped in, mixed with an orange sunset. Well, solving science puzzles could be good, thought Daisy. Then she laughed out loud. *Yeah, I'm too old for that.*

Friendship should be considered, she thought. She'd had a few good friends in life, early in life, during childhood, high school, and at college. None since. A reasonable goal could be experience with a good friend or friends, a drink in a nice bar. Kindred spirits haunting the world's spirits haunts.

Charity, or helping others in general, was a possibility. Daisy had a vague image of grandparents helping grandchildren, biological or simply generational.

Maybe part of the issue is that stage three is an extraneous blip of existence, featuring people past prime reproductive age, with minimal evolutionary purpose. Maybe there is no meaning for this group. Sure, grandparents can support grandchildren but are largely irrelevant in the course of evolutionary history. Until recently, life expectancy cut the third stage quite short.

At the bottom of the mementos box was a pencil sketch of a motel room with the caption: "We are temporary residents." Daisy had drawn it one morning on the what-is-good Northwest road trip that she had mentioned to Glenn and Melinda in Lucerne. *We are temporary residents*, she thought. She'd always liked that phrase. It reminded her that life would end; each phase of life would end; everything you ever did or thought would end; all emotion and consequences would end; everything other people thought or did or experienced would end. These were pleasant thoughts. The sketch's view was from a motor motel's bed, looking out the room's open door onto a slice of a street scene in Yakima. Daisy laid the sketch aside, thinking she would frame and hang it.

The sketch caused her to think of her death bed (perhaps queued by the Yakima motel bed, or perhaps the theme of temporariness) and what her thoughts would be just before her final breath. What would she think of her life in total and of the portion that was in front of her now? Cliché, maybe, but also relevant. Looking back, she was pretty content with her life thus far. Birthing and raising Tom and the motherhood experience was primary. Her childhood was full of happiness; she'd had her share of stumbles and scrapes, certainly, but the overall feeling was one of happiness, security, and freedom. The question was what would come next.

There was a temptation to define what she had already done, or could easily do now, as the correct thing to do, as the meaning of life. Maybe meaning was having a baby and raising the child. Maybe the meaning of life was to treat others well (something she was already doing, for the most part, based on her judgment). And if the temptation were to prospectively interpret meaning as what she already did, the temptation would be orders of magnitude greater on her death bed when no further changes were possible. Or, alternatively, maybe at that point she just wouldn't care anymore, an attitude of "it was what it was" and a shrug of the shoulders, the weak, skeletal shoulders.

The speakers played R.E.M.'s "Orange Crush." Daisy flipped on the TV and muted it just for background visuals. It was a shampoo commercial with male and female models lathering up. Daisy watched. The news came on and Daisy switched the channel. *The Bachelorette* came on with sexy men competing to date a sexy woman. Flip, flip, flip. Sex, love, sports. *Distractions*, thought Daisy. Flip, flip, flip. Pundits, sports, love. She toggled to Netflix; the lauded AI algorithm failed once again as she flipped past offerings: love, sex, adventure, bizarre cartoon, humor with a side love story.

The R.E.M. playlist had reached their more poppy phase, "Shiny Happy People." Daisy switched over to the radio, KEXP 90.3, the college music station at the University of Washington. She didn't recognize the song but took some comfort that the DJ was curating a music stream for her.

Daisy thought she needed to define exactly what she was trying to decide, no suffering lazy, vague thinking. No spirituality mumbo jumbo. Was she deciding what to do for the next year, the next few years, the rest of her life? Or was it something larger, trying to decide the meaning of life, or the meaning of her life, or the value of her life, or the purpose of life, or something like that? The question of the meaning of life always struck Daisy as ill-defined by presupposing that life had some inherent meaning. What is the meaning of red? It is a difficult question to answer because it is a bad question. Unask the question; it stuck in Daisy's head that the Japanese word "*mu*" meant this, unask the question. *So mu.*

Perhaps only a simple shift is needed: what makes life meaningful? That seems about right. Or better: what makes one's life meaningful? What makes my life meaningful? The answer she sought wasn't a hobby to occupy her time, wasn't a distraction to make the days go by, wasn't entertainment to kill time. Time was limited, trying to get rid of it was clearly not the right path. She looked at her pencil sketch again and remembered another phrase from that period of her life: "Paths are personal." *We are temporary residents, and paths are personal*; those still rang true to her.

She defined her goal: *I'm seeking meaning*. She settled on her path to find it: *I'll pursue experience.*

4

Butterflies flew in Daisy's stomach for the first time in years. Strange metaphor, that. It didn't really feel like butterflies, and in other contexts butterflies are generally thought of as pretty, summery, and overall happy creatures. Does nervousness feel like butterflies flapping their wings?

Daisy sat in the bar of the Sorrento Hotel, waiting for an interview with the bar manager. Waiting was always the hardest part, the nerve-racking part. Once in action, she could enjoy the moment.

Following up on her chosen path, she was actively pursuing experience. Maybe the millennials are right, she thought. Maybe experience is the primary value. She knew if she weren't forced to get out and interact, she would tend not to. And she had a lifelong romance with alcohol. What, then, could be better than tending bar in hotel bars? She would interact with a constant flow of people from all around the world, all walks of life. She could engage and learn from customers who seemed to have a spark of insight, those who lived well. To the rest, she could serve draft beer and carry on. Hotel bartending might be peak experiential labor, if she applied herself.

A man in his early thirties, with shaved head and full beard approached her. "You must be Daisy," he said, extending his hand. "Mike Wilcox, bar manager." Daisy thought the manager would be younger than she was, but it was still a little disconcerting to be interviewed by someone so much younger.

After chatting for a few minutes, the manager said "Okay, let's see what you've got." Behind the bar, he pulled out a rocks glass and a liquor bottle filled with water. "Give me an ounce pour." Daisy grabbed the bottle by the neck, forefinger slightly on the pour spout's stopper. *One, two, three, four* she counted silently while pouring. The manager poured the water from the rocks glass into a shot glass with measurement lines and her pour was spot on. "Nice, let's see one-and-a-quarter ounces," he said. *One, two, three, four, five.* Spot on.

"Okay, let's try a few drinks. Pretend I'm a customer." He went to the drinking side of the bar and sat on a stool. "What can I get you to drink today?" Daisy asked, smiling.

"I'll have a gin and tonic."

Daisy glanced at the liquor bottles, saw the top shelf varieties, and asked, "Would you like to go with Hendrick's, or the house gin, or something else?"

"I'll go with the house gin, thanks."

Daisy grabbed a highball glass, filled it with ice, and poured the gin over the ice. She saw the bar had a soda gun but didn't know if tonic water would be in it. "Does the soda gun have tonic water?" she asked.

"No, we use a bottle in the fridge, right there," the

manager said, reaching over and pointing below the bar. Daisy finished the drink with the tonic, a quick stir with a swizzle stick, one lime slice in the glass, and one on the rim. She set a coaster in front of him and placed the drink on it. "Your G and T."

"Okay, now the moment of truth," he said picking up the glass. The presentation was good. He sipped, paused, and a puzzled look crept across his face. He took another sip. "So, it tastes a little off, a little too strong. But fine for not knowing our standard ratios.

"Next, how about a mojito." Daisy muddled the mint leaves and produced the drink. Once again, "Passable, good enough to keep someone drinking," he laughed.

"Okay, Tony said I had to give you the job unless you were a disaster, so you're hired," he said with a smile, reaching out to shake her hand to seal the deal. Tony Brubeck was the CFO of the restaurant group that operated the bar, along with several others in the area. Daisy had worked for Tony for several years as an accountant in the Pacific Northwest region.

Tony had put in the good word for Daisy but made her promise to continue her accounting role in at least a reduced capacity. It sounded like a perfect fit to Daisy: continuity, stability, new experience, and an endless flow of new people.

"Feel free to drink one of those if you want," the manager said, standing to leave.

"Are we done?" asked Daisy. "I never drink on the job," she said, winking at the manager.

"Yep, I'll text you when we get the schedule set up."

Daisy sat at the bar, drinking the gin and tonic,

satisfied with the day. She wondered how gin made it into the pantheon of liquors: whiskey, vodka, tequila, rum, brandy, and gin. Juniper berries. All the others are strong pillars, except maybe brandy. Brandy is the sexy stepchild. But gin, with its juniper tinge, is just so specific. Maybe it gets a pass given its U.K. heritage, maybe Daisy just needed to hear London calling on foggy nights at locals.

She had practiced free pouring at home, working on counts, one count per quarter ounce, until she could hit the mark even with some bottle-level flair. She memorized the top fifty drinks ordered in the types of bars she was targeting, which ranged from upscale hotel bars to a neighborhood tavern. Old fashioneds, Manhattans, whiskey sours, martinis, margaritas, Negronis, mules, Sazeracs, bloodies, Collins, and the impossible Long Island iced teas, impossibly combining vodka, tequila, rum, and gin into something that's actually drinkable.

What could be better to get to core meaning than serving drinks to and chatting with an assortment of drinkers from a broad cross section of society? Locals at the Fremont Tavern, business travelers at the Sorrento, W, and Panorama hotels. The Fremont was a neighborhood beer joint, out of character with the rest of the company's properties; it had been acquired as a favor in a bailout scenario. The W was a modern hotel in the middle of Seattle's financial district. The Sorrento and Panorama were older hotels on the outskirts of the downtown core.

Daisy had also practiced the perfect beer pour,

forty-five-degree initial angle on the glass, quick pull on the tap, gradual turn of the glass to upright, close tap with the head still rising, serve on coaster with the head just tipping over the rim in one spot, signaling to the customer that he is among friends and not in a sterile environment. She had gone through a pony keg of Roger's Pilsner over a couple months perfecting the motion, having rigged the keg to a tap.

She had hosted a party at her house in order to practice tending bar. Attendees were friends from her accounting job, a few old friends from high school, college, and early work, and some friends that were parents of Tom's friends and sports teammates. She had a reasonably fully stocked bar, complete with lemon, lime, orange, and for those fruity guests: pineapple wedges, maraschino cherries, Angostura and Peychaud's bitters, simple syrup, and oversized ice with minimal air bubbles. She had a menu of drinks for the novice drinkers and a challenge to stump the bartender for the veteran drinkers. A few did stump her. She didn't know the Pimpinella (grappa, St-Germain, lime juice, anise syrup, rosemary sprig garnish), nor did she have grappa on hand. Not stumped, but she didn't have cocktail onions for a Gibson. The Bone stumped her, but she did have Tabasco on hand to make it when the guest shared the recipe: bourbon, lime juice, simple syrup, and Tabasco. A retired librarian asked for a Bee's Knees, and Daisy delivered with flair: gin, lemon juice, honey, shaken, served with a lemon twist.

* * *

The dinner crowd was barely hanging on at 8:00 p.m. on a Tuesday night in early December at TRACE, the bar in the W Hotel. The hotel was on Fourth Avenue in Seattle's business district, with the stadiums to the south; the waterfront and the Pike Place Market to the west; Amazonia, Lake Union, and Daisy's house in Wallingford to the north; and Capitol Hill, Seattle's counter-culture hub, to the east. There were no regulars at TRACE; there was only a regular type: business traveler staying for a night or two, maybe a week, tired, either alone or with coworkers, thirty to fifty years old, eighty percent male. Daisy pulled IPAs and crafted old fashioneds. The décor was a dizzying mix of linear and cylindrical features, somewhat jarring, with cafeteria type seating. The rainbow-colored lighting and the ice-blue bar itself redeemed the otherwise uninspired drinking arena. Hits from the sixties forward provided the soundtrack.

A man in his late forties or early fifties sat at the end of the bar. He was Asian, but Daisy couldn't place the nationality. White hair crept up his head, having already infiltrated the territory near his temples and ears. He had the proper uniform for the bar: rumpled suit, no tie, patterned dress shirt. "Welcome," said Daisy, "what can I get you?"

"Are you new here? I haven't seen you before," he asked.

"Fairly new. I've been here for about a month but only one or two nights a week. I fill in at a number of bars."

"You look like you have a good perspective on drinking. So let me ask you, what do you want to sell me?"

"Are you saying I look like a drunk or I look old?"

Daisy asked, winking. "Well, help me narrow it down, what are you in the mood for, broadly?"

"Okay, a drink to fit this theme: dark rainy days, newspapers, political battles, and corporate co-opted art." From many, this would have come off as a pretentious little bitch move, but this person had clearly been through the battles for years, slogging out weeks, grinding out an income and a life, winning many battles, losing some, and ending the night with a drink either way.

"Hmmm, okay, that's my first request for that specific combination. Well, dark rain rules out tequila and rum. Politics and newspapers, could be many interpretations, maybe it calls for a stiff drink, maybe something old school as newspapers are dying. Scotch could be an option for the base, but I associate that with gale force wind-blown rain on a northern coast rather than our Seattle rain. Maybe gin, fits rain and newspapers given its London feel, but I'm not your woman if you like gin. So co-opted art, how does that fit in? Something inauthentic? Maybe a little sickeningly sweet, or overly influenced by the latest trend, so maybe a sweet bourbon drink? I've got it. Okay, so you need to turn around or something, don't watch me make it, then taste it blind, see if I hit the mark."

"Okay, I'll be back," and he went to the restroom.

When he returned, the drink sat in a highball glass on a coaster at his seat at the bar: yellowish brown, a little cloudy, on the rocks, garnished with two olives and a maraschino cherry on a plastic spear. "Wow, okay, let's give this a try," he said. He sipped the drink. He recoiled slightly with a flat, disbelieving smile and wide eyes. "Yeah, that's really bad," he laughed, "really, profoundly bad. I'd say you nailed it."

"May I?" Daisy asked, grabbing a cocktail straw to sample the drink.

"Be my guest."

Daisy sampled the drink, capping the straw with her finger then sucking it out. She shrugged with a slight pout of her lower lip, "I've had worse."

"What is it?"

"Bourbon, a muddled olive and a little brine, bitters, and ... wait for it ... Rainier."

"Ha, well, yeah, I can accept that as a worthy effort."

"Here," Daisy said, reaching for the drink, "let me get you something else."

"No, no, no," he said, swatting her hand away. "That would be alcohol abuse. I ordered it and I'll drink it. I embrace the experience. I'm Jim Cooper," he said, extending his hand to shake, "but everyone calls me Coop."

"Daisy," she said, shaking his hand. "Pleased to meet you Coop."

The night progressed, and the bar slowly emptied. Four college kids drank Mac & Jack's and Jägermeister shots at a corner table. Other than that, the vibe was very chill, contemplative drinking. Coop had switched to vodka sodas after the first Dark Intrigue, vodka soda being a drink that was hard to screw up. The television above the bar showed an NBA game.

Daisy came over to check on Coop, and he pointed to the TV, "That's one of mine." Daisy followed his finger point, confused. A Pacifico commercial was on the screen.

"One of your beers?" Daisy asked.

"One of my commercials, I'm in advertising," Coop

answered.

"Another vodka soda?"

"Yep, still thirsty." It was his third.

The commercial revolved around models in their early twenties at an impromptu party, good friends only, on a laid-back weathered deck at what looked like a Mexican beach somewhere. Lots of bikini tops and cutoffs. One bro tossed a beer to another bro, then a female model settled into his arms and took the beer. The commercial ended with a close up of the beer between her breasts, with the focus on the beer bottle and the breasts just slightly blurred, nipples vaguely visible.

Daisy delivered the vodka soda, found the remote, and rewound to watch it again with Coop. "This is really deep stuff, Coop," Daisy poked.

"Whatever works," he responded. "Advertising is pretty simple. There are only a few basic approaches; all the creativity is to stand out within that limited repertoire. A common approach is to portray a lifestyle and hook your product to it. So here the lifestyle is laid-back sexy, hot bods, romance, beach, friends. My beer will get you there. Why this approach? It works. I kind of want a Pacifico, you?" Coop asked.

Daisy did want a Pacifico. "Yeah, I actually do, damn you. But I don't drink while I work, and we don't even have Pacifico. Impressive work though. I do want to drink Pacifico on a sunny dock with beautiful people.

"Any qualms about influencing people to buy something they otherwise don't want or need?" asked Daisy.

"You're not pulling any punches, are you? Well, to tell you the truth, a little bit. A little bit, Daisy. But a couple things that you have to consider. First, everyone is constantly changing into someone else, buffeted by their experience. Yes, advertising pays to be part of their experience stream and to change them a little bit going forward, but they're going to change regardless, the only question is in what direction. No one ever stays static. Now, if I were selling Nazism or something clearly evil, then yes, that would be bad. But if I'm selling a beer, eh," he shrugged. "People may well be glad they changed to want a Pacifico a little more. And despite the billions spent on advertising, it is a pretty weak form of mind control. In most situations, it helps drive choices between products rather than the ultimate choice for a product category. So, I'm sitting in a bar and wanting a drink, I'm a bit more likely to order a Pacifico than a Corona."

"Aren't both Pacifico and Corona owned by Constellation?" Daisy asked.

"Nothing like cornering the market," Coop said.

"So, your mind control is acceptable because it's weak?" Daisy asked.

"Well, relatively weak, but also benign."

The college kids stumbled out the door, leaving Coop as the bar's only patron. With no busser on duty near close, Daisy cleared and wiped down the kids' table.

"Alright, last call Coop, another drink? Are you staying here? Something to take to the room?" Daisy asked.

"I am staying here, but no, I'm good. I've enjoyed talking with you tonight." He drained the last swallow of his vodka soda and swiveled on his stool getting up to go. "Say," he said turning back around "there's no one here, after last call, that's pretty damn close to off work for you. How about one for the road? Jägermeister shot like the kids, to be young again?"

Daisy poured two tumblers of Lagavulin 12 year. She slid one to Coop. "Cheers," she said, raising her glass. Coop clinked glasses. "This one's on me," she said. "But not to be young again. To be old for the first time."

"Cheers.

"But really? old?" he asked.

"Well, third stage. Empty nest," she said.

"Alright, I need to hear more about this, are you working tomorrow?"

Teased by the Lagavulin, once home at her Wallingford house Daisy poured a glass of Gewürztraminer and settled into her well-stuffed porch chair. *One drink deserves another*. The chair was worse for years of wear in Seattle's weather, even in its protected alcove on the deck. The deck was large and covered, painted the same dark greenish blue as the house, with square cream-colored support columns accented with beveled moldings. The neighbor's cat, a fat tabby, padded up the porch stairs and lay down next to Daisy.

The waxing gibbous moon provided mood lighting. Daisy had just recently learned the moon cycle, with transitions moving from right to left. She hadn't thought too much about it before, appreciating a crescent moon for example, or a full moon, and thinking how the angle of the crescent moon changed as she travelled latitudes, but not paying attention to the complete cycle. From no moon, the crescent starts on the right side, filling toward the left to half-moon, full moon, then disappearing from the right to half-moon and the western crescent. The right-to-left motion produced cognitive dissonance with Daisy's concept of western script, reading left to right.

The sweet Gewürztraminer wine partially matched Daisy's sweet reflective mood. Daisy's sweet reflective mood partially matched the reflective waxing gibbous moon. The bartending had been engaging, even if more drudgery and routine than she had originally imagined. So many people were so uninteresting. So many margaritas, in Seattle, in non-Mexican cantinas. So many cosmos and Sea Breezes and mojitos. Patrons at different places than Daisy on all of life's continuums: where they were in careers, how wise (or unwise) they were, what they experienced as fun, whether and how they reflected upon life, what they expected from sex, their level of concern for human hierarchies, and on like that for any human experience that came to mind.

But there were others, Coop for example, who could hold her attention. She had no sexual attraction to Coop but recollecting the night's conversation made her smile. She appreciated his perspective; he had the potential to say something that she hadn't thought before, or at least his perspective on even worn-out thoughts seemed insightful. Perhaps more importantly, his perspective seemed consistently cheery, optimistic. And not because he led a charmed life, but just because that was who he was. It seemed likely he'd lived through his share of challenges, carried his share of burdens, but he focused on the upside. He laughed it off. He would wear aloha shirts on stormy days.

5

The next evening at the W, a typical crowd of hotel guests and downtown workers chatted over drinks. Daisy worked six to close. As she entered, she noticed the smiling Asian in a Hawaiian shirt in the last seat at the bar, and smiled. "Coop," she said, tying on an apron and pulling her hair into a ponytail, "you're back. Are you going to start off with a theme drink tonight, or was that a one-time thing, an audition to serve as your bartender? Your alcohol curator. Your alcohol cure tender."

Finishing his chicken-fried steak with mashed potatoes in country gravy, Coop dabbed his lips with his napkin, breathed deeply, and said, "Okay, far be it from me to guess a woman's age, but I'm guessing you lived through at least a lot of the seventies and eighties, so how about a Cold War Colada."

Daisy laughed and Coop chuckled. "Okay, just to be sure, that is not a real drink already, right?"

"Right."

"Alright, well, Cold War suggests vodka, Stoli, definitely, and what for America, maybe Jack? So, colada, we could go pina colada mix, but that seems so uninspired, could go coconut water—but you did say cold war not millennial—okay, coconut milk, and what else, some seventies flavor," she paused, thinking. "I've got it," she said, as her index finger pointed up in a success reaction. "I'm not sure we'll have it, but let's see," she ducked from behind the bar into the backroom. She returned with something in a brown paper bag, to hide it, and proceeded to whip up the Cold War Colada. She strained the shaker into a highball glass and served the pink drink on a new "W Hotel" coaster.

"Pink, now I wasn't expecting that," Coop said. "I thought you might go Bay of Pigs with some rum/bacon inspiration. Let me rephrase that, I was hoping you'd go with a rum/bacon inspiration ..." he trailed off into laughter. "Okay, pink drink it is," he said, sipping. "Not bad ... not too bad ... not good, but ..."

"Who can enjoy a drink with mutually assured destruction hanging over their head?" Daisy asked.

"Nice of you to incorporate Pepto Bismol to prepare my stomach," he said.

"Do you know the secret ingredient?" she asked.

Coop paused, considering. He took another drink and let it luxuriate on his tongue. "I believe I do, Daisy. I think it's Nestle Quick."

"Damn, you're good," she said.

"Do you have Tang back there too?"

After the Cold War Colada, Coop settled into drinking mules, and the two chatted most of the night. Coop was in his early fifties, a VP in an advertising agency. He had started his career in public relations but early on shifted to advertising, thinking of ads as modern-day poems. He had three children, the youngest of whom, a daughter named Savannah but usually called Savi, was a sophomore in college. His wife had died of a stroke two years ago. With no family at home, he had transitioned to a role in which he was on the road about half time, overseeing production and artistic design teams.

The night proceeded with Coop sharing aspects of his life interspersed with Daisy rounding the bar, filling drinks. Coop sipped mules and half-heartedly watched the college basketball game on the monitor behind the bar while Daisy was serving customers. Toward the end of the night, he said, "But enough about me, I want to hear about your, was it 'third stage'? Your empty nest plan."

Daisy shared her thoughts on childhood and dependence on parents, adulthood and dependence on a partner to have children, and then third stage with no necessary dependence or dependents. Evolutionary freedom, or, pessimistically, evolutionary irrelevance. "After returning from dropping Tommy off at school, I took some time and thought through life's meaning, thought through how to live right now. I came to the conclusion to embrace experience—damn you millennials with your Iceland trips—and how better to have experiences than tend bar, so, presto." Daisy curtsied.

"So you just recently started tending bar, I never could have guessed ..." his voice trailed off, reliving the drinks Daisy had concocted, a manufactured shiver ran down his spine.

He asked how she came to the conclusion that experience was the point, and she relayed her general thought process. Entertainment was just passing time, not valuable. Commercials were not poems.

"Well, it's all in your perspective. Songs are probably today's true poems, but really, what the hell role did poems even have back when anyone read poems. So, I'll stick with ads as poems. Slices of life through a particular lens."

"Anyway, Pacifico boy," Daisy continued. "Love of course is good, but vague and a cop out. Friendship or community could be the point, but reliant on others. Maybe it's fine to rely on others," she explained, "but seems unnecessarily limiting. Helping others is nice, but endless. And then there is the problem of point-in-time versus continuous, digital versus analog. Meaning can't really be a point-in-time achievement, because then at time achievement-plus-one you still exist but no longer have meaning."

"So you just need to die at the moment of maximum achievement," Coop offered.

"I'm pretty sure," Daisy said seriously, "the meaning of life is continuous. It isn't a series of achievements."

"Okay, so you just chose experience. Just gut feeling? No real process?"

"Honestly, I feel like there isn't a lot of content geared at the meaning of life, ya know, beyond self-help mumbo jumbo, religious mumbo jumbo, spiritual mumbo jumbo, love mumbo jumbo."

"Have you read *Man's Search for Meaning*? It was written by a Jew who survived a Nazi internment camp, also a psychologist if I remember correctly. His point, at least what I took as the point and still remember, also clouded a bit, mind you, by the many mules and one Cold War Colada you've served me, but in any case, his point was that a person craves meaning. A person's main motivation in life is to find meaning."

"He's got me pegged."

"Like anything, it probably resonates with some and not with others. The force is strong with you. Maybe too strong."

"What about you Coop? What's your meaning?"

"I'm still a working stiff. In the words of some great pop singer, just working for the weekend."

"Okay, but really, VP ad man, what's your meaning?"

"Daisy, I've just been trying to hold it together for as long as I can remember. Life with Helen, my wife, was hard.

"You figure it out and tell me. Then I'll sell it to the world in thirty-second increments, thirty-second poems. There will be a global awaking. The revolution will be televised.

"Honestly, meaning has never been an issue for me. Not a driving force. Maybe it is more important for some people than for others. I can see meaning as propagating life. Having sex, having kids. Clearly that's the biological imperative, and probably the dominant subject matter for all thought and action."

"In second stage," said Daisy.

"Second and third, I'd say. Yeah, it wanes with age, but still a big driver. Maybe more for men, I don't know. But meaning, for me, I'm just living. Making connections, trying to enjoy the day, trying to be a good father, trying to make enough money to live comfortably, playing golf, watching football."

"Pastimes," said Daisy.

"Okay so not meaning, not your Everest, but perhaps meaning in a sense since it is experience and as you've defined experience as meaning," Coop's head got lost in a loop of object reference. "Anyway, one thing I like to do is experience historical or cultural locations and have a drink at them. History, pop culture, movie scenes, whatever. I like the depth of feeling at those locations, a connection through time. Staying in an infamous hotel room—say a murder scene or suicide. It's always a little awkward to ask for the room," Coop chuckled. "Whitney Houston's overdose in the Beverly Hilton is a big one—I haven't stayed in that room; I think the hotel changed the room number to confound people like me. Janis Joplin's room in which she overdosed on heroin at the Landmark Motor Hotel in Hollywood, they actually advertise it; I have stayed there. Time probably helps ease the awkwardness. Any locations in Seattle come to mind?"

"Death hotel rooms?"

"No, just any specific locations tied to a memorable event."

Daisy tossed out Seattle standards, none of which she had ever visited: Kurt Cobain's death garage (well, a park bench that overlooks the garage); Jimi Hendrix's and Bruce Lee's graves ("Graves only kind of qualify for me," said Coop, "—the physical bones or ashes of the person are there, but not the event in time that makes it more special"); *Sleepless in Seattle* houseboat; Tom Robbin's hangout at the Blue Moon Tavern; there was a coming of age, taming of the shrew movie at Stadium High School in Tacoma; *Twin Peaks* settings out in North Bend.

"Okay," Coop said, "at some point we'll do one or two of those."

The number of drinkers dwindled as the night wound down. Coop was once again the last patron in the bar. Daisy had cleaned up, prepped the bar for the next day, and was riding out the clock.

"Last call, Coop, one more mule for the room?"

"I like your company, Daisy, you're a rare person. I actually changed my flight home to stay here and drink with you for another day, or rather, drink while you serve drinks. Let me share one final thought, and while I do, sure, I'll take another mule for the walk to my room—those hallway corridors, oy!

"One final thought, I know you thought about meaning, and you settled on experience, but I worry about your process. That's what I do, I get people to make shortcut decisions; that's fine when you're choosing which beer to drink, less so when deciding on the meaning of life.

"I think you need a more rigorous process. I'm not sure what that process would be. But still, simply deciding on experience seems like you're shortcutting the process. In most of history, whenever people just believe something for no reason, it is inevitably wrong. And maybe it is not meaningful to talk about right and wrong beliefs on meaning, but maybe it is, and if it is, then you haven't done the work to explore that path. And I don't know what that path is, how to start it or where it goes, but I think you need to find it and explore it. If you think it's important, which you clearly do."

Daisy looked at the happy-go-lucky exterior man and the surprisingly thoughtful interior man, going on middle age, sitting in front of her on the last bar stool, at closing time, in the W hotel bar, with dark, rainy Fourth Avenue out the windows. She poured two shots of Goldschlager. They clinked glasses, "Cheers," and tossed them back.

"Thank you Coop," she said. They exchanged numbers and talked of when Coop would be back in town, which he did not know.

Paths are personal, thought Daisy, as she walked to her car.

6

Days, weeks, months passed with Daisy rotating bartending duty among the four properties. Tom was enjoying prep school in Switzerland; he spent Christmas with his father in Zurich.

The hotel bars tended to draw mainly from hotel guests and therefore had no true regulars. There were a few familiar faces, but they were the exception. The lone free-standing bar at which Daisy worked was a different story. The Fremont Tavern was a beer joint; it smelled of beer and joints. The bar in the Fremont neighborhood definitely had its regulars. Fremont had a small nightlife district, one that seemingly had been on the come for a couple decades but had never really arrived. The bar had live music crammed into the back room occasionally on Friday and Saturday nights, with jukebox selections other nights, one pool table, neon beer signs, exposed brickwork, and exposed airshafts in the ceiling.

On a Thursday in spring, a sideburned regular sidled up to the bar. "Manny's?" asked Daisy, knowing his predilection. She didn't know his name, but his hands were strong, not like the technology hordes, maybe an engineer, environmental scientist, or forestry manager. He nodded, and as Daisy pulled the pint, she asked "What gives your life meaning?" He squinted subtlety, not expecting the question. He gave her a smile, implying that maybe Daisy's question was a (bad) joke, suggesting the beer gives his life meaning. He walked back to his booth. *Okay, that approach didn't work*, Daisy thought.

Heeding Coop's advice to be more thorough and rigorous, Daisy had resolved herself to initiating conversations about meaning with her customers, to get their take.

Take two. Daisy tried a new approach with the next patron who she thought may have some insight. She waited until the woman had had two drinks. The woman was drinking with a friend, another woman. Daisy asked if they wanted another round, they declined and asked for the check. "Let me ask you something," Daisy said. "I'm trying to find the meaning of life. What would you say it is?" The formulation bugged Daisy, she would rather say the meaning of *her* life, but that creates an awkward question, too personal; the formulation she used would better encourage big picture responses, she thought.

The friend answered first, apparently thinking the question had been posed to the table. "Kindness, it all comes down to kindness."

The targeted woman, after a pause, with her head cocked at an angle in consideration, a thoughtful pose, said "I don't really have an answer, it is what it is."

Daisy started to think this drinker sampling would not be fruitful. Nevertheless, she continued. If nothing else, it created a different level of bond with the person. Maybe some later-visit conversations would be deeper than if she hadn't posed the question.

The questioning was an enjoyable source of tortured facial expressions. From furrowed brows, pursed lips, tilted heads, skyward glances, to Daisy's favorite, the perplexed turtle, one corner of the mouth pulled back with squinted eyes and retracted head as if to say "Did you miss the memo? That isn't even something we care about anymore. Don't we just do what we want?"

Over the next few months Daisy got lots of love, but only in the form of answers. Love, love, love, love. "It really all comes down to love."

Experience was a popular answer, so Daisy's initial instinct was widely shared—perhaps instilled as part of the modern zeitgeist. Also popular were variations on "Just live." Many badly sung answers proved that song lyrics were the modern-day poems, not ads.

One person was keeping score on net worth; you can bet he wasn't a forestry manager. All possible takes on the virtues of alcohol were offered. Several earnest offers to discuss God and to go to church. Odes to enjoyment, such as the classic "Enjoy it!" were common, and the more thoughtful exhortations to be present, be in the moment, achieve flow, and/or achieve transcendence. Certainly, some oddities were proffered, "Be treelike," "The honeybees," and more crude replies than were worth enumerating, such as "Eating beaver." There was a positive correlation with the number of drinks a person had had and the creativity of the answers, as well as the crudity. Drunks and children are the most honest people, someone had once told Daisy; in these cases, though, the drunks seemed to first get in a joke—or at least an answer colored by the evening and the alcohol, but then got down to the serious answer, "But really ..."

Friendship might have been the number two answer, behind love. Or friendship variants like community or finding your tribe. These were usually accompanied by physical touching of the members of the drinking party, an arm around shoulders or a hug if the positioning were not too awkward, high fives and fist bumps for those with more testosterone in their bloodstreams. The setting of drinking with friends clearly had a priming effect on producing the answer of friendship.

The meaning of life question did prove to be a remarkable pick-up line. It opened the door for the next step in the flirt. The first requirement, of course, was interest on Daisy's part. Then, anything like "A beautiful woman's eyes," or "Waking up next to a feisty woman," or the efficient "Sex," or the direct "You," or the only slightly less direct "A woman like you" (Daisy followed that one with, "Well, I'm like me," and a weekend in the San Juans). The art of the flirt was to open the door, the dance partner needed to take the next step.

Happiness was high in the rankings, as were "Fuck negative shitheads" and "Mean people suck," (Daisy started the flirt dance with "Well, I suck," but it somehow fizzled at that point). Joy scored well. While vague, goodness placed on the leaderboard, and really, who can argue that goodness isn't good. Meaningfulness did not place though, even though it seems clear that meaningfulness is meaningful.

Over time, Daisy gave up asking anyone who appeared to be under thirty-five. Only clichés such as

"Enjoy it" and love/sex were offered up, the youngsters were too busy scouting for partners for the night or for longer. She gave it up, that is, unless it was opening the flirt door, no age restrictions there.

Freedom collected some mentions, both in the form of "Not letting anyone tell you what to do," and in the abstract notion of freedom, often followed by "man," "Freedom, man." Art and creativity scored well among those with two or more appearance affectations (unnaturally dyed hair, extreme hairstyle, high tattoo volume, facial piercings other than ear or nose, ear hoops, overly niche clothes, etc.). Music and painting were more popular than writing; advertising poetry was never mentioned. More generally, expression and free expression were not uncommon answers.

Mu was a standard response from the science types, unask the question, not in those words (or, really, that word) of course, but something along the lines of there is no meaning. Meaning is just an illusion; there's just the physical universe; religion and larger meanings are just self-perpetuating concepts due to social selection; religion and larger meanings are just ways that rulers control people. Science is all that really matters, finding the truth. Why do you care about finding the truth? Okay, finding the truth is meaning, or rather getting closer to the truth, since we all know we'll never really find the truth of everything.

Daisy noticed a natural divide between lawyers and scientists—her categorization, not their actual vocation. Lawyers defined meaning as rules for interacting: kindness, freedom, justice; in theory a social structure could be created with rules that fostered meaning; meaning was created. Scientists tried to discover meaning: truth, joy, love, beauty; meaning was found or discovered.

Parents focused on kids, providing, creating life, raising the next generation, being a link in the chain of life.

A few specific interactions stood out. A woman, about Daisy's age had entered the Cloud Room in the Panorama alone, around 5:00 p.m. on a weekday, dressed in office attire, clearly a white-collar worker. The Panorama was an older hotel that embraced and charged for its age. The Cloud Room, on the top floor after a slow elevator ride, featured décor that would have been considered futuristic in the 1960s, Jetsons chic. The window views looked out over the downtown cityscape and slices of Puget Sound between buildings. The woman ordered a cosmo; Daisy pegged her as an amateur drinker, as she did with all cosmo drinkers. Taking the first sip, the woman asked, "Is this really a cosmo?" with a frown creeping over her face, but she endured. Two friends soon joined her, and they ate dinner and drank a couple of rounds. Eventually one friend left and then the other, but the woman remained. Daisy approached and asked "Anything else I can get cha? Another drink?"

"Sure, one more," said the woman.

When Daisy returned with the drink, she launched her usual intro "Let me ask you a question. What do you think is the meaning of life?"

"That's a big question. Existence, thought, emotion." She sipped her drink. "Language, communication, expression, childhood/adulthood, friends, enemies, everyone else." Sip. "Time, increasing entropy, decreasing energy. Love, hate, sex, anger, lust, ambivalence, boredom, power, transcendence. God, the devil, angels, and demons. Yin and Yang." Sip. "Travel—okay, that's not really the meaning, but can help one to get to meaning. Music, flow, dancing, drum rhythms, bass lines. Consciousness, learning, drinking, drugs, flavor." Sip. "Emotional release, orgasm, cycles."

She downed the half of her cosmo that remained in one swallow. "You know, just everything, just all of it."

Daisy upgraded her to a professional drinker.

Another that stood out occurred in the Sorrento's bar. The Sorrento, overlooking the city from Capitol Hill, was a luxury hotel from the early 1900s that had transformed into a boutique hotel as the idea of luxury morphed to require more space. The red brick exterior housed dark wood paneled walls in the brass-filled bar. A man in his late twenties sat alone at the bar, overweight, overwrought, self-consciously scanning the room. He drank PBRs in sixteen-ounce cans. He had been in the bar a few times while Daisy was working, always alone. He never tried to engage Daisy or anyone else, bartender or patron, in any conversation. *What the fuck*, thought Daisy, *he's three beers in*, and she asked his take on the meaning of life.

He looked down at his beer, avoiding Daisy's eyes. He spoke words softly, so softly that Daisy could not understand him, despite it being a fairly quiet night in the bar.

"I'm sorry, I couldn't hear you," said Daisy.

The man nodded, forced a smile, and looked down and away, seeming to signal the conversation was over. Later in the evening, Daisy checked back with him, "Another PBR?" He nodded.

"Your drinks are on me tonight, sweetie," Daisy said. The man smiled momentarily. Daisy never saw him again in the bar.

Another memorable interaction was at the Fremont. A man in his midforties, Daisy's age, drank beer with two friends, a man and a woman. They appeared to be work friends out for drinks at the end of the day, dressed in jeans. The two men drank Hop Bombs, an IPA from a local brewery; the woman drank a blonde lager. Over time, the friends left, and the man sat alone in a booth. His hair buzzed close to his scalp, he seemed as if he'd fought the good fight for years. Daisy was tending bar, and Ali, a waitress, had the table responsibility, but Daisy winked at Ali and approached the table.

"Ali's tied up, your waitress, so I wanted to check on you, can I get you anything else?"

The man made weak conversation, "I saw you tending bar, any personal favorite drinks I should try? Anything you like to make?" As he asked it their eyes met and Daisy felt like she was looking in a mirror. She wasn't seeing another person; she was seeing herself in another body.

"I make a mean, um ..." and no drink came to Daisy's mind. Daisy waited for some drink to pop into her mind. The pause grew, Daisy still waiting. *Scotch and soda—no that's terrible, who can't make a fucking scotch and soda.* Daisy kept waiting but became increasingly focused on how long the pause had become. *Okay, this pause is really long now, let's go brain.* Finally, "Ya know, to be honest, everything I make is really good."

"Okay, surprise me," the man said.

With the pressure on, Daisy thought about what she would want to drink. Bourbon/cranberry?—strong candidate. But he's been drinking IPAs, what would she want after IPAs?

She came back with a seasonal sour beer. He took a sip and puckered; it was true to its name.

She asked him the meaning of life.

"So much for small talk, chit chat," he said. Daisy explained her situation and survey of bar patrons. "Well," the man said, "I don't have a great answer. But my guess is consciousness plays a central role. Meaning seems like a judgment, or an emotion, or a thought; something in that realm. And that is all consciousness, not physical. Well, you know, consciousness probably has physical aspects, but big picture, it is different. So, I'd say something consciousness related."

"I like that," said Daisy.

"And one aspect of consciousness is its individual nature," the man said. "It coalesces at the personal level; a person has one conscious experience and that is separate from another person's conscious experience. Even edge cases like schizophrenics tend to have one experience at a time, I think. So that might open the meaning of life to being personal, or a personal choice, potentially different for everyone. So, I'd say the meaning of life is probably related to the personal experience of consciousness, not some universal truth for everyone." He took a gulp of the sour.

The mirror man thanked Daisy for the question, paid his check, and left.

7

March arrived and Seattle broke out of its winter gray drizzle into its spring breezy drizzle. Tom returned from boarding school for a two-week break. He and Daisy ate at Ivar's fish and chips on Lake Union, just down the hill from their house. The restaurant's dining room smelled of deep-fried cod and salt. Their specialty, well, their quirky offering, was clam nectar—served hot like tea. Tom dared Daisy to drink it and she would not.

On Thursdays, the W opened at 3:00 p.m. for the happy hour crowd, followed by the dinner crowd. Daisy opened the bar with a few random groups of drinkers. Later, a group of five slim, shaven-head Asian monks in orange robes walked in from the hotel lobby. They were there for dinner. All had vegetarian dishes.

Oh my, what a golden, er, orangish opportunity, thought Daisy. She observed the monks were talking among themselves, so they were not bound by vows of silence. Daisy approached the table and made small talk. She learned they were Buddhist monks from Japan, in town for a multi-faith conference titled "Hands Across

Faiths." *Who could care that much about multiple religions to throw a conference about it*, thought Daisy, *or to attend it?*

After establishing rapport, she asked what they thought was the meaning of life. One who looked to be the oldest responded. "We try train our minds to be present every moment. We find dat produce, kind of, inner light, inner harmony, quiet mind."

"Enlightenment?" asked Daisy.

"If you like."

"Is there a shortcut route?"

"Most important step, meditation. Focus da mind. Quiet da mind. Live well, meditate."

The monks were polite, but not verbose, and they weren't drinking so Daisy couldn't work her usual two-drink timing for a more revealing answer. The monks left shortly after finishing their dinner.

At 10:30 that night, one of the younger monks came back still dressed in the orange robe. He was with another young Asian man dressed in jeans and a graphic tee with the caption "The Loneliest Monk" and the jazz legend in a monk's robe cross legged floating in the air at a keyboard with notes flying off in all directions. The graphic was in gray scale except the robe was bright orange and the notes were bright rainbow colors. They sat at the bar.

"Hello Miss Daisy," said the monk. "Have you practice meditation, yet? Achieve Nirvana?"

"I like you, Chip," said Daisy.

"What Chip?"

The friend laughed, "That's you chipmunk."

"I am Hoshi," the monk extended his hand

somewhat awkwardly, and Daisy shook it.

"What can I get you guys?" Daisy asked.

"Harvey Wallbanger," said Hoshi. His friend ordered a Manhattan. Daisy was surprised that the monk was drinking, and her face betrayed this. "Rules, am I right?" said Hoshi. Daisy returned with the drinks, garnishing both with a maraschino cherry and orange wedge. They chatted with Daisy throughout the night. The non-monk, named Haru, explained that he had been in a Buddhist monastery for two years, but left in order to come to America and study computer science. He was now a student at Western Washington University in Bellingham. The two had been in the monastery together. Daisy asked why he had left.

Haru explained that he found it overly prescriptive. Too many numbered lists. They had 227 precepts to follow, the eight-fold path, the four noble truths, the three jewels. And the meditation got boring.

"I did not want to extinguish desire. I did not view the world as suffering. I went into monastery, at first, I think, to make my mother happy. Her family had tradition of monks in family, strong Buddhist belief. My father, not. I learn after two years my reason not good enough."

He explained that while Buddhism focuses on the development of the self and doesn't posit an external god, one must still have faith in the process, and that the process will lead to a better place. For him, he could not believe this. He also disliked the environment in the monastery: normal human hierarchical power struggles were alive and well. And the idea of reincarnation seemed a silly sidetrack, but yet played a key role in the official dogma.

"For me," the monk said, "it's about balance, balance in all things. Yes, Haru is right, reincarnation is silly. But I take what works and ignore rest. I like da focus on improving da self. All other religion is god-centric, Buddhism is self-centric. I think I become better person."

"The Western religions, and some Eastern religions, are god-centric," said Daisy. "You say Buddhism is self-centric. But really in the West, we have abandoned both god and self, in the sense of the self being something other than a physical being."

"You asked about meaning earlier," the monk said to Daisy, "unusual question for bartender. What is reason?" Daisy filled them in on her path. "Maybe you Buddhist and do not know it," the monk laughed. "Similar. You seek meaning. I seek quiet mind. People say end of suffering, end of desire. For me, is balance. Balance mind lead to enlightenment, lead to meaning, Daisy, for me, I think. Lead to experience every moment. Almost inner self different than outer self, inner self always laugh dat outer self exist in human situation."

"If you come to Japan, I teach you my approach, beginner," Hoshi offered. Haru described the monastery in the mountains north of Kyoto. He also described a series of eighty-eight temples on the Japanese island of Shikoku. Haru had walked the entire 750–mile circuit after leaving the monastery, a way to work through his decision and his direction.

"An acquaintance of mine walked the Camino de Santiago in Spain," Daisy said, "a Catholic walking pilgrimage. I don't know how far, but something similar to the seven-fifty you describe. He wasn't Catholic but wanted to experience it. He said that the thing that struck him was being around so many people who were there seeking to experience God, together."

"Kind of like monks and bartender talking about meaning of life, together," said Hoshi.

"Yes, I've heard of that pilgrimage," said Haru. "And I appreciate the community seeking their god. Even Buddhism, we work on the self, but we do it in groups. Ha."

The monk and computer science student had finished their drinks. Daisy poured three shots of Wild Turkey. "I propose a toast to our paths and happiness that our paths have crossed," Daisy said.

"Cheers." Glasses clinked. Shots shot.

8

Coop sat at the desk in his Tucson home, a bottle of Buffalo Trace bourbon and a rocks glass in front of him populated with rocks and spirit. *When did they stop showing Saturday morning cartoons?* he asked himself, flipping the TV off. The last decade had been hard for Coop. Fifty-two, empty nest, and deceased wife. No Smurfs on Saturday morning.

Married at twenty-three to the last girl he dated at the University of Arizona, their first child was taking midterms in nine-month preparatory school when the wedding bells rang. After Coop's own graduation, he started working in public relations for an Arizona gubernatorial candidate and subsequently, governor. After two years, he was drawn to the more creative opportunities in advertising, telling a story rather than spinning a story. He had worked for two advertising agencies since. The first, specializing in print ads, for only five years, followed by twenty plus years at his current full-service agency.

Their first daughter, Samantha, was born when Coop was twenty-three. Next up came Tabitha when

Coop was twenty-five. Savannah rounded out the power-pop trio when Coop was thirty-two.

His wife, Helen, was a 4.0 student at UA, with a major in political science. She was an accomplished partier as well, holding her own at quarters (thumb master was her go-to rule) and fuzzy duck. After graduating, she had been accepted to Harvard Law school, but decided to defer enrollment when Sam was born. The deferral eventually became a cancellation when Tabitha was born.

Coop, following the Buffalo Trace, remembered the good times he shared with Helen in the early days of their relationship, at football games, at parties, at bars, a weekend in the snow at Tahoe. He remembered the events, some of the events, but no longer the emotion. Or rather, he knew he had enjoyed it, but he didn't feel the joy or the love in the memories. The last decade had drained the last drop of love juice from him. Even through Savi's early childhood, his relationship with Helen was healthy. But when they hit about thirty-five, it seemed to have become clear to Helen that the life of mother was not all that she wanted. She turned Coop into her punching bag.

"We really should have had me go to law school and you stay home with the girls," she would say anytime money was tight or a decision was constrained by finances. Never mind it was Helen who had originally wanted to stay home and raise the girls, not a plan by Coop to derail her career.

Helen threw herself into one effort after another, each pursued more intensely and passionately than the prior, then abandoned for the next. The family in general, and Coop most of all, got the inverse of that passion. Tennis was the first that struck Coop as odd. They had played in mixed-doubles tournaments for a time at their club, for fun. But Helen became obsessed, practicing three hours every day, taking private lessons, spending the entire weekend at the club playing, practicing, scouting. Coop drove the girls to soccer and basketball games on the weekends while Helen played tennis.

Then came the cupcake business, operational just long enough to buy equipment and rent commercial kitchen space, before being dumped. The animal rescue and wine-making phases followed.

As time progressed, Coop's opinions became idiotic, his style was sloppy, his motivation was lacking, his parenting was permissive, his friends were degenerates, and his dog shed too much.

Coop escaped into work and movies and television. Not an advertising superstar, but no slouch either, rising to VP of creative content and a comfortable salary and bonus. "Why do you watch so many movies?" Helen asked. "It's not like you make anything creative like that. You sell shoes. You try to sell shoes. Didn't you guys lose that account? Didn't Al Bundy sell shoes?"

"Yes Peggy," as Coop slouched on the couch, hand in his pants waistband.

Sex had stopped in their early forties, just as Sam was leaving for college (paid for by Coop's mediocre earnings), Tabitha was in high school, and Savi was navigating fifth grade.

About that time, Helen started her political career on the school board. "Coop, you're not trying hard enough to get to know the parents." She advanced to the

Tucson city council and endless receptions, "Coop, just be less like yourself and more like me at these things."

Coop began to look forward to his work road trips, extending stays when feasible. Three-day trips turned into week-long ones, spanning a weekend. The road was a reprieve. Airports, once something to endure with restaurants that seemingly strived to provide the worst service imaginable, became portals to freedom; the restaurants still sucked.

But he stayed at relatively nice hotels, and their bars were his oasis. On an expense account but not a lavish one, the hotels were not luxury level by any means, more upper midmarket. He favored older hotels that had some history, or new hotels that repurposed older buildings. He avoided Courtyard Marriotts and the like when possible; not that he minded them, but they didn't have the aura of age or link to history that provided a spark of joy for him. And their bars were strictly utilitarian and often untended. The older hotels had nicer bars, carved wood, sturdy stools, embellishments authentically collected over the years rather than imposed by an interior designer. The bartenders had a wider range and perspective. A well-crafted drink in an interesting space was his respite.

As Savi entered high school, with the older two daughters already out of the house, Helen changed from parent to wanting to be Savi's best friend. Helen would push to hang out with Savi, go shopping, talk about boyfriends. She would buy beer for Savi's friend group and then drink it with them on the patio, the only adult in the group. She strove for MILF status.

Coop and Helen attended Savi's high school

graduation in Desert Valley High School's football stadium. "Don't you think you should wear a suit?" Helen asked as they left the house. The next week, Coop was on the road meeting with an insurance company in Boston. Helen suffered a major stroke and was rushed to the hospital in an ambulance called by Savi. She died in the hospital twelve hours later, shortly after Coop had arrived at her bedside. Tests revealed she had suffered a series of small strokes over several years.

Coop added another three fingers to his drink and a new batch of ice cubes. He swirled the bourbon to cool it, then sipped. He hadn't lived the life he had imagined, although, truth be told, he told himself, he had never really imagined what his life would be like. It was what it was. He was glad that Helen was dead.

* * *

Seattle in early April was a wet, sparkling emerald. The first pink and white dogwood blossoms provided contrast to endless shades of green. Yards were dotted with purple, yellow, and white crocuses and the wilting remnants of daffodils. Daisy sampled the seasonal taps at the Fremont Tavern after work one Friday, her shift having ended early.

Shortly after 6:30, Coop walked in. He was in town for the week, and he and Daisy had arranged to meet. "What are you drinking?" he asked.

"Rogue Rhubarb," she said, "sessionable with a blast of flavor. I sampled all of the seasonals. Clearly the best for my mood today."

"That a girl." He ordered the same when the

waitress came by.

They talked about paths and the last few months. Coop had been in town one other time since they had first met, including drinks served up by Daisy. Daisy filled him in on her meaning-of-life patron-survey research and in particular that she had been researching consciousness and its implications for meaning. "Rigorously, just like you advised," she said.

"You're a bulldog on meaning," Coop laughed, rubbing his temple. "That's good; that's how you get the bone. That's how you find the truth, your truth. Rigorously." He spun his coaster to its flip side as he took a drink. "On the other hand, have you considered that your need for meaning might just be a mental illness? Maybe your ancestors were wise men and mystics, and now you carry that on in the modern age," he smiled.

"Yeah, certainly could be," said Daisy. "I'd say that's the mainstream scientific viewpoint, as religion has waned, meaning is scoffed at. It's seen as an evolutionary adaptive trait to make societies cohesive, a shared meaning to bind and control communities. A false premise, but a practical one. But, even if that is true, I've still got to experience what I experience."

"I want to tell you about my family, and my wife," Coop said, changing the subject. He told of meeting Helen at a party in the house he rented with five other guys, watching the sunrise with her from the roof outside of his bedroom window, smoking Camels and drinking Coronas. He talked lovingly about each daughter.

"The reason I bring this up, well, it's two-fold I guess," he said. "The obvious reason is we're friends and you tell your friends things like this. But the other reason has to do with relationships with other people. You see, when Helen died, I was secretly glad. Living with her was miserable. She was unhappy with how her life had unfolded, I think, and she took it out on me. You know you would hope someone you're with every day would be a net positive factor in your life, a partner to commiserate with. At the very least, a marriage could be survivable if it were just neutral, with no real value created but also no negative. But when it is a constant drain of positivity, it's really unbearable. But I didn't want to hurt my kids, and so really didn't ever consider a divorce; maybe I'm not selfish enough. Instead, I got philosophical. And this is why I bring it up, it relates to your thinking on personal interaction and love.

"People change. People constantly change. On its face, this should be obvious. Everything always changes. Physically, say, the physical world, structures always change. With our time perspective, seeing someone every day, we don't notice the change. Even with our own kids, from one year to the next, seeing them every day we don't notice a change. And then we look at a picture with a one-year time lapse and the physical change is striking. The mental change would be even more so if it could be photographed. With kids, though, we embrace the change. Yes, we yearn for the snuggles of the infant, but that infant no longer exists when the girl is going to prom. With adults, though, we often don't recognize and appreciate the change, but adults are constantly changing too. Not as fast, not nearly as fast as kids, but changing every day regardless.

"So I look at the woman I'm married to at age fifty

and don't recognize the woman I married at twenty-five. And of course I don't. Not only is she different, but I'm different, by twenty-five years. Some marriages, perhaps by happy coincidence, perhaps by hard work, who knows, the spouses change in complementary ways, and you get a sappy love story, or a flavor piece on the local news 'couple still in love after seventy years.'

"But see, for the last decade I was mad at Helen. I didn't accept who she had become, I wanted her to be what she was, or what she was combined with how I had changed. She had become a social-striver and a politician. She loved city council meetings. I'll say that again: *she loved city council meetings*. I don't even understand how, but she did. She would tally up favors granted and work the political math to calculate the power she could exert on an issue. In retrospect, I realize I didn't really know my wife at all anymore. And, truth be told, I didn't really want to know her because I didn't really like her anymore. But here's my point. She had changed. And there is no point trying to blame her or me or anyone, because change just happens. Change is mandatory. I just had to accept who she had become.

"Now, she also should have accepted who I had become. Instead, she was always trying to change me, make me into more of a clone of her changes, who she had become. And of course, that didn't work and just made me frustrated."

"You're a perceptive guy, Coop," Daisy said.

"So in my case, we learned that she had had a series of small strokes over the years. Now, it's tough to say exactly what mental changes those strokes caused, but surely they impacted her personality. So that is clear physical change with time. But that's an extreme example. Everyone, every moment is changing, and honestly, mainly in ways that are beyond their control. Just riding rocket-ship Earth, brains changing, often deteriorating. Bombarded by cosmic rays, blasted by muons. Who's to blame? As you like to say, *mu*! Unask the question! No one's to blame. That's life.

"So, if Helen is someone who I don't like anymore, well, that's okay. It's only not okay if I let it get me down, or if I need another person to give me value.

"Now, sadly, take a meth addict."

"Huh?" asked Daisy.

"C'mon, keep up flower-girl. Take a meth addict, your child say. Not Tommy. Your hypothetical child. The parent hurts so badly wanting to get the child past the addiction. But also thinking of the child *before* the addiction. That before-child doesn't exist anymore. There is no going back. You can never go back. You have absolutely zero chance of going back. The best you can hope for is a future that changes in a more positive manner than the current, but that child you remember is gone forever, as surely as your snuggling infant is gone."

"If I knew you were going to go deep tonight, Coop, I'd have selected a different beer."

"Where is that waitress? The quality of the staff in here is sketchy. We can always switch it up, given our drinking aptitude."

Daisy went to the bar and came back with another round of Rogues.

"Another rhubarb?" asked Coop.

"What can I say, it's good."

"So, getting back to your path for meaning, the

reason that I drag you through this, it seems to me the love goal is largely just a random chance, at least in terms of a long-term relationship with the same person, or a series of short relationships," Coop said.

"Then why does the media, and advertisers, push love so hard?" Daisy asked, rhetorically. "Could it be the purchasing power of stage two? Or that everyone who makes the media is in stage two?"

"But I had one more thought along these lines," said Coop. "All those years, the years in the past, at this point in time, don't matter. They aren't a failure that I need to keep living; they're just gone. Over. Done. They don't saddle me with negativity now, unless I let them. But they shouldn't. Time. Whether past success or failure, on whatever measure, judged by whatever judge, just doesn't matter now. Unless you let it matter. And really, future success or failure might not matter much either. Yes, we need to prepare for the future, but it has to be a balance, right, between preparation and enjoying the now. Every day is judgment day, judged by yourself. Every moment."

"What about right ... now, Coop?" Daisy laughed. Coop nodded. "And ... now, now, how about now?

"Alright Coop, seriously though, let me make sure I understand. So, what you're saying is people change?"

"Last time I drop insight on you," Coop smiled, and chugged his beer.

* * *

The next evening, in the Cloud Room at the Panorama Hotel, Coop sat at a table overlooking the cityscape. The bar was short staffed and crowded with pre-event concert goers; Chris Cornell was playing across the street at the Paramount Theater that night. Coop drank IPAs, watching the city and watching the aging crowd, most of whom had cut their hair and gotten jobs since the time Cornell was screaming life with Soundgarden. The concert goers emptied out shortly before 8:00 p.m., leaving Coop and a few other dedicated drinkers. Coop migrated to the bar to chat with Daisy.

"I came across something that may interest you," Coop said. "Every two years there is a consciousness conference in Tucson, 'The Science of Consciousness.' It's a mishmash of academics, scientists, philosophers, head cases, wackos; you'd fit right in. Everyone trying to make progress on understanding consciousness, what it is, how it can be probed, how science can interface with it—things like that." He nibbled on complementary bar pretzel sticks. In an earlier conversation, Daisy had suggested consciousness seemed likely to play a key role in meaning.

"When is it?" asked Daisy.

"Coming up—late April."

"What do ya think about consciousness, Coop?"

"Well, I'm not sure how to answer that. I like it?"

"So, consciousness has what's known as the Hard Problem," said Daisy. "Most scientists today are physicalists, they think that physical matter is all that exists—and include in that fields and forces, gravity, electromagnetism, things like that. But the experience of consciousness is unlike physical items. You feel pain and joy. You see colors; you see red; that's the classic example. You experience redness. You feel emotions. The

Hard Problem is how conscious experience can exist in a physical world. How can atoms and forces combine to create first-person experience?

"And for my purpose, finding meaning, it seems to me that the physical is largely irrelevant, and the conscious experience is likely what matters, what produces meaning and value. Really, even the word value implies a conscious person to bestow that value, it seems to me." Daisy looked at her watch, eager to get off work so she could join Coop in drinking an IPA. "So, in the past, there was belief in dualism and souls, you had both physical matter and non-physical souls or consciousness, but the latter has proven totally intractable to science."

Daisy pulled out her phone and pulled up The Science of Consciousness conference website. She scanned the confirmed presentations: Evolution and Consciousness; Conscious Intention and Free Will; Anomalous Conscious Experience; Knowledge Argument, Explanatory Gap and Conceivability; Panpsychism, Idealism and Metaphysics; Vibrations, Scale and Topology; Ketamine and Anesthetics; Implications of Psychedelics.

"HOLY FUCKING SHIT, COOP!" Daisy's jaw dropped open, staring at her phone in disbelief. "Autism and the Consciousness Gestalt – Bianca Zanone. That's my old college roommate! We're going to this Coop!" When Daisy's shift ended at 10:00 p.m., she and Coop retired to a table at the window to experience the light rain falling with the evening, and Daisy told of her experiences with Bianca.

Book Two: Bianca

9

The small bedroom on the third floor of the Theta Gamma Phi frat house just north of the University of Washington smelled funky, a mixture of bong water, old socks, spilled beer, and unwashed sheets. It was the start of summer in 1992 and Daisy had just completed her junior year at the university. She was renting a room in the fraternity for the summer but started to have second thoughts as her olfactory system flashed warning lights, albeit strange that the sense of smell would use the sense of vision for alerts. The room's price was right at $250 for the whole summer (with the requirement that she attend the frat's parties, *twist my arm*), and she did need somewhere to stay during the summer before the apartment market opened up for the next school year. She was working nearby at a smoothie shop on the Ave. The low rent and full-time work would enable her to save some money for her senior year and perhaps beyond.

There were two beds in the room; Daisy tossed her duffel bags on the one nearest the window, the sill of which was covered in wax of various colors, the remnants of candles having burned down. The window overlooked a small courtyard with a volleyball court staked out in the grass. She started to unpack but scanning the condition of the chest of drawers in the room, thought better of it, only hanging a couple of summer dresses and a few shirts in the makeshift closet, which was just a recess in the wall with a hanging bar.

"Hi, roomie," a woman entering the room called out. She was dressed in black from head to toe: black hair, potentially dyed, falling well below her shoulders with a natural wave; copious amounts of black eyeliner; fitted black tank top covering a lacy black bra that poked out here and there; black jeans tucked into black leather calf-high boots. "I'm Bianca." She tossed her backpack on the unclaimed bed and hugged Daisy. Her body, including her face, had an angular quality, sharp lines with a default sneer and ice-green eyes. Bianca's angles contrasted with Daisy's curves.

Daisy's style leaned toward the grunge bohemian look dominant in Seattle's youth culture at the time, blue jeans with frayed knees, tee shirt, flip flops or Chuck Taylors, flannel shirt and long johns when the temperature cooled. Bianca had a goth, underground vibe.

Bianca had just finished her sophomore year, majoring in chemistry and considering a double major with physics.

"God, this room is a dump," said Bianca. "But I love it, it's our dump. We'll have a blast."

A few days later, on a Friday, the frat had a small party to welcome all the summer residents. The group was a collection of seasonal nomads including several members of the fraternity and university students sticking around for the summer. The keg was tapped at around 4:30 and day drinking from red plastic Solo cups commenced in the large common room. Daisy and Bianca had prefunked in their room with *dos manos* tequila shots, a suck of salt from between thumb and forefinger, a shot of Cuervo, and a lime wedge; *dos manos* because one hand was dedicated to the salt and lime wedge while the other handled the shot.

Neither Daisy nor Bianca lacked male attention, but they tended to stay close to one another as the social relationships of the summer crew were still forming. They joined into a game of turbo quarters that evolved into a series of drinking games as participants came and went. As the evening wore on, the drinking spilled into the courtyard, soaked up the last rays of the early summer sun, then sprawled throughout the house into the early morning. Around 1:00 a.m., the crowd had dwindled, and a group of about fifteen people were in the common room, sprawled on couches. One boy with side-parted hair had been persistent in his flirting with Bianca and continued despite the lack of any reciprocation from her.

Daisy and Bianca were playing foosball with two other guys, arguing whether spinning was allowed. One of the guys noted there was no rule against it in soccer. The Bianca/boy team scored the winning goal, a ricochet shot launched from the back row defender.

The night dragged on and people defected to sleep. Daisy sipped her beer, sitting on a couch with her foosball partner, who drank rum and Coke from a rocks glass. Bianca sat across the room, looking sleepy but dedicated to finishing her drink, still with her pesky suitor hanging on. Suddenly, Daisy seized the half-full rum and Coke and fired the glass across the room, hitting Bianca's suitor squarely in the chest.

"What the hell!" he said, as the surprised partiers turned their attention to the situation.

Daisy strode across the room, grabbed Bianca's plastic beer cup, and held it out to the boy. "Drink the god-damned drink," she said. "You drink this, mother fucker."

"What the fuck is wrong with you, bitch?" he said, looking around for support, but the crowd would not commit.

"There's nothing wrong with me, but there will be something wrong with you after you drink this, pass out, and get worked over by me and a broom handle," Daisy said. "I saw you slip something into her beer. What was it? Rohypnol? Date rape? Fuck you. Drink the god-damned beer."

The boy who had been talking with Daisy, with a god-given physique that he couldn't achieve thirty years later if he worked out twenty-four/seven, had stood up after Daisy threw the glass and now provided the judgment of the room, "I think you need to drink that beer," he said to the boy.

"You guys are all crazy," the boy said. He grabbed the beer and chugged it, then went off to his room. The surge of excitement declined gradually in the room as the frat-mandated music mix of Bob Marley and Jane's Addiction played on. The boy woke the next morning with permanent marker decorations, some might say improvements, all over his face and body, but no broom damage. He moved out and wasn't seen again for the summer.

"You've got a pretty good arm," said Bianca the next day, squeezing Daisy's bicep. "Thank you."

* * *

September in Seattle was a slice of heaven. Indian summer's warmth mixed with hints of autumn on the breeze, footballs in the air, Mariners long since eliminated from contention. Daisy and Bianca moved into a two-bedroom, second-floor apartment together for the following school year. It was up north on University Avenue, the Ave, near Ravenna, near the Knarr Shipwreck Lounge. That made for a longer walk to campus, but the pair didn't mind; it also made the rent a little cheaper. The apartment building looked like a motel, with covered exterior walkways.

Ravenna Avenue, with a park-like tree-and-grass-filled median, snaked its way from their apartment to Green Lake, and the two regularly jogged around Green Lake and back, turning young men's heads.

Daisy had turned twenty-one the previous summer; Bianca was still twenty but possessed a flawless fake ID. Thursday nights were spent at Dante's, a sprawling college bar, for dollar-pitcher night. Pitchers of PBR, or maybe MGD, or maybe Oly were lined up on the bar and were yours for a buck. Everyone drank directly from the plastic pitchers. Daisy and Bianca played pool, pop-a-shot, college boys, Frogger, and Ms. Pac-Man. After last call, they would stumble back to their apartment together, pepper spray at the ready.

Tuesdays were pool tournaments at the Knarr. The dive bar was perched on the edge of the U District, but most of the clientele were blue collar. The bar was Viking themed to the extent it had any theme beyond run-down beer joint. Bianca played in the pool tournament weekly, with Daisy generally cheering her on. Bianca won two games all year: one on her competitor's scratch on the eight ball and the other on her competitor accidentally sinking the eight ball. Winning wasn't Bianca's goal as much as meeting people.

Finals week ended in early June, blue books and scantrons filled and filed. Bianca approached the apartment following her last final with a snippet of lilac in her hand. Wispy clouds sailed by high in the sky. Daisy was sitting on their balcony, which doubled as the exterior walkway, drinking coffee. "Another year in the books. Smell this–June perfection," Bianca said, handing the lilac to Daisy. Bianca poured a coffee and joined Daisy. "Any word on your job hunt?"

"I've got a second interview at IntelliScope.com, looks promising," Daisy answered.

"I've really enjoyed living with you this year," Bianca said, pouring Baileys into both of their coffees. "You're the closest thing to a sister I've ever had."

Momentarily stunned by a sensitive thought from Bianca, Daisy choked on a sip. "Wow, from you, that's really something. I love you too. Best year of my life."

"Let's do something to commemorate it. Our sisterhood. Your graduation and becoming an adult."

"What do you want to do?" asked Daisy.

"Tattoos!"

They bussed to Pine Street on Capitol Hill, Seattle's counter-culture center, to get their virginal tattoos. Daisy went first, with her eponymous flower on her inner-left forearm, white petals, yellow center, and green foliage outlined in tattoo-blue. The white petals were faint and subtle on her skin.

"Does it hurt?" Bianca asked as Daisy was under the needle.

"You'll like it," answered Daisy.

Bianca flipped through the sample books, eventually settling on a cartoonesque, sexy she-devil: Hot Stuff's hot stuff. "Where is the most painful location to get a tattoo?" she asked the tattoo artist.

"It varies person to person, but generally the top of the foot, the ribs, or any personal sensitive areas," he answered.

"Okay, let's go with the ribs," she said, and got the tattoo on her right side, midtorso.

10

The new lab glistened in its stainless-steel technological prowess. Located on a leafy side street just off the Cal Berkeley campus, it featured state-of-the-art equipment, leaving Bianca wanting for nothing. Even the lab mice had their choice of Cheddar, Swiss, or Havarti; no trailer park Velveeta mice allowed. Bianca ran her hands over the machines, dials, beakers, petri dishes, automatic latte machine, spectrometer, calipers, syringes, science. The lab was a night-and-day change compared to Dr. Olmstead's on-campus lab that Bianca had worked in last year, with its broken HVAC system, broken-down equipment, and worn-out inspiration. A Golden Bear compared to a gaunt grizzly.

Bianca was pursuing a PhD focusing on molecular neuroscience, researching pharmaceuticals to influence the brain. Her advisor, Dr. Samuel Olmstead, had produced ground-breaking new anti-depressant and anti-anxiety drugs decades earlier. During their initial interview to assess whether he would be her advisor, he mentioned his long history working with and success in developing new anti-depressants. "How's your home life?" asked Bianca.

Dr. Olmstead was nearing retirement and not in demand as a PhD advisor. The world of science had passed him by. He was playing out the string and everyone knew it. A pioneer thirty years ago, he was now content to farm his homestead. Bianca didn't care, though. She just wanted an advisor who would stay out of her way. The affable, balding, tweed-clad, elbow-patched, bespectacled Olmstead fit the bill.

The new lab came as a surprise to Bianca and the other grad students who had worked in Dr. Olmstead's prior on-campus lab. There had been no knowledge among that group of the new lab until just after the spring semester started and even then, certainly no knowledge of the luxury they would step into in the fall. The Olmstead Brain Science Laboratory would cement Dr. Olmstead's legacy in the academic world.

The lab was paid for by Dr. Olmstead's long-time corporate business partner, Scorze Pharmaceutical Research Corporation. Scorze was majority owned by Hee Molecular Sciences but obscured through a series of holding companies with headquarters scattered in countries across the globe. Hee, in turn, was owned by a consortium of pharmaceutical companies of which Green Shoots Investments was a major shareholder. A man somewhere was the CEO of Green Shoots. Thus, the org-control chart, if anyone could ever piece it together, was He-Shoots-Hee-Scorze.

"Sam, how did you get such a great new lab?" Bianca asked Dr. Olmstead one day in the lab. "I mean, Prozac's great and all ..." her voice trailed off. "But this lab is beyond expectations in every way."

"There's great interest in our work, Bianca."

Is there? thought Bianca.

* * *

There hadn't always been so much interest in Bianca's work. Shortly after she started the doctoral program, Cal Berkeley and Stanford had a program in which graduate students could present their research topics to one another as a way to foster a broader intellectual community and help students extend their professional networks. Bianca of course volunteered to participate. On a Saturday morning, she waited in the assigned room in Sequoia Hall on the Stanford campus for others to arrive. No one did. At five past the assigned hour, she double checked her paperwork: right room, right day, right time. At ten past, she was about to leave when a young, wiry, goat-like man skidded into the room, with tight blonde curls flopping about and a scraggly beard. "I'm sorry I'm so late. Hello, I'm Brian Stevenson," he said panting. He extended his hand. "Where's everyone else?"

"It's just us so far. Bianca Zanone," Bianca said, shaking his hand.

After waiting another five minutes or so, they concluded others weren't as willing to give up a Saturday morning to discuss neuroscience as they were. Bianca suggested they discuss the research over brunch, so they walked to a restaurant that Brian recommended near campus.

Brian's research at Stanford involved neural connectome mapping, or figuring out how each neuron connected with all other neurons, and the connectome's information processing implications. He had not intended to present that day, just to listen, but gave Bianca an overview as they walked to the restaurant.

At the egg-centric restaurant, there was no wait despite it being fairly busy. Bianca and Brian scored a window table, looking out on the sidewalk and street. They ordered mimosas to start, and waffles and blintzes to share. They chatted while waiting for the food, getting to know each other. The food came quickly, with a mountain of whipped cream atop a giant waffle and a variety of blintzes. They shifted samples of food from the serving plates to their personal plates.

Bianca launched into her prepared spiel. "My research is aimed at influencing the brain's interpretation of stimuli, specifically emotional interpretations. Among other things, if successful this could result in a quantum leap in treatments for depression and anxiety relative to today's brute-force pharmaceuticals. Currently, the most effective anti-depressants on the market are based on flooding the brain's synapses with serotonin. These are selective serotonin reuptake inhibitors, or SSRIs. Serotonin, of course, plays a key role in happiness and mood; by flooding synapses with serotonin, mood improves, anxiety lessens, depression departs. Prozac, Paxil, Lustral, citalopram—all of these are SSRIs that work in this manner. On the illicit side of the drug trade, MDMA, aka ecstasy or molly, has a similar modus operandi.

"But human physiology isn't simple; increasing serotonin doesn't just increase happiness. Serotonin modulates a wide range of neural activity. Side effects occur.

Suicides increase, for example. SSRIs are a blunt tool to tweak the most complicated machine in the universe, like whacking the brain with a rubber mallet and hoping for the best. Like getting drunk by bathing in wine."

"Like getting a video game to work by blowing on it," said Brian between bites.

"Ha, yes! We used to have to jam a VCR tape on top of the video game cartridge in the old Nintendo to get it to work.

"So the question is, can we influence the brain's interpreted emotional state in a more subtle manner, without the brute-force SSRI approach? And also, can we target a wider range of emotions in a way with few or no side effects?

"Science has known for many years that the brain's interpretation of an arousal is important to the subsequent course of the body's response. For example, wandering the African savannah, a human sees a lion. The human's stress response kicks in with a shot of adrenaline into the blood steam, enabling a fight-or-flight reaction, elementary-school science. But in the grade-school version, the process is a one-way street. The brain sees the prowling lion, interprets it as a threat, instructs the adrenal glands to release adrenaline, and then, prepped for action, figures out whether to fight or run. Classic fight or flight. Reality isn't so simple, though."

"It never is," said Brian as he refilled his plate.

"First, notice the arousal mechanism: a shot of adrenaline; and the reaction: quickened heartbeat, increased blood flow to muscles, quickened breathing, dilated pupils, perspiration, suppression of digestion. These are similar for a vast range of underlying causes.

The initial glimpse of the lion produces similar *initial* arousal as other stimuli: a pornographic image say, or needing to slam on a car's brakes to avoid rear-ending someone. The physical reactions are not identical, but close, different shades of gray. Once the initial arousal is triggered, even artificially with, say, a syringe-administered dose of adrenaline, the rest of the body's arousal-response system kicks in with a cascade of reactions.

"But why is the body aroused? The brain is tasked to supply an interpretation. The body demands an interpretation in order to continue its reaction. The brain, having not triggered the arousal in the case of an artificial stimulus via an administered shot of adrenaline, tries to come up with a narrative that fits the situation. Cute boy over there? Okay, I'm feeling sexy. Asshole at the next table hassling the waiter? Okay, let's go with anger. Snake in the grass? Okay, fear it is."

Bianca had been picking at her food while she spoke but noticed Brian was ploughing through the food. She recalibrated her estimate that there was no way they would finish the whipped-cream mountain to an even-money proposition.

"Now here's the kicker. Even when the stimulus is natural rather than artificial, the neocortex generally doesn't interpret the situation *before* the brain calls for an arousal response. That is, a person isn't consciously aware of the lion before the adrenaline is released. Instead, the amygdala—which, I'm sure you know, is a very old part of the brain evolutionarily speaking, common to most brains in the animal kingdom and buried deep beneath humans' wrinkled neocortex—the amygdala triggers the arousal cascade before cognitive interpretation.

The amygdala acts first, calling for the release of adrenaline, and the amygdala is generally thought to not play a significant role in conscious awareness. So we feel the arousal *before* consciously interpreting the reason for the arousal.

"Instead of 'see lion, consciously interpret threat, release adrenaline, fight or flight' the real sequence is 'see lion, release adrenaline, consciously interpret threat, fight or flight.' That is, the arousal comes *before* the conscious interpretation. The 'see lion' step only precedes the 'release adrenaline' step in the sense that the visual system captured the image—so the brain *saw* the lion—not in the sense that the person consciously saw the lion. So, the arousal comes before we know a lion is there (if we define 'know' to mean to be consciously aware of the lion).

"The time gaps between steps are very small, of course. So people naturally think they are scared because they consciously see a lion. But really, they are suddenly aroused and then they interpret that they are scared by the lion. The bugle blast of adrenaline forces the brain to focus on the issue at hand and interpret the stimulus. The brain then modulates the initial arousal signal based on the interpretation. So arousal precedes interpretation and then is modulated by the conscious brain's interpretation of the stimulus. In other words, the natural situation is remarkably similar to getting an external shot of adrenaline and subsequently demanding an interpretation from the brain.

"That's where the consensus science ends and where my research begins. My goal is to influence how the brain interprets the arousal. As you know, the brain does not have a central consciousness location where all the various parts of the brain send their input to be interpreted by a poor player who struts and frets his hour upon the stage. There is no stage for the poor player. Instead, consciousness arises from the brain as a whole—somehow. Most brain areas are specialized for a specific type of processing, but consciousness itself, the human experience, is not generated by a specific brain section. It's an emergent function of the whole brain—somehow. Does this sound like a tale told by an idiot?"

"I've got to admit, I'm a little rusty on my Shakespeare," said Brian, as he continued to make food disappear. "That Shakespeare reference was planned, right, not off the cuff?"

"Guilty," said Bianca.

"No, I actually like that it was planned. Well done."

"Okay, so new competing thoughts, or interpretations, bubble up constantly, but through a winnowing process only one is able to rise to the level of attention, of conscious awareness, of feeling. Or, more accurately, not only one thought, but one gestalt of different components of consciousness: abstract thought, emotion, and sensory input. The sound and the fury," Bianca winked. "Certainly, neuronal feedback loops between brain regions play a role in this winnowing process, as do rhythmic brain waves, or gamma waves. The exact process governing the competition to pop into consciousness, though, is unknown. I want to impact which interpretation gets propagated into consciousness."

The waitress brought another round of mimosas.

"Since we're two new friends eating brunch rather than colleagues sitting in a lecture hall, I'm going to go on a tangent, okay?"

"By all means, let's explore tangents," said Brian.

"So, I originally become fascinated with the process of how thoughts take over consciousness while doing sensory-deprivation meditation. A friend had a practice space for his industrial-goth band with severe soundproofing in a basement, and no windows. The room shut out virtually all light and sound. A black void. He let me use it for meditation sessions. Initially, my goal was a quiet mind, balance, peace, blah, blah, blah. But within the first few minutes of the first session, I became fascinated with the process of thoughts popping into my head. Initially I tried to stop thoughts from popping in, thinking that my goal with meditation was to stop thinking, but in fact what was really interesting to me is how the thoughts were popping in. I changed my focus to concentrate on the thoughts. No Buddhist anti-ponderings for me.

"Some came from seemingly nowhere, just some random concept. But more often, they were tangential references to a current thought. So my meditation sessions turned into observational studies on thought percolation. Thoughts chased down tangents, then ricocheted on pattern recognition run amok." Bianca moved her arms through the air at odd angles. "For example, a seed thought might be 'blackness' from my visual observation, then came the bubbling tangents: ... swamp ... Creedence Clearwater Revival ... church sanctuary ... communion wine glasses and tray ... seeded-pattern fruit ... break—why was there a break? Who knows? New seed: tiger—why a tiger? Who knows?—tiger ... tabby cat ... Top Cat ... Cleo ... beret ... raspberry beret ...

raspberry syrup ... the waffle you're gobbling down."

"I should really leave the rest of the waffle for you, but it's *so good*," said Brian.

"Please, finish it. I'm not very hungry," said Bianca, secretly wondering if he would be able to.

"From that meditation experience, I decided that I wanted to understand the process of thoughts taking over consciousness, how does it happen and how can we influence it. Now, in that example I gave, the thoughts were mainly triggered by word association or associated memories. In reality though, there are all sorts of triggers—both in the environment and in your thinking. That experience got me interested in the process of a thought, or interpretation, getting into consciousness. I think the emotional interpretation is a practical first step. Hence, my research agenda.

"Of course, consciousness has a unitary quality, the conscious being feels a coherent, single, mental existence. However, that mental existence is still composed of several simultaneously experienced layers, including emotion; sensory input: visual, auditory, olfactory, taste, hunger, touch; and abstract thought. For example, you might be happy, smelling ocean air, and thinking about where the nearest coffee stand is. You experience these in an integrated manner, but you can also break them into component parts of the whole. Each element of the gestalt competes to get into consciousness. Potentials bubble up from the neural spaghetti bowl and compete to enter conscious experience for a shimmering moment of stardom. I want to understand that process for emotion. I want to *control* that process for emotion."

"Do you think we're anywhere near the point of

being able to do what you're suggesting, affecting conscious interpretation in a refined manner? I mean, I agree it is fascinating, but aren't we decades away from that being even remotely tractable? And I assume you don't want to wait that long to get your PhD?" asked Brian, scratching his scruffy beard. "There's so much that needs to be understood first, starting with even a remote idea of how consciousness works."

"Well, we'll find out," said Bianca. "I don't think we necessarily need to understand consciousness before we can effectively affect which thoughts or emotions propagate into consciousness. After all, hundreds of thousands of people undergo general anesthesia every day, and we don't know why or how it shuts down consciousness. We just know it works."

Bianca saw that the serving plates harbored only a few remaining crumbs.

"We do know how food comas work, though. I can't believe we finished all that food. And by we, I mean you," said Bianca laughing. "My god, how are you so skinny? Hey, since you clearly like to eat, would you be up for an occasional dinner with friends?"

11

Bianca's research regimen progressed nicely during her first three years at Berkeley. Experimenting on lab mice, she tried to affect which emotional interpretation would bubble up and take momentary control of consciousness. Functional magnetic resonance imaging, or fMRI, could reveal which parts of the mouse brain were more or less active at certain times. It was difficult, though, to know what the mouse was interpreting, what the mouse was feeling. So Bianca targeted lust and anger, both of which could be inferred by the mouse's behavior—did the mouse slap tail or tail slap?

With fMRI and behavioral views, Bianca would then flash-freeze the mouse in a vat of liquid nitrogen to fix its brain chemistry in its then-current state. She would measure the neurotransmitters and other chemicals present, in which parts of the brain, and in what quantities. She read the mice's minds. That gave her some chemical targets, some levers to pull and dials to turn, neurotransmitters to wiggle and hormones to waggle, to try to affect the emergent interpretation by using a drug cocktail of agonists and antagonists for the various chemicals. Bianca's attempted interventions did not target the brain wave aspect; she hoped that the electrochemical intervention would be sufficient, and the rhythmic synchronization of gamma waves that seemed to be critical for an interpretation to expand and enter consciousness would take care of itself.

After months of failures, in which the lab mice were more interested in drinking sugar water than in either sex or fighting, Bianca eventually found some target drug combinations that had weak but statistically significant effects. And critically, when she flash froze and examined the chemical brain states, there were similarities to mice who naturally grew lustful or angry. *Eureka*, she thought upon discovering the first target. *Eur-fucking-reka.*

It would be easy to administer existing conventional drugs that would make the mouse lustful (just a little alcohol in its feeding tube) or belligerent (just a little alcohol in its feeding tube). But those conventional drugs were akin to flooding the brain with serotonin, bathing in wine, but even more extreme, flooding the body with hormones. Bianca's approach was subtle, affecting only which emotional interpretation bubbles gained momentum and emerged victorious as the brain's interpretation of the stimulus.

* * *

Enjoying a double tall from the new lab's automated latte machine, Bianca took inventory of her life of trying to influence mice to get off. She sat on a wooden bench outside the lab's entrance with a view toward the Berkeley campus, waiting for her once-a-semester check-in with Dr. Olmstead in his office within the lab. Young college students walked by wearing backpacks, blue jeans, and sweatshirts. The rays of California late-summer sunshine matched her mood, but not her midnight-inspired lab attire. A few more years, likely, to finish her dissertation and receive her PhD, and then she would attempt to get a professorship at a respected school. A lifetime of research, teaching, and publishing awaited. Consciousness provided the ultimate scientific challenge, a tough nut she could try to crack, or contribute to cracking. What an opportunity, she thought. A monumental scientific challenge that intersects with the core of human experience. Consciousness understanding consciousness in a self-referential loop.

"Miss Zanone, how are you?" Dr. Olmstead asked, striding in. "Ready to get your hands on this shiny new equipment? The Olmstead Brain Science Laboratory has a nice ring to it, yes?" They walked through the lab to Dr. Olmstead's office. Sitting down, they discussed Dr. Olmstead's summer travels and the outlook for the current semester's research. They reviewed the classes that Bianca would teach as a TA. At the end of the conversation as Bianca rose to leave, Dr. Olmstead removed his glasses and fiddled with the nose bridge. "Oh, one more thing, Bianca, I'm going to need bi-weekly status reports on your research: experiments conducted, experiment design, drugs tested, outcome observations, everything—err on the side of over-reporting."

"Every two weeks? Why so frequent? At that pace the status will usually be a jumble of half-conducted trials and non-verified results, half-baked interpretations. Do you really want to see that? I'll be spending all my time on reports. I'd prefer to keep our existing cadence." During the prior three years, Bianca had submitted progress reports quarterly that documented her early successes in affecting the brain's emergent interpretation of emotion.

"I'm afraid I must insist. Our process has been a little lax," he said, putting his glasses back on. "We need to be more rigorous with our documentation and status reports going forward. Your research is generating attention. I know the reporting is a bit of a pain, but it will help me to keep everyone informed and provide guidance to you on likely drug candidates and next steps."

Everyone informed? Bianca thought. *You provide guidance to me?*

* * *

Two weeks later, Bianca walked down Telegraph, stopping for a beer at a pizza place's back patio. Remnants of patchouli from the sixties wafted by. *Do I build the atomic bomb, or not?* she asked herself.

Until recently, perhaps naively, she had pursued her research primarily as personal and scientific curiosity, as well as the obvious next step in career building. But it seemed clear now that others, with deep pockets, were interested. Her work, if successful, would be one of the first concrete steps in mind control. Extrapolating not too far and not too wildly could lead to severe world-changing consequences. A government could cause feelings of nationalism or loyalty to out-compete thoughts of justice and freedom. Advertisers could have their day, causing feelings of need or want to triumph. Different formulations could be crafted for different purchasers, if they had the money. Autonomy of thought would start to erode.

On the flip side, thought-control drugs promised potential personal freedom too. Thoughts of strength and health could beat down thoughts of drug addiction; yes, other physical symptoms would need to be overcome, but the mental victory would be a huge step. People could take a formulation to feel more confident, or more aggressive, or yes, happier, without the side effects of the current brute-force anti-depressants. Or a drug could make people more creative; a formulation could assist more random, tangential, or abstract thoughts to propagate into consciousness, while avoiding the side effects of other creativity supplements like marijuana. These were all decades away, she thought, but that first step was the most important.

Sitting in the shade of a giant evergreen on the restaurant's back patio, the autumn breeze gave Bianca a slight chill. She pulled on a sweater from her bag. The patio's heaters were not turned on. The waitress brought Bianca another beer and a slice of veggie pizza. Cold beer on a cool day.

Bianca thought about the modern world. It had become so complex and interconnected that hidden systemic risks could reach extreme levels before being identified and could be almost impossible to remedy. Decentralization helped limit the scope of failure, but also stymied effective countermeasures. It remained to be seen whether the Y2K bug would wreak havoc across the world's software landscape. Pathogens have long flourished in unprepared ecosystems, either aided or unaided by human consciousness. Smallpox was a scourge to Native American tribes, aided by infected blankets. Viral pandemics have repeatedly swept the globe: the Plague killed over one hundred million in the years around 1350—over twenty percent of the world's population. More recently, the Spanish Flu of 1918 and HIV/AIDS invaded unprepared ecosystems. The Irish Potato Famine showed the vulnerability of a society dependent on a single factor, healthy potatoes. Scores of financial crises and bank runs over the centuries demonstrated the problem with systems built on confidence when that confidence wanes. Self-reinforcing cycles especially, within complex systems, were a recipe for hidden disaster.

But all of these paled in comparison to the biggest systemic risk of all, mind control. Stripped of the ability to combat the enemy with thought, humans could be controlled en masse with little expense. *Is there any reason to think mind control could not sweep through the human population? What defenses would we have?* she thought. The only limiting factor would be drug delivery, how to force, or trick, everyone to take the drug. If that were solved, whoever controlled the drugs would control the world. Sure, there would be biological differences among people such that some people could not be mind-controlled effectively, but the world's brains are far more similar than dissimilar. Armies could be raised with complete loyalty and blood thirstiness; mental slaves could push labor production to extreme levels. Hope would be gone, replaced by whatever interpretation the controllers wished, maybe artificial happiness. Humans' natural tendency to mimic peers' beliefs and actions would exacerbate things: things seem okay to everyone else, so they seem okay to me, too.

If I can develop these drugs, though, and choose not to, someone else surely will, she thought. She wasn't so vain as to think these were just achievable by her brilliance. At best, she might have five to ten years on the next researcher, given the state of the science. So, then the question became should Bianca perform and control the work or allow that role for someone else.

Bianca drank her beer and admired the evergreen under which she sat. It must have been hundreds of years old. Berkeley grew up around it. The modern world grew up around it. Complexity mushroomed around it. Complexity hides risks, and trees. The tree went on, converting carbon dioxide and sunlight into oxygen, energy, and biomass, oblivious. One day it will die, and the complexity will devour its small patch of earth too.

* * *

"Who paid for the new lab?" Bianca demanded of Olmstead, bursting into his office, her black hair falling out of a loose ponytail. He had been playing Tetris; the geometric shapes quicky topped-out to failure as he looked up.

"What's the meaning of this? It's not like you to just barge into my office. Is something wrong?" said Olmstead, reacting, his face starting to flush.

"Be straight with me, where is the money coming from? This lab cost a fortune. Why now?"

"Most of it is from Scorze Research. It is a company that oversees R and D in academic settings, interfacing with the pharmaceutical industry. They've supported my work for at least twenty years now; we've done some work-for-hire for them over the years, too. They wanted to honor my legacy with this wonderful lab and surely to cement their relationship with others after I retire. They're interested in your work too Bianca—you have a very bright future. Is something wrong? Maybe you preferred the old lab?"

"What information do you give to them? What are they paying for?" Bianca continued.

"Well, that is a gray area. Of course, the work-for-hire results were their property. But with our normal research, as you know, we publish some results for all to see, but other results we don't. I do keep them apprised of what is happening in the lab, and frankly, that helps open doors for my students, like you. It's how academic science works: we get funding from industry; industry gets our pure science output."

"Do you trust Scorze?"

"I do. You have to realize, they're a business. I think they want to help the progress of science, but they also want to make money. Nothing evil about that. The American way. But they've always been fair to me."

"Who's your primary contact at Scorze?"

"Look, I really don't appreciate this inquisition. I assure you, Bianca, the arrangement is above board and very typical in academia. The lab investment was approved by a university committee that oversees relationships with industry. You would prefer to work in the old lab, huh?"

"You already said that. Stay with me here. Who's your contact?"

Olmstead was a clown, and Bianca could have ripped him apart intellectually, but that was not her move. She had searched public records and found that Scorze had indeed paid for the new lab and had paid Olmstead seventy-five-thousand dollars in honorariums and consulting fees over the last year. Earlier work-for-hire projects were noted, but no dollar amounts listed. Trying to untangle the maze of holding companies to tie Scorze to its parent companies proved much more difficult, though. Bianca faced one dead-end after another.

She knew Scorze was willing to pay a huge amount of money, somewhere between one to two million dollars, she estimated, for the lab and incentive payments to Olmstead, and that certainly wasn't for any research her fellow grad students were doing on slug nervous systems, vision processing defects, or neuron mapping. Mind control was the goal. And Scorze clearly didn't want meddling kids tracing its sponsors upstream.

Needing information, she met one of her more shadowy acquaintances, Serge, for cocktails. They met in an upscale bar on Kearny in San Francisco's financial district as office workers streamed toward happy hours. Serge was the type who emerged from dark rooms filled with computers only to source new equipment, a Silicon Valley castoff. White hat, black hat, no one really knew; sometimes one, sometimes the other; probably a dungeon master earlier in life. Bianca needed to hack into Olmstead's email. She needed concrete details as to whether Scorze was dangerous. "Can you hack into Olmstead's email?" Bianca asked.

Serge sipped his Grey Goose and Red Bull, which had elicited a condescending sideways glance from the handlebar-mustachioed bartender when ordered. "You know Cal Berkeley is public, right? Accessing public entities' systems hardly qualifies as hacking; they basically put their data on the curb with a big 'free' sign on it."

"Okay, Serge, I feel you. And impossible to track back to us, right?"

"Bianca, please."

They took BART across the bay to Berkeley and went to the undergraduate library. Settled in an alcove near the back of the second floor, protected by a flank of studious Asian girls, Serge had Olmstead's email account pulled up in fifteen minutes. "People still use all these physical books?" Serge asked, looking around at the shelves full of bound paper, yielding control of the terminal to Bianca.

Bianca dug through Olmstead's emails and got the name of Olmstead's contact: Brett Goodwin, VP of Business Development for Scorze. Olmstead had multiple strings of emails with Goodwin, stored in a "Scorze" folder—apparently not concerned about getting hacked. It seemed the seventy-five-thousand dollar publicly disclosed amount, technically for lectures and consultations, was backed up with an additional two-hundred-and-fifty-thousand dollars under the table.

Olmstead had sent Bianca's periodic lab progress reports to Goodwin. "Argh, that is unbelievable! Who the fuck does he think he is? That has to violate ethics standards." She took photos of the emails.

"Serge, can I get continued access to Olmstead's email, without him being aware?"

"Sure, I can build you a backdoor. Just access it from a burner tablet that you don't use for anything else, and only from public wi-fi spots, got it?"

"Got it."

Bianca also engaged a Wall Street–analyst friend to better understand Scorze's shadowy tentacles. Its ownership structure was exceedingly difficult to ferret out. The company was primarily used as an intermediary by several pharma companies to keep an arm's length distance from certain dealings. But Scorze had more ominous connections, too. An apparent sister company had significant dealings with an Iranian company known to have ties with Iran's chemical weapons development program. Another company linked by a common ownership group had ties to the Gaddafi regime in Libya, and a Scorze-owned affiliate had significant transactions with a company believed to be a shill for the North Korean state. *These guys are not boy scouts*, thought Bianca, *or maybe they are*—remembering scouting sexual-abuse reports.

The next day, Bianca logged into the lab's network and subtly but effectively falsified all the data on her past research, including the back-up copy on a separate server. The lab had laughably little security against internal sabotage. She maintained multiple encrypted copies on her personal laptop and an external hard drive.

12

For the next year and a half, Bianca took full advantage of all the lab had to offer. She dutifully filed her biweekly status reports. Sadly, progress on drug combinations to boost targeted emotional interpretations into consciousness stalled. An Olmstead-initiated retrospective review of the prior successes conducted to shed light on why the progress had stalled suggested confounding variables had not properly been controlled for in the earlier work, and the initial results were spurious.

After several months of non-progress reports, Olmstead called Bianca in for a talk, worried about the direction of the research, curious about the abrupt change of luck. These discussions increased in frequency and urgency throughout the year. With the increased urgency, Olmstead pored over the lab reports and experiment results. The discussion shifted to call into question whether Bianca could publish a dissertation given the current status of her research. "Look, Miss Zanone, I don't know what game you're playing, but this is not your best work."

"Kind of like using a four-bar horizontally?" Bianca asked, seeing the reflection of Olmstead's paused Tetris game in the window. His office was newly rearranged to shield his monitor from visitors.

"Huh? Never mind that. Some of my colleagues think there are curiosities with your research. I of course defended you, but I must admit, this is a head-scratcher. They think the lack of results is suspicious."

"Which colleagues? Do they know science is a process of trial and error?" Bianca asked.

"No matter," Olmstead replied. "But the ice is getting thin, Miss Zanone. We all expect your best work."

"I was thinking of switching to a new research topic," Bianca said. She swept a semi-circle on the floor with her foot.

"No, that would be a very bad idea. We all have faith in you, you are on to something critical. Just break through. Switching now is not an option. Persevere!"

Toward the one-and-a-quarter-year mark: "Bianca, my legacy is on the line here, can you find nothing but dead-ends? You need results and you need them soon."

At one-and-a-half years: "Your future in this program is in serious jeopardy. If you want to graduate, you will need some new research success and it better start damn soon."

Bianca monitored Olmstead's email regularly. Olmstead passed her reports on to an increasingly frustrated Goodwin. There was a discussion of a planted student to keep an eye on Bianca. Bianca thought through her various lab mates, not having suspected any of them of complicity.

Goodwin had leaned hard on Olmstead. "I'll teach

that bitch a lesson if you don't, Sam, she's playing us for fools. I need results!!! This isn't a fucking game—we've got serious commitments. My clients aren't the type who smile and say nice try."

Toward the end, Goodwin wrote "You know that little cunt is hiding things, falsifying things, damn it! Take control of your god-damned lab." The SSRIs kept Olmstead on a more even keel, it seemed. Goodwin finished, "You're going to get us both fucked."

Hmmm. That gives me an idea, thought Bianca.

* * *

Bianca resigned from the Cal Berkeley PhD program, walking away with encrypted files on her laptop that solved the first step of mind control. Nine months later Olmstead retired, the lab was renamed for a flourishing research professor, and Olmstead's other graduate students had to move back to the run-down campus lab.

Bianca's next step wasn't clear to her. She could apply to a different PhD program, but she wasn't motivated at the moment by any other research idea, at least any research she was willing to let anyone else see, and she liked the idea of a bigger change. She had several connections in the pharmaceutical industry and could easily land a high-paying job, but that seemed a little too career-oriented.

She decided to do what she did best: expand her network. Bianca travelled the world, flying ultra-economy and couch-surfing to save money when possible, building relationships with every neuroscientist who would meet with her. Neuroscience was a small, close-knit professional world, unlike the organ it studied with its billions of neurons and trillions of synapses. The papers Bianca had published while at Cal Berkeley were more than enough to open doors.

She also built relationships with people from organizations one might not list on a resume: some targeting to expand consciousness with new and interesting drugs, some combating governmental mind control, some working on artificial consciousness. And then there were the consciousness philosophers, the least wholesome of the lot.

Bianca was everywhere and got to know everyone, embracing connections both in the legitimate academic, scientific, and business worlds, and in the more shadowy, underground variety. When there was a topical conference, Bianca was at the happy hour, making friends, then making friends of the friends' friends and so on. She had a near photographic memory, which she would say doesn't exist, and could recall names and life stories with ease. Her mouth had a natural sneer, a look of disdain, but her eyes shined with a sparkling intensity that drew a person in. The combination led those she met to think they were in her inner circle, the two of them sharing a fight against the idiocy of the rest of the world.

After close to a year of penny-pinching travel, Bianca was ready for the next step. She went to work for a pharmaceutical company located in Santa Barbara working on Alzheimer's drugs, PTSD drugs, and autism drugs. A breakthrough on any of these would be a life-changer for many people, she told herself, not to mention a cash cow for her company. But it was the mission that attracted her. Imagine the cumulative parental anguish she could eliminate if she developed a drug to materially eliminate the effects of autism—it could be among the largest eliminations of suffering produced by one person in the history of the world. The mission, the stability, and the salary, not to mention the lab equipment and access—it made sense.

The company made some progress over the next decade plus, and Bianca made wads of money rising up the ranks like ecstasy-fueled dance-floor energy. Of course, being Bianca, she built relationships with everyone she met, and her network continued to grow, as did her dinner roster.

* * *

Three years after Bianca had withdrawn from Berkeley, Brett Goodwin, then a Senior VP at Scorze, made numerous week-long trips to Austin, Texas. He had two purposes. First, he was developing and expanding Scorze's relationship with University of Texas scientific faculty. He showered the community with steak dinners, speaking honorariums, and consulting fees. A pharma company that Scorze was newly affiliated with was also located in Austin, and Goodwin was tasked with expanding the collaboration between the two companies. When in town, he usually stayed at the Cactus Flower Hotel, a boutique hotel located between the nightlife of Sixth Street and the UT campus, not far from the state capitol. The hotel's bar was small, with seating for no more than twenty patrons and did not have a discernable name other than that of the hotel. The décor was Texas chic:

longhorn horns, neon cacti, Modelo signs, white-leather upholstered stools and booths, and turquoise touches. Goodwin often ate at the bar when not wining and dining Longhorn laboratory laborers. And regardless of his dinner establishment, he invariably ended the evening with a prickly-pear margarita in the hotel bar.

As Goodwin took the first sip of his second margarita, the glass's rim wasn't the only salty attraction. A beautiful woman in her midtwenties, hair in a ponytail and glistening with sweat from a just-finished workout approached the bar next to where Goodwin was seated and ordered a Tito's soda with lime. She wore matching workout bra top and shorts, with the shorts ending at her uppermost thigh, body hugging—completely inappropriate for the bar—leaving nothing to the imagination. She downed the vodka soda in two swallows, took the lime from the rim, and held it up toward Goodwin. "Who wore it better, the vodka or the tequila?" she asked, nodding to his margarita and motioning to clink limes, which Goodwin did, and then the woman bit down on her lime wedge. "God, I shouldn't be in here dressed like this," she said to no one in particular, although Goodwin was the only person within hearing range. "*Uno mas, por favor*," she called and motioned to the bartender. "And a Patron shot for *mi amigo*." When the drinks came, they clinked glasses, "Cheers," and threw back. They chatted for a few minutes. "One more cowboy?"

Goodwin, enjoying the situation, breathing in the pheromones, brain kicking in its million years of sexual alertness training by filling consciousness and body parts, said "Of course," and signaled for the bartender.

"Another round, please."

The woman put up her palm as a stop sign to the bartender. "I've got a better idea," looking at Goodwin. "Give us the rest of that bottle of Patron. Put the drinks on my room, my friend's too." She grabbed a cocktail napkin and pen that was on the bar, wrote her room number, printed and signed her name, grabbed the Patron and Goodwin's hand, and led him off. "Navel shots," she said, "with my little salty rim." Goodwin could have said no, but his married life had not been a sexual bliss of late, opportunities like this never happened, and what the hell anyway.

When the video came out online, there had been no blackmail demand to keep it private. The woman had been hired by Scorze as an administrative assistant two weeks prior to the hotel pow-wow. The video included power-differential reinforcing lines like "Tell me what you want me to do," "You're so powerful," and the capper: "So you won't fire me for that scheduling mishap, right boss?"

The blood drained out of Goodwin's face (and another key organ) when he heard that, but that reaction didn't make the final cut. He was fired and effectively unemployable for any professional management job.

The woman shot Bianca a text: "He came, they'll see, we conquered."

13

About twelve years into Bianca's tenure at the pharma company, a professor in UC Santa Barbara's Dynamical Neuroscience graduate program asked if Bianca would teach a series of seminars for the grad students. Bianca's employer loved the idea as a form of community outreach and for the potential to recruit promising students for employment. Bianca also loved the idea—getting back to academia, even as a guest lecturer, felt right. She taught a single one-hour class every two weeks each quarter. The classes covered multiple topics related to the content of the rest of the seminar series, providing a pharma perspective.

One of Bianca's classes focused on theories of episodic memory stimulation and recall and related pharmaceutical interventions. Bianca had done extensive research on memory as part of the R and D for the PTSD and Alzheimer's compounds her company was developing. Memory recall was also of particular interest to Bianca as a critical element in the spontaneous popping and subsequent spreading of ideas into consciousness. "A pattern is perceived in current stimulus that triggers a memory with a related pattern from the past, and the triggered memory cascades through the brain, grabbing momentary control of attention, of consciousness, then is tossed for the next, and the next," Bianca explained to the class. The dynamic was analogous to emotion interpretation but on declarative-memory content. Could drugs modulate which memories popped and made it into conscious awareness? Judging by the time the students spent on their phones compared to being engaged by her slide deck, Bianca concluded the students were somewhat less fascinated by the topic.

The auditorium-style lecture hall had a seating capacity of 175 students, but the graduate seminar series had far fewer students enrolled than that, with typical attendance of around thirty students. Bianca never understood the reason for the lecture hall location, probably bureaucratic ignorance. That quarter, her time slot was Friday at 3:00 p.m., suboptimal for student engagement. The memory recall talk fell on Halloween, a double whammy. The class lacked interaction and pace.

A gentleman whom she did not recognize sat in the top back corner of the hall, near the exit. It wasn't unusual for UCSB faculty to sit in on these lectures, so his presence wasn't unusual, although his solitary seat removed from all the others was out of the ordinary. He was older than the students, most likely in his fifties or sixties, overweight, wearing a Portland Trail Blazers baseball hat pulled down over his forehead, glasses with tinted lenses, and a windbreaker over a button-up shirt, untucked.

The lecture finished. "Okay, it's over guys, you leave now," Bianca told the class a few minutes earlier than normal. The auditorium lights were on throughout the lecture so there was no lighting cue for students who were less than fully attentive that it was time to transition. "Get your costumes on; start your parties; get out of here." The students filed out and Bianca gathered her materials, somewhat disheartened. The man from the back row approached the stage.

Bianca recognized the man as Allen Paulson, software mogul and co-founder of the largest software company on the planet, a billionaire several times over, ranking near the top on the list of wealthiest Americans. "Allen Paulson," he said, extending his hand, which she shook. "Are you free for a bite to eat?" He spoke softly, stammering somewhat.

"Wow, Mr. Paulson, it's an honor to meet you. Unbelievable really," Bianca stammered back.

They walked to a seafood restaurant near the beach. Clouds had blown in from the ocean, but the weather was still pleasant. The situation didn't seem quite real to Bianca, strolling with a legend in the tech industry, not to mention a billionaire. Over appetizers, Paulson spoke of his Brain Institute in Seattle. His vision was to bring the best scientists together and make progress on understanding the brain, from brainstem to cerebral cortex, from axo-dendritic synapse to dendro-somatic synapse.

"I talked to the scientists at the Institute," he said. "They told me you were the brightest up-and-coming brain scientist of your generation. They told me you dropped out of the Berkeley PhD program and went to work for pharma, wasting your talents, like Mozart building pianos rather than writing music. They told me I should recruit you to the Brain Institute. Naturally, I'm a little bit skeptical, not that you are talented, but of the hyperbole of the title of brightest neuroscience mind of her generation. If this is so, why is she not pushing the boundaries of neuroscience? So I reached out to my friends on the faculty at Berkeley, and they subsequently asked around to understand why this rising star had dropped out. The feedback they heard was that your advisor had had a sweetheart deal with pharma, and you didn't like it. Or perhaps that you objected to pharma's access to your work. My contacts said the sweetheart deal was specifically for your research, and then mysteriously the research proved unfruitful, very suddenly."

The world spun around Bianca. Paulson—Allen Paulson—had pieced together her past, events that had long ago receded from her own rear-view mirror. Why? She twirled her spoon around her clam chowder.

"You seem to have made quite an effort to research my background, Mr. Paulson, I'm flattered." She couldn't believe she was having a meal with Allen Paulson. She knew several relatively well-known people, perhaps some who would qualify as famous, and would converse with them like she would her neighbor, ignoring the imagined hierarchical social structure. But Paulson was different. An icon. Alone here, for the sole purpose of talking to her—providing a synopsis of her grad-school experience. It threw her for a loop. "Beyond flattered, quite frankly I'm shocked to be eating lunch here with you right now."

"Please, call me Allen. And, yes, I do value information, but you are surprisingly well-known for someone running in the rather ordinary pharma rat race. I take it you are active in several, say, underground communication networks. I don't mean to imply anything illicit, I'm not the most articulate man, just communication outside of the normal staid world of science. Speculative theories that border on sci fi, unconventional ideas, partial data/knowledge extrapolations, dancing on the knife edge of research, guessing at what it all means.

"So, Ms. Zanone, let me get to my point. Please come to work for the Brain Institute. As I'm sure you're aware, we have ample funding, the latest technologies, the most powerful computing support, several scientists who already respect you and would welcome you onto the team. You would have wide latitude in your research scope. Let's get you back to working on science."

"I'm honored," said Bianca. "That is a great opportunity. And based on the depth of your research, I'm sure you already know I have roots in Seattle, having done my undergrad work at the University of Washington."

"Yes, Go Dawgs."

They finished their light meal and strolled along the beach back toward campus. Groups of costumed students were roaming, prepping for an Isla Vista Halloween. Despite the overcast skies, the community buzzed with electricity.

"So I'm flattered that you came down to talk to me and still can't really believe I'm hanging out in Isla Vista with Allen Paulson—do you know how many times Excel has crashed on me, by the way? But I don't think you would be here just to give me an employment offer?"

"Right you are, Ms. Zanone," Allen said. "I do have another objective." He paused from walking and threw a small rock into the waves. "You see, I need your help.

From what I gather, you are the only person on the planet who can provide what I need. And of course, the employment offer stands regardless of this additional request."

They resumed walking, heading inland toward the school. "And I am presuming a bit here, but I'm pretty sure you spiked your doctoral research. Beyond that is mainly speculation, but my guess is that the reason you agreed to work in pharma for a decade was for the lab resources you could secure in order to continue your research with no need to publish results.

"My niece is in trouble, you see. I need your help, Bianca. I need mind control."

* * *

"Been talking to Paulson about me?" Bianca pressed send on the text while sitting in bed, watching a streaming show that was too complicated to half watch, half surf her phone, so the show would be abandoned a few more episodes in. The text wound its way through air, wires, air again, and to Brian Stevenson's phone, in his pocket, in the Brave Horse tavern in the South Lake Union neighborhood of Seattle. Amazon and Mr. Paulson had bought and redeveloped broad swaths of the neighborhood over the last decade, transforming it from rundown, small-scale, single-story retail: auto-body shops, guitar shops, pawn shops; into a tech hub with mixed-use buildings for tech bros to live and play: restaurants, bars, labs, server rooms. Property values had tripled. Tech bros tippled. Grunge had been toppled. Chief Seattle had been trampled.

A streetcar ran to and fro between downtown Seattle and South Lake Union. It was named South Lake Union Transit, and its advertising beckoned people to "Ride the SLUT." That summed up South Lake Union: newly prosperous, overly prosperous, an area that had entirely lost its edge and tried to manufacture a new, artificial edge.

The Brave Horse was one of the new bars. Long wooden tables and benches filled an expansive open space, encouraging groups to collide and interact rather than be siloed at smaller tables.

Brian had received his PhD from Stanford and was now a lead scientist in the Brain Institute's effort to produce neural maps of mouse and human brains. Science had thus far produced a complete mapping of the roundworm's nervous system. Roundworms are one millimeter in length and have between three hundred and four hundred neurons. The human brain has about eighty-six billion neurons. Each neuron averages about seven thousand synaptic connections with other neurons. Brian's job was a big one.

The Brain Institute was only a few blocks from the Brave Horse. It sat on the southwest edge of Seattle's urban Lake Union. Across the lake to the north was the Wallingford neighborhood in which Daisy's house was tucked.

"Hola Zanone" Brian texted.

"Well?" - Bianca.

"Yeah, but Paulson knows everyone and everything. Yes, he talked to me. I said hire Zanone" - Brian.

"But I'm sure he heard about you from others too. He has resources $$$" - Brian.

"So, did you get recruited?" - Brian.

"By the man himself" - Bianca.

"Yowsa! Seriously? Jealous" - Brian.

"You're not exactly secretive about your work, you know" - Brian.

"The underground meshes with above ground" - Brian.

"When do you start?" - Brian.

"Still considering" - Bianca.

"Seriously, great place to work. Labs, technology, computing, brilliant people. Seattle. Why the hell wouldn't you come?" - Brian.

"Not sure the world is ready" - Bianca.

"So you've got something!!! I knew it" - Brian.

"I'm worried about unleashing a monster. Lots of potential abuses. Big systemic risk" - Bianca.

"On other hand, I'm worried it could be an arms race. If other, less scrupulous people develop these first, watch out. Maybe better to sprint now to take the lead" - Bianca.

"It's like this, who do you trust? Pharma? You're nuts. Government/military? You're wacko. The world's best brain scientists and one of the world's richest men who shuns the spotlight and power? Bingo" - Brian.

"Thanks B, we'll see. gn" - Bianca.

"Night" - Brian.

"You're a fast texter for a scientist, btw. Better lay off the speed" - Bianca.

Bianca lay back in bed, her head buried in an oversized pillow, absorbing the magnitude of the opportunity in front of her. Life didn't offer crossroads like this often, she thought. When one comes, it's best to take it.

And this opportunity was so perfect. *There is no way I can't walk down this road. It's barely even a choice. I would be crazy not to do this, and my life would hinge on the missed opportunity. I'd always be looking backward, rear view mirror.*

So she loaded up a truck, and she moved to Jet City, Queen Anne Hill that is, left-wing fools, Tesla cars.

Her apartment faced west to collect sunsets over Puget Sound with the Olympic Mountains in the distance, and an easy commute to SLU.

14

"So y'all aren't still wearing flannel and torn denim?" Bianca, dressed in black faux-leather skirt, midnight-blue silk blouse, and black pumps asked the room in general.

"Come as you are," retorted the man sitting at the head of the conference table. He looked ex-military with a muscular build and short cropped hair. He introduced himself as the project manager. Also in the room was a woman, midthirties, wearing blue jeans, tee shirt and blue-rimmed glasses. Her auburn hair was cut short and asymmetrical.

They sat in a conference room in a South Lake Union building owned by Mr. Paulson. No signage existed that would signal the company or office's purpose. The conference room's windows overlooked Lake Union. The boardroom-style table, perhaps mahogany, was far larger than the three attendees needed. They clustered toward the end with a large video screen.

"Julia Bronson, now twenty-five years old," the man spoke authoritatively, advancing to the first slide in his deck, which was a picture presumably of Julia Bronson.

Her strawberry-blonde hair curled inward to frame her round face, not quite pretty, but not ugly either. "Julia entered the Kansha Kokoro compound in June 2013, about a year and a half ago. Kansha Kokoro, or Thankful Mind, was started in the early 2000s by Masaki Kami, who claims to be the brother of Jesus and Buddha by way of some difficult to follow time/soul/reincarnation theory. The compound is a sprawling five-hundred-acre campus in the shadow of Mt. Fuji, sixty miles southwest of Tokyo. Julia is Allen Paulson's niece, although we suspect the cult does not know the connection. She hasn't been heard from since entering the compound."

The presentation rolled through a series of reconnaissance photos of the complex, taken by drone. "We are able to see Julia in reconnaissance photos and she appears to be physically well. We estimate the compound houses approximately five hundred people, most of whom never leave. The perimeter is enclosed by chain link fencing topped by razor wire. People are theoretically free to come and go, but it is viewed as a spiritual failure to interact with the world outside of the cult. The razor wire is claimed to be required to keep the compound safe from outsiders and Japanese authorities, although the cult doesn't seem to be breaking any laws, other than low-level drug use. There is no evidence they are dabbling in chemical weapons or planning attacks. Japan is naturally nervous of cults since the famous Aum Shinrikyo sarin attacks on the Tokyo subway in the midnineties.

"While people are free to leave in theory, there are a series of guard posts that one must pass to actually leave. At each point the guard questions the member's integrity and spirituality if they choose to leave. The guard instructs that they are possessed by an evil spirit and offers a healing ritual the member should perform. In the course of our surveillance over two years, we've only seen two people make it through the guards and leave the compound on foot. Thirty-two have approached the first guard, seemingly intending to leave. Once out, a person would face a six-mile walk to the nearest town or an attempted hitchhike on a country road with minimal traffic. They would have no money, no identification, and only the clothes on their back.

"Julia was in Tokyo teaching English, after having graduated from the University of Oregon. She was living in an apartment with two other American women. She started attending 'meditative yoga experiences' hosted by Kansha Kokoro. They offered a wide array of sessions, from beginner yoga to hot yoga to a disorienting yoga with fog machines, light show, and blaring sound effects. All were said to strive to unlock personal enlightenment, to create a thankful mind. Her roommates reported that Julia really enjoyed the various sessions. The last one she attended was an invitation-only class. Participants were blindfolded and lead through a series of passageways in a human chain, holding the hands of other participants. Finally, they reached a room filled with light and the sounds of a fountain.

"Still blindfolded, they were spaced out and began yoga poses combined with mental focus exercises. The leader repeated phrases such as 'You are ready,' 'You have been chosen,' 'Realize who you are,' 'Claim your enlightenment,' 'Push yourself.' At one point, it was said that the cult leader, the Glove of God, Masaki Kami, entered the room and walked through the rows of participants. 'Can you feel him?' the yoga leader repeated. 'He is among us. The Glove of God.' The blindfolds had electrodes that aligned with the participants' temporal lobes. We believe these were activated in an attempt to produce a spiritual epiphany the moment the leader supposedly walked past. We doubt that the leader was actually there.

"In any case, it worked on Julia. The next day she emptied her back account, packed some clothes and a few items in a backpack, and disappeared without a word to her roommates. They got worried eventually and reported her missing to the police. Apparently, this isn't unusual, and Kansha Kokoro regularly reports new soul seekers, as they call them, to the authorities. It behooves the cult to stay on good terms with the police.

"About a year after she entered, we sent in an ex-special forces operative, Mina here," he motioned to the woman in the room, who nodded, "to attempt to extract Julia. The operative went through the same yoga process and was actually able to pocket the blindfold which is how we learned of the process and the electrodes. She made it into the compound.

"There is a strict hierarchy within the compound. New recruits are assigned to one of several lowest-level work duties: vegetable gardening; animal farming: goats, cows, chickens; janitorial; maintenance; kitchen; or laundry. Work duty is performed in groups of three—all male or all female, with monthly rotation of members among the three. Communication with members outside of one's immediate trio is severely limited outside of sanctioned events. Mina was required to leave for repeatedly trying to communicate with others, attempting to get in touch with Julia. The entire compound is bugged for sound and video by the cult's leaders.

"Every evening there is a worship and teaching session that all members generally attend. Members are seated, either on the floor or folding chairs, with their work-duty trio. Usually, the Glove of God addresses the members, walking among the groups. If he isn't there, another leader takes his place. There is singing, chanting, and preaching. All in all, not too unlike a church service here in the States, other than the seating.

"Every three days there is a celebration of life. Nine members, all male or all female, meet. Beer, sake, and marijuana are available, and music plays. Every nine days, this is replaced by a celebration of spirit, in which nine males and nine females meet. All of these meetings begin at sundown and end at sunup; of course many members opt for bed before sunup, and that is fine. Sex is optional at the nine-day parties; beds in alcoves are provided, but couples are not allowed to leave the gathering—the only option for leaving is to return to one's sleeping quarters.

"Every full moon, the nearest three/nine-day celebration is replaced with a compound-wide bacchanal. All rules are essentially off from sundown to sunup. Members can talk with whomever, sleep with whomever. There are three primary rooms: one with a rave/club vibe with electronic dance music, dancing, lights; one with a drum circle; and one with a meditative vibe, incense heavy in the air. Alcohol and marijuana are available, maybe other drugs to a lesser extent. The leaders and other high-ranking members have private bedrooms—they select partners to sleep with.

"Julia was assigned to vegetable-farming duty for her first six months in the compound, then has worked in the school for the compound's children for the last year or so."

"Can you tell me which of the three rooms she usually attends on full-moon hoe-downs?" Bianca asked.

"We can't tell by drone recognizance, as they are all in the same building. Mina was in the compound for one full moon and at that one, Julia was primarily in the dance room, then spent some time in the meditation room before returning to her sleeping quarters."

"Are beer and sake only available at the three day/nine day/full moon events?"

"They are available nightly in moderation; one drink is encouraged daily."

"And does Julia partake?"

"She regularly has a glass of sake."

"Does she partake in any of the drugs?"

"We've seen her smoke marijuana. Sometimes the events are outside. We've never observed her doing other drugs, but we don't have visibility on most of the full-moon celebrations, as they are typically indoors. Mina does not think Julia used drugs on the full-moon celebration she attended."

"Do you have constant drone surveillance?"

"We did for about one year. Now we send the drone up when we expect to see people outside. Their schedules are very regimented."

"Can the cult members or leaders see the drone?"

"It is visible to the eye, but we fly very high. It is not like the drones people play with here that are loud and obvious. It just appears as a small dark speck in the sky. We have observed people point at it but haven't observed any signaling or messages intended to be seen by the drone. Nor have they tried to shoot it down or stop the surveillance in any way. It is possible they could suspect Japanese police surveillance given the history of cult attacks on the public in Japan. It's possible they welcome the surveillance to demonstrate that they are not breaking any laws.

"The Japanese government does send in a delegation occasionally. Government officials speak to all members as a group and ask if anyone is being held against their will. We don't have perfect visibility on how many members have left via this route, but we think it is minimal, if any."

"What about audio monitoring? Are you able to eavesdrop on conversations?" asked Bianca.

"Unfortunately, no. All of their buildings have been soundproofed. We could pick up audio from outside, and we did for a while, but very little was ever said. We did pick up the audio from the guards blocking the exit when we were monitoring. In general, though, interpersonal communication is very limited within the compound, at least outside."

"And no outside media or communication makes it to the members?"

"None at all."

* * *

Excited monkey shrieks rang out as Bianca entered the enclosure, the sounds as out of place in the Pacific

Northwest forested foothills of Mt. Rainier as a sockeye salmon swimming up the Congo. The unmarked warehouse was surrounded by a fifty-yard wooded buffer zone and a security fence topped with razor wire and monitored twenty-four seven. The site belonged to Green Forest Products, Incorporated, the company that housed Bianca's work. While Bianca was officially employed by the Brain Institute, the drug development was handled in this separate company in a non-visible manner. The company was hidden through a series of holding companies such that very few people even knew it existed, and of those who did most probably thought it sold lumber or firewood or ferns. In fact, GFP, with Bianca's work, was far and away the leading company pursuing mind-control drugs worldwide. Bianca hit play on an Apple Music Chill House playlist and cranked the volume with the beats filling the facility. She got to work.

When she first arrived in Seattle to begin work, her first month was spent with the operative who had been in the Kansha Kokoro compound, Mina Carew, and the project manager for the niece extraction, Harrison Wainwright, Harry, who had presented the initial debriefing. The three spent days in the conference room in Paulson's unmarked SLU office building, providing Bianca background on the cult and brainstorming options for the next rescue attempt. Bianca tended to sit so she could look out the window, watching the boats come and go at the Center for Wooden Boats on Lake Union.

"Is the feeling in the compound one of authoritarian rule or more a communal spirit?" Bianca had asked.

"Honestly, it is hard to generalize," said Mina. "There certainly is a rigid hierarchy in place, and a progression from lower to higher levels within the hierarchy. Julia has progressed from the lowest-level farming to a higher-level school teaching. And we have observed a material number of people who seemed to want to leave. But when I was there, I did not get a sense of widespread discontent. But it wasn't a happy wonderland, either. More a newly defined way of life, solitary for long stretches of time, few close contacts—really only the three people who share sleeping quarters could be said to be really close. Other interactions are just understood and accepted to follow a rigid structure—the celebrations and the worship/teachings."

"Do you think Julia wants to be there?"

"I can't answer that. I couldn't get close enough to her to judge. I can say that most people who I spoke with did seem to genuinely want to be there, but their thinking was so muddled by admiration of the Glove, Masaki Kami, love for the leader, worship of the leader. Honestly, it was bizarre. So the personalities that I saw did want to be there, but I have to believe those people have other personalities and have been brainwashed somehow."

"Do we know if Julia has a lover?" asked Bianca.

"We believe not," said Harry. "We have never seen her involved in any romantic gestures on drone surveillance. Monogamous relationships are frowned upon. They aren't forbidden, but the cult teaches that they prevent a person from reaching one's true self. The three-person sleeping quarters are partially to discourage relationships. If a relationship is reported, it is likely the two would be separated into different sleeping quarters. She may be having sex during the nine-day celebrations or the full-moon celebrations; we do not have visibility on that."

"What is the cult's core teaching? For example, if I'm a member, what is it that is getting preached at me over and over?"

Mina fielded this one. "Reject, accept, merge. Reject, accept, merge. We heard it every day. Reject the modern world; it only distracts people from their true self; it distorts perceptions; it instills artificial desire. Most importantly, reject money. The modern world uses money to quantify value. Money corrupts one's quest for true value.

"Accept the world of Kansha Kokoro. It's a life more in line with human experience over the centuries: farming, living in nature, living in a relatively small community. Living without monogamous relationships they claim is a more natural state.

"Merge the self with the spirit. And the spirit incarnate is the leader Masaki Kami, the Glove. 'Merge' definitely had a sexual interpretation with Masaki sleeping with many of the cult members, but also 'merge' meant to pair the physical self with the spirit self, to pair the spirit self with the infinite, or the universe, or god, accessed through God's Glove. 'Reject, accept, merge' should lead to an enlightened state, something like a Buddhist elimination of self and quiet mind, an appreciation of existence."

Book Three: The Art of Being Conscious

15

The character-to-normal-person ratio in the lobby of the Tucson Ventana Canyon Resort was about two-to-one on the Monday evening before The Science of Consciousness conference was scheduled to begin. The conference attracted many of the world's preeminent neuroscientists, and the presentations were limited to serious material—or at least material created by serious scientists and philosophers who were encouraged to tend toward the speculative. The subject matter, though, did also attract a broad swath of eccentric pseudo-scientists, new-agers, and outright kooks. There was statistically significant overlap between the philosophers and the kooks.

Daisy, Bianca, and Coop sat in a bar just off the lobby. The bar sunk two steps below the lobby level, the steps being the only demarcation between bar and lobby. A patio extended the bar outdoors, overlooking a pool complex opposite the resort's main entry. Beyond the pools, a lush golf fairway, green, and tee box defied the desert. Beyond that, rocky scrubland stretched to the hills in the distance. The group, which also included a friend of Coop's named Willis Towner, sat around a small tile-topped bar table. Willis was an executive with Netflix, involved with content procurement. He sported a shaved head, probably to hide partial balding. He and Coop had played golf regularly for the last five years.

"So big sis, you want to know about consciousness and its implications for meaning?" started Bianca. "Well, I can help with the first part, but drink quickly, because the answer is science knows very little about consciousness. I'll share the science highlights, but I'm going to mix in my speculation and observations too, which, I dare say, may be more relevant in a personal quest for value."

Bianca spoke quickly, energized by the topic and the company of her long-lost friend.

"So, Daisy, tell me what you're conscious of right now."

"Well," Daisy said, putting her IPA down, "I'm in a hotel bar, drinking beer, talking with my old college roommate, my friend Coop, and my new friend—what's your name again?"

"Willis."

"Wha choo talkin 'bout," Daisy laughed, pointing her finger at Willis.

"Ah, yes, the glorious age of sit-coms," said Coop.

Daisy looked around the room. "I'm aware I'm alive; I'm breathing; I see a table, chairs, people. I smell the desert air. I feel the dryness. I hear a piano cover of 'Girls Just Wanna Have Fun.' I'm thinking about what I'm conscious of."

"Fair enough," said Bianca. "So to sum it up, you're conscious of an interpretation of your surroundings, or more generally, an interpretation of your situation, which wouldn't necessarily include your immediate surroundings. Now, you already know consciousness is somehow created by the brain, mainly by electro-chemical signals. So all of your sensory inputs, visual, auditory, olfactory—right smell, proprioception, touch, are all translated into electro-chemical signals, and interpreted. So, at its most basic level, consciousness is an interpretation.

"Now, keep in mind, using vision as an example, your consciousness doesn't really see the photons that strike your eye, for example. Those get translated to neural information, and then consciousness arises from those neurons. Hearing, same story, the sound waves are translated to neural signals. Touch, everything, same story. So your brain translates all inputs into electro-chemical patterns, and those give rise to what you see, hear, feel in consciousness. So, emotions, right, you feel those just as real as you feel a physical touch, because emotions also are interpretations of electro-chemical patterns. And further, with vision, your brain disassembles the photographic image into components that are more relevant to the organism. So it identifies edges and movement, for example. It separates brightness and color. These are processed separately, and then reassembled into the visual image you see."

Bianca's hair, with a natural bounce, kept falling into her face as she talked. She ran her hand through it over her head, which momentarily solved the problem.

"So, my opinion, not scientific consensus mind you, but my opinion is that consciousness is really just an interpretation. Now, as an interpretation, it isn't necessarily a true representation of reality, whatever that is. What I mean is, what you see or hear is influenced not just by your sensory inputs, but also by what your brain expects to see or hear. The brain's interpretation, that is, your conscious experience, is always colored by what is expected. Most undergrad psychology students subject themselves to grad students' experiments for extra credit, and half of these deal with priming since it's such a robust and easy-to-demonstrate attribute of our consciousness. Where am I going with this?" Bianca took a sip of her dirty Belvedere martini. "So, for example, in your visual consciousness, you don't really see bits of green and yellow with brown running through the center, you see a tree with those constituent parts. You can't help but interpret the visual field into objects that are more meaningful for how you interact with the world. You see a tree. Recognition of faces is very important to us, so we are primed to interpret anything remotely like a face as a face. Well, this isn't really true priming, this is evolutionary priming, so to speak.

"You've all seen the picture that can be interpreted as either an old hag or a young lady, depending on which way you look at it. You don't just see the image, the pure shapes and colors, which are of course static, you see it as either an old hag or young lady. Also those Magic Eye optical illusions, with images that pop out at you if you can kind of look through the page. Whether you see the intended image or not, the shapes, patterns, colors, the pure photon-transmitted visual is constant, but sometimes you perceive the intended image and sometimes you don't. So your conscious experience is an interpretation, not just a representation of reality.

"The same is true for sound. You generally can't hear a word in your native language without simultaneously comprehending its semantic meaning. Horse, right, it could be an interesting sound, but you consider it as an equine reference and the pure sound gets somewhat lost. Not so with foreign languages, there you hear the true sound of the words. *Mo ippainomu.* Beautiful, right? That means 'have another drink' in Japanese, but you could only hear the sounds of the words. Sometimes you can get to that point with a word in your native language, especially a word without a concrete representational meaning, a preposition for example. Let's use 'of.' If I say 'of' over and over, I can usually eventually get to a point where I'm only hearing the sound and almost forget the semantic meaning of the word: of, of, of, of, of, of, of, of, of, of, of, uhf, uhf, uhf, uhf, uhf, uhf, uhf, uhv, uhv, uhv, uhv, uhv, uhv, uhv, uhv.

The waitress came around and asked if the group wanted another round. Everyone consented.

"Where am I going with this? Since our consciousness guides us around this physical world, it's a fair bet that consciousness does a very good job of producing a reasonably accurate interpretation of the world, or at least the world that we can interact with. Right, string theory posits ten or eleven dimensions, but we can only interact in three spatial dimensions and time. But does the world really look like what our consciousness sees? That's an interesting question. And just using vision as an easy example, the same is of course true for other senses. Right, we look at this tabletop and we see blue, or as the resort would like us to say lapis lazuli, or at least lapis style. But what is it really? Well, it's a molecular structure that reflects certain frequencies of light. Is it really the blue we perceive—who can say? I'd say, not really, it's not really any color. It's just kind of a shimmering mix of matter that reflects certain frequencies of photons. I think of Predator, or Terminator, whichever was the freaky liquid metal or see-through guy."

"Terminator was the metal guy, Predator the see-through guy," said Willis.

"Okay, I'm not a huge movie fan, but the point is all we can ever know is our interpretation. Blues, pinks, greens, right, it's all just our interpretation, corresponding to information in the world, but in a format that is useful to us from a survival perspective—or, as you all know from public school, God bless America—from a reproductive-fitness perspective.

"So, that's a little bit mind-blowing, and you are all taking it in stride, so show a little more amazement. My sexy cocktail dress isn't really black, we just perceive it as black. All we can really say about the external reality, or the information content, is that the dress reflects a certain wavelength of light, giving it the color we perceive. This Men at Work cover doesn't really sound like we interpret it, its sound, its information content, is just the frequency and amplitude of sound waves. It's just information."

Coop obliged by motioning with his hands that his mind was being blown.

"Much appreciated, Coop.

"Okay, so if consciousness is just an interpretation, as I'm suggesting, you might ask what about higher-level thought, logic, reasoning, mathematical thinking, etc. A couple points here. Which animals are conscious? We of course don't really know, but it seems highly likely that a lot of animals are. To make it easy, let's get far away from edge cases and just focus on mammals. It seems highly likely a dog is conscious. The good boy has eyes, ears, smell, lots of similar brain structures as humans, and acts like he's conscious. But he clearly doesn't have all of the intellectual talent of a human. He doesn't have language, and very likely doesn't have abstract-reasoning ability. So, you might be more inclined to grant me that a dog's consciousness is just an interpretation, but humans, with our big cerebral cortexes and abstract thinking—that is, thinking about things that are not in our immediate experience, reasoning as well—is a different ball game. And certainly, it is a huge difference. But at a meta level, it is still just taking information and interpreting it. That information isn't limited to perceptual information; it can include prior learning of trigonometry, for example, but it is still an interpretation. It all gets represented electro-chemically in our neurons before being interpreted. Just like vision."

Daisy sucked down the last swallow of her IPA and looked hopefully for the waitress with a trayful of drinks. "What was that Japanese again? *Mo ipanamu*? I'd like to have another drink."

Bianca cleared her hair again and cocked her head to the side.

"Another cool point that you may have never thought of. And isn't it very rare to have a thought at our age of something that you haven't thought before? So the cool point: consciousness is the only thing in the universe with aboutness. Thoughts are about something else. Your thought is about that tree, or my dog. Well, information content created by consciousness also has aboutness. You'll hear this referred to as intentionality, but just think aboutness.

"How cool is that? Really? The only thing that exists in the universe, as far as we know, that is about something else is consciousness. That's mind-bending to me. It seems like that could have something to do with meaning and value." She nodded toward Daisy.

"I'm thinking about my beer," said Daisy.

"Where am I going with this? Well, you'll hear over and over here at the conference about the Hard Problem. Everyone here is giddy about the Hard Problem, and with good reason. It's pretty rare in science that you get such a fundamental problem that can be easily understood by everyone and with such huge consequences. So, the Hard Problem. One prep step first. So, modern scientists are by and large physicalists, or materialists. Madonnas. Material girls. Right, so they believe in and do research on the physical world. Molecules, atoms, subatomic particles, electrons, photons, forces—strong and weak nuclear, electromagnetic, fields. And they've pushed the science to the point that it is very difficult for anyone to understand, but with great success—success in being able to predict how physical items will interact. However, the Hard Problem is 'How can the physical world give rise to our conscious experience?' How is it remotely possible that physical neurons produce conscious experience? The classic example is an experience of redness."

"I told ya, Coop," Daisy interjected, thinking back to her discussion on consciousness with Coop. The waitress came around with their drinks.

"So, the experience of redness," Bianca continued, "or a qualia as it's called, a subjective experience of color. And maybe there has never been a more apt name, that is a hard problem. So hard that no one has any good idea. Or, I should say, any idea with any scientific evidence backing it up.

"One school of thought tries to solve the problem by denying that consciousness exists. And, if you think about it, that is really funny. The only thing anyone has ever experienced is their consciousness. Ever. From the first animal that sensed a twinkle of light—maybe through its pineal gland for our third-eye fans—to all of us today. We only directly know the interpretation of our consciousness, every touch, pleasure, pain, the smell of a rose, or lilac, smashed up olive taste." She sipped her dirty martini. "But this school of thought tosses that out and says it doesn't exist, and instead only the physical world exists. We just misunderstand consciousness they say. You can probably tell I'm not a student of this school of thought.

"But, if we accept that consciousness exists, then we are stuck. How does it exist? And that is what no scientist can tell you currently. Most neuroscience now focuses on the neural correlates of consciousness, or studying what physical brain regions and states are correlated with what conscious states. There's a widespread belief that the physical brain causes the conscious states, but science struggles to understand even what a conscious state is, it's nowhere near to understanding how the physical brain causes it. The Hard Problem."

Bianca's speech increased in rapidity and volume as she gained momentum and her cumulative vodka level rose.

"There are lots of speculative outs, but none with any scientific evidence. My personal favorite is to consider that consciousness could be a fundamental aspect of reality, just like a field in physics, say an electromagnetic field, or a force like gravity. The universe has this fundamental aspect of consciousness that emerges. This doesn't answer the Hard Problem of how it emerges, but instead it sidesteps it. Consciousness exists just like the physical world exists, just as part of reality. The more we learn about physics, the more the interaction of fields with particles and waves becomes important. For example, the Higgs field is now needed for particles to have mass; mass is created by particles moving in a Higgs field. Perhaps there's a consciousness field—a Zanone field perhaps?—that creates consciousness when certain information passes through it. Wild speculation of course, but not crazy. Given that consciousness exists, it doesn't strike me as too outlandish that our universe is somehow tilted to enable consciousness. Of course, the physicalists would howl.

"If I were a textbook at this point, I'd have to go into all the boring history of dualism, physical and mental, blah blah blah. Without fail, books always feel they need to recount the dated thinking of hundreds of years ago. Anyway, this worldview could be considered dualist.

"But here's the part I like. Not why does consciousness exist, the answer to that is that's just how our universe is, but *when* does consciousness exist? The answer to that ... anyone, anyone?" Bianca motioned to her three drinking mates for a response. No one volunteered an answer. "Consciousness arises whenever anything is interpreted. Now, all I've really done is define an identity. I've defined consciousness as interpretation, and interpretation as consciousness. But this sets up a worldview, or universe-view, that I like. The universe is composed of information and interpretation, and that's it. That's the yin and yang of the universe. Everything the physicalist scientists study is information. Everything mental is interpretation. Information and interpretation. Interpretation and information. You can't have one without the other.

"It's an interesting question, though, can you have one without the other? Mainstream thought is that consciousness only exists in animals and it evolved, meaning the universe existed from the big bang for billions of years before the first consciousness popped into being. Who knows? Maybe it's a one-way street, maybe you can't have consciousness without information, but you can have information without consciousness. But at that point, the information wouldn't be information, it would just be ... I don't even know what to call it ... data? Or maybe the whole universe was just in some massive quantum superposition, meaning in all possible states, until the first consciousness came along and collapsed the wave function. And possibly something that is in all possible states doesn't hold any information content. This is just drinking speculation and certainly wrong, but these are the reasons you have so many people off the street at this conference, it's fun to think about. It's fundamental to our existence. We consider ourselves quite advanced scientifically, but science is still blind on this one."

"I like that," Daisy said. "Information and

interpretation."

"Think of general anesthesia," said Bianca. "General anesthesia doesn't block the nerve signals from getting to your brain, it blocks the brain from being conscious of the signals, blocks the brain from interpreting the signals. In the surgery, cuts are being made, the body still sends pain signals via nerve impulses to the brain, but they are not interpreted. The information still occurs, but not the interpretation. Or maybe the information doesn't occur, but only the physical impulse occurs—if we want to try to draw a distinction between physicality and information.

"So maybe it's just a matter of perspective, a matter of the lens through which you view reality: the physical lens or the consciousness lens, with information/interpretation being the dynamic through the consciousness lens. Maybe somehow reality has these alternate aspects that are both true but don't really intersect at all.

"Okay, one more thought to add here. Why did consciousness evolve? What does consciousness add to our evolutionary fitness that the pure information and the processing of that information does not? That is, consider our brains processing all of the information that they do now but without the epiphenomenon of consciousness arising. These are referred to as zombies in the philosophical jargon; they have all the information but none of the subjective experience, no interpretation. In terms of behavior, a zombie would be indistinguishable from a person. That would mean consciousness adds zippo from an evolutionary standpoint.

"Now, there are a few outs. Perhaps, it is easier for this level of information processing in animals to evolve in a manner with a conscious element than without; still, the consciousness serves no purpose, but it would be feasible that it could evolve despite having no purpose. It's just easier, in the universe we live in, than the same amount of information processing without consciousness. Now on its surface that seems curious, since it still involves all the same information processing, but perhaps if consciousness is a fundamental aspect of reality it comes with some information processing advantage.

"A common route folks take here is that consciousness is needed in order to make decisions, in order to have a free will. But this is very problematic. Just what entity do we want to assume has a free will? You, of course, but what you? Presumably not your physical body; it's pretty clear that everything in the physical world follows physical laws and there's no room for free will. So then how about your mental self, which is what common sense would dictate has the free will. But what exactly is that? It would seem odd to suggest that this mental state could in any way affect the physical world, and if it can't affect the physical world, then it clearly doesn't have free will in the way most of us think of it. Also, go back to my information and interpretation worldview. If consciousness is just interpretation, it is not in the decision-making business, it's just interpreting what's going on with the information. So basically, free will is out the window."

The sun had set, and a purplish dusk settled over the desert beyond the golf course. Banks of lights clicked on at the tennis center.

"Okay, hopefully your minds are reassembled from the prior blowing because I'll aim to reblow them here.

Daisy, you just reached out your hand and grabbed your glass. Here's the amazing thing: your brain sent the nerve signal to initiate that action before you were consciously aware that you would make the motion to grab the glass." Now Bianca mimicked Coop's earlier mind-blown hand gesture.

"To me, that is incredible. Did you all catch what I said. The nerve signal comes first, meaning the brain decided to move the hand, not that Daisy consciously decided to move her hand. All Daisy's consciousness did was interpret the signal, interpret the information. She saw and felt her hand move toward the glass and came up with an interpretation that fit the situation, that she had decided to take a drink. And in a sense, she would be right: her *brain* did decide to take a drink, but her *conscious self* did not; her conscious self only interpreted her physical brain's decision. Even the word 'decision' in this context is a little odd because it implies a different decision could have been made—but it seems like the physical brain does not have such latitude.

"So, consciousness just interprets actions after the fact. At least that's what some very sophisticated experiments suggest. Free will would mandate the conscious decision comes first. As it is, it sure seems like consciousness is just along for the ride—the interpreter. And if you sit back and contemplate it, at least to me, it does feel like most decisions just happen, they just pop into your consciousness. Even if I'm actively, mentally, weighing pros and cons, at some point a decision just is made. It doesn't feel like I actively make the decision, but rather that I feel a decision has occurred. I interpret the brain state that reflects the decision."

"I actually have an example," said Coop. "An example of consciousness providing an interpretation, not of this sequential timing issue. A few years ago, I started using a CPAP machine for sleeping; I have sleep apnea, so I would stop breathing about twenty times per hour. For years before I started using the CPAP, I would have dreams that I needed to urinate but couldn't find a suitable location. I'd find a urinal in my dream, but it would be overflowing; I'd find an empty field, but the wind would blow so hard back towards me that I couldn't pee without getting it all over me; I'd find a bathroom, but it would be so crowded, jam packed with people, that I couldn't pee without getting it on someone. Then, when I started with CPAP, those dreams just stopped. I think what was happening was my dreaming brain was interpreting the lack of oxygen—as I stopped breathing in the real world—as some equivalent stressor in my dream. My body probably released some stress hormone, and my dreaming brain tried to figure out why.

"There were other stressed dreams too. Sometimes I would need to hit a golf ball, but the ball wouldn't stay on the tee, or I couldn't get a full backswing because a person was in the way, or a clump of earth was interfering with where I wanted to strike the ball—really crazy problems. Or I was dribbling a basketball but couldn't control it because I was wearing gloves, and I couldn't take the gloves off. All sorts of interpretations of the lack of oxygen from the apneas. All gone when I started CPAP."

"That's a great example, Coop," said Bianca. "I had not heard that effect before, but I think your assessment is spot on."

"Alright, I've made my contribution to the conference," said Coop.

"I have one too," said Willis. "When a name or word won't come to you, all you can really do is wait for it to pop into your head. It's not like you can systematically instruct your brain to work toward an answer, you just have to wait for it, then suddenly it pops into your consciousness. So perhaps behind the scenes your brain recovered the information, then it popped into conscious interpretation."

"Nice," said Bianca.

"So, to wrap-up, what can the pure scientific consensus really tell us, at a high level?" Bianca continued. "First, there is not one part of the brain that is the center of consciousness. It seems to be spread across multiple areas of the brain. That isn't to say all parts of the brain are equally privileged to the production of consciousness, they aren't; some are demonstrably more important. But there is no little homunculus—you have to hand it to scientists, everyone refers to this little brain guy as a homunculus, I don't think I've ever heard of a homunculus in any other setting—maybe my gay uncle (ba da boom)—" Bianca motioned the classic comedy drumbeat, "but really, there is no central stage of consciousness. The experience of consciousness isn't really different depending on which brain region is the then-dominant active region.

"Second, consciousness requires a certain frequency of brain waves to ripple through the brain. Brain waves are electromagnetic waves caused by billions of neurons firing rhythmically, in a synchronized manner. At a slow frequency, say below four hertz, that is, four cycles per second, a person is asleep and not conscious. As the frequency increases, you're conscious but relaxed, meditative. Gamma waves in the range of around forty hertz are associated with attentive consciousness. They seem to bind parts of the brain together to direct attention. Also, feedback and feedforward loops between the cerebral cortex and the thalamus seem to play key roles in consciousness. So, there you have it, what science knows: no homunculus, gamma waves, and cortical-thalamic feedback. Consciousness. Oh, the brain-wave amplitudes could play a key role too, but that's more speculative. How or why these lead to conscious experience, no one knows."

"I thought it was information moving through a Zanone field," said Daisy, winking.

The group fell silent for a moment, each taking a drink of their respective beverage: Bianca martini, Daisy beer, Coop margarita, Willis old fashioned. Bianca checked messages on her phone and excused herself to make a call.

16

The lobby bar had become crowded with conference attendees. The tables were all occupied. Daisy's group enjoyed the prime table real estate they had staked out early on with its view of the darkening hills out the patio. A sweet dusty scent blew in on the breeze from the desert.

"You two as college roommates would have been trouble," Coop said.

"Yeah, it was good times, for sure. We lived together my senior year, her junior year. Seattle is still recovering," said Daisy.

"So, Daisy, Coop tells me you're looking for the meaning of life," said Willis.

"Well, I'm sure as hell not going to find it watching Netflix," Daisy winked. "Unless the meaning of life is love. How much has love paid you guys, anyway? Would it kill ya to produce a little variety? Coop's advertising is just as guilty, except more tilted toward sex. But everything, and I mean everything, is interpersonal. Everyone's value is dependent on someone else. Why? My theory is there are three life stages: childhood in which one needs their parents, adulthood in which one needs a lover, and third stage in which one finds personal meaning. You need to produce content of third stagers finding meaning, and not meaning from another person."

"You know I like that, Daisy, but here's the problem. Your demographic doesn't watch much content or spend money. They don't consume. We don't consume," recognizing all at the table were solidly third stage.

"If I spend some money and buy your drinks, do I get a stage three show?" asked Daisy.

"And in our culture, younger people will not watch a show about older people," Willis said. "So you're right, obviously. Themes are recycled and beaten like dead horses. But that's what is demanded by the audience. Excluding children's programming, which is its own genre, probably eighty-five percent of content focuses on characters in the thirteen to thirty range."

"And mainly their loves," said Daisy.

"Mainly their loves," agreed Willis.

"It becomes a chicken-and-egg question," said Daisy. "Is love so in demand as subject matter that you programmers need to focus on it, or does the love barrage of content convince viewers that love is the key to life? Probably a lot of traffic both ways. So not really chicken and egg, but a self-reinforcing cycle."

"How powerful is the media Coop?" Willis asked.

"Strong enough for me to earn a living."

A man in his late thirties or early forties approached the table, sturdily built, dressed in jeans and golf shirt. The bar had a cocktail-hour-mingle feel with conference attendees milling about, and Daisy had noticed this man standing nearby while Bianca was talking. "Hi folks," the man said, extending his hand first to Coop, then Willis, then Daisy. "My name's Mick Walker. I don't mean to intrude, but I'm here alone and you've got an empty chair. Can I buy y'all a round of drinks?" Shaking his hand, Daisy admired his strong hand and forearm, practically strong, as if from physical labor.

They welcomed him and his drink offer to the table. The conversation turned more prosaic: jobs, the conference. Mick was a fishing guide and a consciousness enthusiast.

About thirty minutes later Bianca returned. Mick recognized her as part of the group and stood up, offering Bianca her chair back. He and Bianca exchanged greetings; he wished the group well and returned to the cocktail-hour crowd.

"I had one more thought I wanted to share," said Bianca. "This is obvious, if you think about it, but pretty incredible nonetheless. Consciousness is a unitary experience." Daisy elbowed Coop, bragging about their prior conversation. "You experience one consciousness. But to produce it, billions of neurons work together. One experience of consciousness emerges from the billions of neurons. Why not a billion consciousnesses? We have two brain hemispheres that are largely redundant, not entirely, there are specialized areas only in one or the other hemispheres, but the structures are largely symmetric. Why not two consciousnesses? The neural connections and gamma-wave synchronization produce one emergent consciousness. You can add neurons and get a much more complex consciousness, say from a bird brain to a human brain, but it is still a unitary single consciousness. It doesn't take too big of a conceptual jump to think of combining multiple brains together into a new consciousness, which would likely then be a single consciousness. We're light years away from actually doing it, but conceptually easy-peasy. It's so easy to fall into sci-fi dreaming about consciousness.

"But I bring up the unitary nature for two reasons. First, it's just really cool to have an emergent unitary phenomenon, with many inputs leading to a single output. But second and more relevant, we're not going to be doing mind-melds anytime soon. So in this universe for now, you are alone in your head. Even if we did mind-melds, you'd still be alone, you'd just be a different you, assuming the unitary nature remains. When it comes down to it, based on consciousness, you have to be alone. We are starting to be able to read minds, a tiny bit, based on neural activation patterns, but only things like 'You're thinking of an apple,' not 'You're hatching a complex scheme to overthrow Canada, fucking Canucks.'"

They talked and drank too late into the night, eventually turning in for sleep. Daisy and Bianca had rooms at the resort while Coop and Willis returned to their homes.

Daisy woke the next morning to a bird song with which she was not familiar, a series of low-to-high swooping tweets. She had left her balcony door open during the night to enjoy the desert air. She slipped into the resort-provided white waffle-cloth robe and stepped onto the balcony, looking for the tweeter, but she couldn't locate it, seemingly obscured by palm trees and shrubbery. She made herself coffee from the in-room pod system and sat on the balcony. The air was refreshing in the shade, with just a hint of the warmth that was yet to come in the day. The rocky brown landscape in the distance was so different than the wet green she was used to in Seattle. She closed her eyes and breathed it in deeply. Life was progressing nicely. She was on track, or at least on her personal path. Paths are personal.

The birdsong continued, suuweep, suuweep, suuweep. Daisy appreciated it. She appreciated her forty-five-year-old physical body. She appreciated her mental self. She thought of her family, growing up, and her son Tom. She thought of lovers. She thought of friends, including the ad-man poet Coop. "Suuweep, suuweep to you birdie."

The conference provided a buffet breakfast for registered attendees served in one of the hotel's ballrooms. With a yogurt and scrambled eggs on her plate, Daisy scanned the room looking for an isolated seat. Coop and Willis weren't actually attending the conference so neither was at the breakfast; they were golfing that morning. Daisy saw Mick, the man who had bought a round of drinks the prior night, sitting alone.

"Mind if I join you?" she asked.

"Please," Mick said, gesturing to the empty place setting with an upturned palm.

"You know," said Daisy, "if you hadn't told us what you did yesterday, I still might have placed you as a fishing guide. Your forearms suggest casting prowess." Mick had a stocky build that suggested he didn't turn down twenty-ounce steaks but would have worked out earlier in the day to offset it. His sandy-blond hair, parted on the side, clumped together in a natural style. Daisy found him quite attractive.

"Do they? I'm not sure about that. Guiding is half of what I do. I also work as high-end security, protecting politicians and dignitaries and the like. Mainly because you can't fish year-round, and I need to pay the bills."

They chatted about the day's sessions they planned to attend. The conference was a virgin experience for them both. It ran five days, with plenary sessions during the days and smaller concurrent breakout sessions in the evenings.

The conversation was a little awkward; *attraction not cushioned by alcohol?* wondered Daisy. The discussion wound back to fishing. Mick guided anglers in various locations throughout Colorado, Wyoming, and Montana, but his security work took him throughout the US. Daisy caught Mick's eyes lingering on her between bites of scrambled eggs.

"Excuse me, I'll be right back," Mick said, standing up and walking off.

He returned shortly with two mimosas. "Cheers," they both said and clinked glasses.

"What do ya think of the OJ to Champagne ratio?" Daisy asked.

"Well, I asked for heavy on the Champagne, so I can't complain."

"A man after my own heart."

"So how do you know your friends from last night?" Mick asked.

Daisy explained her friendship with Coop and that she had just met Willis that night.

"How about the woman? Was it Bianca?"

"Yes, Bianca. We were actually college roommates

back at the University of Washington. I hadn't seen her for twenty years. Then actually Coop saw an ad for this conference and brought it to my attention because we'd been talking about consciousness and such, and I saw that Bianca was presenting."

"Oh, so Bianca didn't know Willis or Coop before this?" Mick asked.

"Nope."

"I saw Bianca's presentation is titled 'Autism and the Consciousness Gestalt.' A neuroscientist, a Netflix programming executive, and an advertising executive is a potentially scary trio. But I guess the world is safe for now."

"What's scary about it?" Daisy asked.

"Well, I don't know, if she were into mind control, for example."

Daisy and Mick hung together for most of the day, with Bianca flitting in and out connecting with everyone at the conference. By the end of the day, Daisy was ready to spring her pick-up line, "What do you think is the meaning of life?" but it seemed like that would play better in a bar after drinks than after a day of presentations on quantum consciousness and the potential consciousness of plants. Instead, she went with "What kind of gun do you carry on security duty?" It didn't really work, but following dinner the two did sit out on one of the resort's patios talking until the early morning, drinking Sam Adams. The sexual attraction was obvious to both.

"Are you married?" Daisy asked.

"Divorced," said Mick. "About eight years ago, now."

"What happened?"

"Lots, actually," Mick said. "We were married pretty young, at twenty-four; well, maybe that's not young. I'd spent four years in the military, then went to college right afterward. We were married when I was still in school; she had just graduated. Then we started careers. At the time, I was travelling a lot for security work, and a lot of it was confidential so I couldn't give her details of where I was or exactly what I was doing. We grew apart. Then we weren't able to get pregnant; we both wanted kids. That was probably the relationship killer. The love had faded. The dew on the rose had evaporated, the bloom wilted. And there were no kids to keep us together. We were together eight years altogether, so it took a while. Finally, one morning we woke up and looked at each other thinking, 'Why are we still together?' It was an amicable break-up."

They talked about Daisy's bartending, about experience, about the meaning of life, and about Tom. They talked about Seattle and Denver, where Mick currently lived. They talked about consciousness, and why Mick had an interest in it—personal curiosity. They talked about the Berlin wall falling, about where they were when the space shuttle Challenger exploded, about where they were when the World Trade Center collapsed on 9/11.

A little before 1:00 AM, Daisy stood up and said she'd better call it a night. Mick, standing too, offered to walk her to her room, and she declined.

"I'd take a kiss, though?" she asked, reaching for his hand.

"Yes," he said. "You have my consent." She stretched on tiptoes to reach his lips. They wished each other good night and went to their respective rooms. Daisy wondered where the suuweep bird was sleeping.

17

The next morning, Daisy met Bianca, Coop, and Mick for breakfast in one of the resort's restaurants. It was situated one floor below the lobby bar in which they had drunk the first evening. They were seated next to the window with a view of one eager family with kids already in the pool.

"Was there a love connection last night?" prodded Bianca. "Two lonely souls meeting at a conference dedicated to determining the existence of souls?" The four sipped coffee, turning the menus over.

"What's this?" Coop perked up.

"My room has a view of the pool deck and patio. These two were chatting it up pretty late."

Daisy ordered eggs benedict and changed the subject. "Your presentation on autism went well yesterday, Bianca."

"Thanks, glad you enjoyed it. I find the topic fascinating, how in autistic people we see lower brain activity in regions that indicate thoughts of the self. So when most of us think of a concept, say 'a kiss,' there is a component in our conscious gestalt that considers how we relate to the kiss. This kiss is happening to us, interacting with us. The autistic patient has materially lower activity in the brain regions that relate to the self, so they just think of an objective kiss, with no personal content. I wanted to see if I could create a drug that would knock out the 'self' brain regions, to simulate autism, but I didn't get any traction.

"I didn't talk about it in the presentation, but another thing that's really interesting is that autistic minds tend not to habituate to repeated stimuli. For example, most of us have high brain activity when we see an object for the first time. Or, say, a commercial—maybe one of yours Coop," Bianca nodded at Coop. "But then with repetition, our brain activity decreases each subsequent time we view it. We've learned what the object is, and it has no novel attributes that we need to really pay attention to. This actually may be part of brand building that advertising accomplishes. We get to a level of familiarity with the brand and don't need to scrutinize it anew, at a neural level we trust it. But the autistic person's brain doesn't habituate nearly as much, so their attention is constantly drawn to items and events that the rest of us find uninteresting."

"I want to hear about this love connection," said Coop, not done with the prior conversation topic. "Mick, you know Daisy has sworn off of love, right?"

Mick gave a dead-ringer performance of a strong, silent type, emphasis on silent.

Daisy backhand punched Coop in the shoulder. "We actually did talk about it a little bit, or a tangent. We talked about the media bombardment of love and interpersonal value." The waitress brought the food, impressively balanced on her arms in a manner that struck Daisy as a waitressing throwback.

Eyeing Coop out of the corner of her eye, Daisy said "I haven't sworn off love. Or friendship, for that matter, Coop *my friend.* But I don't think anything interpersonal is the answer to the meaning of life—or rather, the answer to *my* meaning in life. And I do think too many people just assume it is, because of the media or because of lingering biological echoes—I really don't know which is more powerful. They both contribute.

"If your meaning is tied to someone else's affection, or behavior, or opinion, you've ceded control. People change. Coop, you know that better than anyone, as you've told me about your wife. Everyone mature knows that love fades in the best of conditions. If your value depends on it, where are you when it exits. Or friendship. And so what happens, you become someone that you think the other person wants you to be in order to hold onto the love. And maybe they do the same. Then you're both missing out on who you really are, and resenting the other person for it, and starting to hate the other person. Or worse, you become someone who will fall apart without the other person in order to guilt your partner into staying in the relationship.

"No, I'm open to love, but I'm also open to leaving someone behind. Love isn't my path. It isn't my value. And now that we're on the topic, note what Christianity has done to get out of that dilemma; they've transferred the love relationship to God, about whom you can believe anything you like. God will always love you. All you need to do is love God. Hey, if that works, I'm not wanting to be critical. It can genuinely give meaning to lots of people. But as a culture, we're moving away from religion, and many are trying to replace that unwavering love with very much wavering love and affection from other mortals."

Daisy sipped her coffee. "I should have warned you I was going deep."

"Damn it, Daisy, it's too early for your meaning talk," said Bianca drinking her coffee.

Daisy continued, "I really like Warren Buffett, but one thing he likes to say is that you should judge your life by how many people love you when you die. I just think that's really misguided. Kinda like his bet on US Air. That sentiment is more along the lines of accumulating wealth, accumulating love. I've also heard him state it a little differently, as how many of the people whom you want to love you actually do. And I get his point. But I still think it is misguided. It relies on others' opinions for your value.

"So, no Coop, I haven't sworn off love, or friendship, but it also will not define me.

"Also, I think the unity of consciousness plays into my view, a bit. A couple nights ago, Bianca described how bigger, more complex brains made consciousness more refined, more capable, but still outputting just a single consciousness. Now, that's just a statement of fact. But, if we take the leap that meaning resides in the mental, or at least the non-physical, it is interesting that it is necessarily a solitary experience, forever alone. Physical bodies come together—I'm talking about sex, Coop—but souls don't. And if they did, presumably it would still be a single entity experiencing a single consciousness. Alone."

"You're love drunk this morning," laughed Coop.

"Maybe I am," Daisy winked at Mick. "But, my last point. If we agree that there is no exogenous meaning, and I think we do, and I think Western culture agrees as well, then we're left to define meaning for ourselves. I think we agree that meaning is in the non-physical realm. No amount of money, wealth, possessions, body physique, even health, none of these are going to define meaning for us. So we're left with consciousness. I, for one, will take Bianca's view on consciousness—that is, it is an interpretation. Information and interpretation, physical and consciousness—see, I was paying attention Bianca. So if we care about meaning at all—and that's a personal choice, I guess, although it seems like human nature is preconditioned to care about meaning—if we care about meaning it is up to our own singular consciousness to interpret it. That is, we interpret our own meaning.

"It's possible to adopt some ready-made meaning as your own, religion, say. Or really even sports fandom, the love-cult, hippiedom, all sorts of ready-made meanings. But we have the potential to define it for ourselves. And if we interpret it as such, then it is. Consciousness is interpretation. If we interpret something as meaningful, then it is, within the unity of our own consciousness."

"You always were a thinker, Daisy," Bianca said.

"Yeah, you're right about that," said Daisy.

The group talked about their travel plans. The conference ran through Saturday, but Daisy was flying back to Seattle the following morning, on Thursday. After the conference end on Saturday, Bianca was headed to Los

Angeles to meet with a neuroscientist at UCLA. Mick was headed to Denver, but then to DC shortly thereafter for a security job.

"Who will you be protecting," Bianca asked.

"Sorry, I'm not at liberty to say."

"Loose lips sink ships? That kind of thing?" Bianca asked, eyebrow raised. Mick drank his coffee.

"Damn it Daisy, I'm glad we reconnected," said Bianca. "I'll check out your Seattle bars."

"I'm glad too," said Daisy. She looked at the flower tattoo on her forearm, then at some ink on Bianca's arms. "It looks like you've added a few tattoos."

"Yep, but nothing like the first time," Bianca said, patting her ribs.

Following breakfast, Daisy went for a six-mile trail run, racing cacti and jack rabbits, coyotes and road runners, lizards and lingering doubts. The temperature was forecast to reach the low eighties, but during her run she guessed it was in the midsixties. Perfect.

Once again, Daisy and Mick hung out during the day at the general sessions. Bianca was here and there, sitting with Daisy and Mick for a short while, popping into the lobby to meet with someone, then someone else, and on like that.

A panel of bigwigs in the consciousness science and philosophy community were on the stage discussing the evolution of consciousness and opining on which animals are conscious. Apparently there was quite a controversy over whether honeybees are conscious. On one end of the spectrum, a panelist held out hope that even plants are conscious at some level. Another argued bees have a kind of hive mind or collective consciousness. Most came down in favor of bees being normally, but not collectively, conscious, although some argued against bee consciousness outright. To Daisy's novice mind, it seemed the definition of what would constitute consciousness varied among the panelists, limiting the value of the discussion. Many did clarify what they meant by consciousness, but the details were onerous to follow.

The ballroom in which the session was held was unbelievably cold for a resort in the middle of the Sonoran Desert. Daisy went to her room and grabbed a blazer. When she returned, it wasn't clear if she had really missed anything, as the panel was still discussing striped stingers' souls.

Daisy had always thought it self-evident that virtually all animals were conscious at some level, that they had an experience of the world: visual, auditory, tactile. They were not automatons. It would seem very unusual for parallel structures, like eyes, ears, nerves to not give rise to some type of experience.

But just four years before, in 2012, a group of prominent neuroscientists released "The Cambridge Declaration on Consciousness," a two-page synopsis on animal consciousness, that concluded with: "We declare the following: The absence of a neocortex does not appear to preclude an organism from experiencing affective states.... Consequently, the weight of evidence indicates that humans are not unique in possessing the neurological substrates that generate consciousness. Non-human animals, including all mammals and birds, and many other creatures, including octopuses, also possess these neurological substrates."

The declaration was included in the presentation materials. It spoke to the state of consciousness science that there was no real consensus as to which animals were conscious, and only four years earlier it was considered necessary to assert that many animals were conscious.

Daisy had had all the brain talk she could handle. Following the afternoon session, she retired to the pool deck, eating a grilled-chicken sandwich for dinner from the poolside bar, then lounging by the pool, lying in the desert heat. Mick stuck it out and attended one of the conference's breakout sessions following dinner.

Daisy lingered poolside. She watched the pale color scheme of the desert gradually shift as the sun set, starting with a washed out yellow, transitioning into pink and then lavender and blue. The saguaros stood lonely guard—keep your golf balls on the irrigated grass or else. Better the cacti than the rattlesnakes. Daisy watched birds flying into and out of a cavity in a nearby saguaro. After the sun finished setting, Daisy retired to her room and packed her bags in preparation for a morning departure. She sat on her balcony and drank a Budweiser from the mini fridge. She listened for the suuweep bird, but no luck. She flipped through all the television channels despite a frustrating delay between changing the channel and the channel actually changing. Nothing was worth watching.

"Whatcha doing?" Daisy texted Mick.

"Watching *Cannonball Run*" - Mick.

"What room are you in?" - Daisy.

"212" - Mick.

Mick, newly cleaned up, sat on his bed watching the movie. There was a knock at his door. He opened it to find Daisy in the hotel-provided, thick, white, waffle-cloth robe. An ice bucket in one hand filled with ice and a few beers from her mini bar.

"Looks like I'm overdressed," said Mick, welcoming her in.

"Me too," said Daisy, slipping out of her robe and onto the bed.

Later, they sat in bed against the headboard, watching *The Late Show*.

"I had an interesting thought today, poolside. A thought I'd never had before. It goes back to that animal-consciousness presentation," said Daisy.

"Yeah?"

"Think of the very first time any inkling of consciousness arose. Some slug feels a poke say. Or the first precursor to vision, the first glimpse of light. So probably in some sea creature. Before that first bit of consciousness, there was nothing in existence that could at all understand what was coming. There was nothing that could sense anything. There was nothing that could think or feel. At all. Then pop—and wow—okay consciousness.

"So think of it now, what could pop up next that we have no possible way to think of. Not just that we can't think of what it would be, but that it requires an attribute that we don't possess to even comprehend it. We don't even really have a verb to describe what it could be—not until it happens.

"That first conscious thing was the first thing that

had any ability to feel. The attribute requires itself to even be contemplated. Could something new be around the corner? It feels like no, but it also seems like at least once in history, there was a pretty incredible something new around the corner."

18

At home in Wallingford on the evening of the summer solstice, Daisy sat on her porch, generally reflecting on life, missing her son Tom who was staying with Glenn in Switzerland for the summer. The day had been classic Seattle June gloom: high sixties and solid clouds; a tenuous sunshine filtered through producing an eerie kind of yellow light. Daisy thought how disappointing it must have been for ancient cultures that had built elaborate structures to coordinate with sunlight on the solstice when it was cloudy on the day. Earlier in the day, she had walked down the hill to Gasworks Park and climbed the park's man-made hill to the sundial on top.

She felt like she needed to pull all of her thoughts and feelings on meaning and value together. It had been ten and a half months since she had dropped Tom off at the boarding school, and she'd made a lot of progress in her thinking. She'd had experience. But her initial hunch of experience as value rang a little hollow in her current interpretation. The idea of a pilgrimage to pull everything together appealed to her. She thought back to the monk Hoshi and the ex-monk Haru and the Shikoku Buddhist pilgrimage route. Japan was appealing with its Buddhist flavor. But she watched some YouTube videos on the pilgrimage, and it struck her as tedious and, maybe not quite commercialized, but co-opted by the official Buddhist experience rather than a genuine experience. Not like walking a route of eighty-eight temples found via an ancient scroll, but like following a tourist map to eighty-eight locations. The pilgrims, or *o-henro* as they're called, wear ugly white smocks with some official logo on them. The words of Hoshi came back to her: "Rules, am I right?"

She rewatched *The Way* about the Camino de Santiago, or the Way of St. James, the pilgrimage walk ending at the Santiago de Compostela in Galicia in northwest Spain. Her Christian background would make it a natural, in a sense, although she wasn't Catholic. And walking through Spain sounded fantastic. Daisy's heritage was primarily German, but she had never spent much time in Europe, and the experience was appealing. But, like Shikoku, she feared the idealized version in her mind wouldn't resemble the actual experience on the ground. Probably too many hyper-religious walkers who lacked insight.

She certainly didn't want to walk through the Arabian desert under the scorching sun to Mecca in July or August (or, really, any other time) for that flavor of pilgrimage.

I'm down with the walking, just not other people's silly interpretations, she thought. *I just want to walk and think*. She remembered backpacking with Tom a couple years earlier, hiking to alpine lakes and camping.

They had been on a kick for the summer: hiking, camping, fishing. Tom's goal was more the camp part, but Daisy preferred the hike. *Really, the key to a pilgrimage,* thought Daisy, *is the physical exertion and the search for meaning.* For some the camaraderie of other pilgrims may be important but not for her. *I don't really like most other seekers, and I don't want to interact with them.* For her, the other people would be a distraction.

When the idea popped in her head, she knew it felt right. With one of hiking's most iconic trails, the Pacific Crest Trail, so close to Seattle, the decision was easy. She would hike a section of the PCT, by herself. It was mid-June, and she targeted the hike for late July. She started with a trip to REI to buy the lightest gear available. With Tom, he could carry a lot of the load, but now Daisy would be solo. She bought a one-person tent with rainfly weighing 1.5 pounds. Backpack 2.2 pounds. Camp stove and gas 0.8 pounds. Sleeping bag, rated to twenty degrees, 1.75 pounds. She watched YouTube videos and streaming shows on backpacking, and noted how many more shows there were, and how much more informational, than there were videos on meaning. She bought trekking poles with cork handles, 1.0 pound.

The PCT is divided into sections that vary in length but are typically around one hundred miles. Near Seattle, Section K runs southbound, or sobo in hiker parlance, from the North Cascades Highway 20 at Rainy Pass to Stevens Pass on Highway 2, a total distance of 127 miles. The guidebooks called it a challenging section. Section J runs from Stevens Pass to Snoqualmie Pass on I-90, a distance of seventy-five miles, and is also a challenging section, although less so than Section K. Further south, the trail continues as Section I to White Pass on Highway 12, a distance of ninety-nine miles, but with several miles burned out from wildfires, and according to the guidebooks a generally less remote section, crisscrossed with logging roads and access points.

Section J seemed like a good fit to Daisy. Remote, but also relatively short. As a new backpacker, she did not want to bite off too much. One can only stomach so much dehydrated food. Plus, her first kiss had occurred on Snoqualmie Pass at a sleepover at a friend's ski condo. The friend's brother also had a friend over, and stage two started for Daisy. Fitting then, Daisy thought, to also mark the start of stage three on Snoqualmie Pass. Seventy-five miles, at fifteen miles a day, would be five days four nights. *Tough, but doable,* thought Daisy.

Daisy had about a month to prepare for the hike. She did practice hikes each week, breaking in her shoes, figuring out her water-filtration system, getting the least-uncomfortable fit on her pack, setting up her tent and camp even though she wasn't camping overnight, using her stove to boil water and prepare food. She made several trips back to REI to fine tune her equipment and approach.

She also prepared for the pilgrimage aspect. On her phone's notepad, she listed out all the concepts that she wanted to work through. "Start with what you know," she noted. The list went on from there.

The Cascade Range, through which Section J of the PCT runs, is not too scary in terms of animal predators. Cougars were present as were black bears, but neither would attack humans in normal circumstances. No concerns on the snake or bug fronts–well, no serious harm concerns, there were mosquitos in droves. Very rarely, sightings were reported of a grizzly bear or wolf, but there were no sustained populations in the area that Daisy would hike. There could be people, though, bad people. Hikers were generally no problem: a little smelly, overly hairy, but also friendly. Any other people out in the wilderness were likely a different story. The trail was out of cell phone range for most of the way, and even if a call could be placed, the location would not be readily accessible to police help, should such help be needed. The only somewhat timely intervention would be via helicopter, which would take several hours minimum (if it could even be called, which it generally couldn't be). Some hikers carried satellite communicators, but if Daisy were in a situation that required police assistance, waiting for a hiker to pass who had a satellite communicator and then waiting for the helicopter response seemed less than ideal.

As an attractive forty-five-year-old woman, Daisy feared either a sexual assault or a nutso assault. There was a famous double murder on the Appalachian trail in 1990. A young hiking couple was held prisoner by a drifter who ultimately shot the man then raped and stabbed the woman, killing both. Violence on America's through-hikes was rare, but not unheard of. For Daisy, if she were unprepared, she might fixate on the risk thereby detracting from the trip, even if no direct threat were ever encountered.

"Mick, what is the lightest weight handgun you would recommend for me?" Daisy reached out to Mick over the phone for his advice.

"Have you ever shot a handgun before?" Mick asked.

"Are you asking if I've given a guy a hand job?" Silence. "I'm sorry, I couldn't resist. No, I've never shot a handgun."

They settled on a Ruger .38, weighing a little over 0.5 pound including a laser sighting system. Suboptimal as defense against a grizzly bear but more than enough against a grizzly man.

Mick flew to Seattle and took Daisy to a gun range to practice shooting. The gun packed a bit of a kick and it took Daisy a while to handle it with confidence. They worked on the preferred two hand grip and standing stance, but also practiced a one hand grip, as well as different stances including kneeling.

After the first session, they went back to Daisy's house, drank Maker's with a splash of Galliano on the rocks, and had sex. "You're really hot shooting a gun," Mick said.

"Bang bang," said Daisy.

They returned to the range the next day and Daisy felt much more comfortable with the weapon. The prior day she felt tentative, now she felt aggressive, almost like her mind had processed the experience overnight and was now ready to continue with confidence.

"One more night?" asked Daisy as they left the range. Mick stayed at her house again and would fly out the next day.

Daisy ordered deep dish pizza from The Wallingford Pizza House on 45th Street. Mick went to pick it up and grab beer at the old Food Giant. Daisy was cleaning up around the house when she heard Bianca call out.

"Hey sis," banging on the screen door.

"Hey Bianca, what are you doing here?" Daisy asked, walking to the door. "C'mon in."

"I brought you a little present." She flipped Daisy a small box containing two sheets of pills in metallic-foil wrapping.

"Methylphenidate hydrochloride?" Daisy asked.

"Generic Ritalin. You mentioned you wanted to start painting again but kept getting distracted and couldn't focus. Now you can. Pharmaceutical focus."

"Thanks, I guess. I might be a bit past my experimental-drug phase." Daisy instinctively tried to peel a corner of the metallic foil up.

"Your call. It's really safe. The only side effect is psychosis," Bianca shrugged exaggeratedly. "It bumps up the adrenaline and dopamine in your brain. The dopamine keeps you content and the adrenaline keeps you energized. Combined, they keep you focused. No need to peek at your phone for a dopamine hit, or to sneak a snack for a carb hit."

"Okay, but why? This is a little out of the blue."

"I've been working on drug formulations to help free people from mental structures forced upon them. It just got me thinking. You'd mentioned frustration with modern-world distractions. I thought a little pharmaceutical focus could help."

They sat in the front room. "Do you want anything to drink?" asked Daisy. "Beer? Soda?"

"I'm fine thanks. I won't stay long, just wanted to drop off the pills. Have you painted anything yet?"

Bianca asked, seeing some canvases leaning stacked against the wall. She stood up and flipped through them.

"No, not yet, all blank."

"Well, let me commission one for my office. What's your rate? Your friend rate. A hundred bucks?" Bianca pulled a money clip from her front jeans pocket, peeled off a one-hundred-dollar bill and set it on the coffee table, putting a glass figurine on top of it to weight it down. "Do I get to choose the content or is that solely at the artist's discretion?"

"Depends what you ask for."

"No nude self-portraits? How about an homage to our old apartment on the Ave? To our time there. To us. Earlier. Our early selves."

"Ice cold beer here," came a call from the front porch steps. Mick used his foot to open the screen door, which—following the universe's guidelines for screen doors—was a bit ajar. He entered with pizza and beer in his hands. "Get your ice-cold beer here." Looking up, he was startled for a moment recognizing Bianca. "Oh, hi, um ... Bianca, right? Nice to see you again."

"Uh huh, you too, Mick," said Bianca.

"Are you here for pizza?"

"No, I just came by to commission some art. But if you're offering ..."

The July weather was idyllic, temperature in the upper seventies, a few cumulus clouds blowing across the sky for variety and daydreaming prompts. Daisy brought a table chair out to the front porch to add a third seat. The trio sat, eating pizza with plates balanced on their legs and drinking lemon shandy.

"I'm surprised you didn't get artichokes on the

pizza, Mick," Bianca said.

"Why's that?" Mick asked.

"You just seem like an artichoke kind of guy," Bianca answered.

Daisy looked quizzically at Bianca. "Soft hearted? Big hearted? Spiky armor?" Bianca didn't respond and Daisy let it go. The breeze picked up.

Daisy described the section of the PCT she would be hiking. "You're really going to carry a gun?" Bianca asked.

"Yeah, for peace of mind," said Daisy.

"Hey, a bluebird," said Bianca pointing to a maple tree across the street.

"I don't see it," said Daisy.

"It just hopped to the other side of the trunk. It looked like it's working on some kind of project. A bluebird project."

"Nest building?" asked Daisy.

"Maybe, or maybe a monitoring station—watching the other birds, you know. The crafty crows, sinister sparrows, rascally robins."

"A bird monitoring station?" asked Daisy.

Bianca shrugged with raised eyebrows and a pout, eyeing Mick. "I like your style, Mick. Lemon shandy was a solid choice for this day. A nice *background* drink. Not in your face, just kind of supporting your general welfare."

"Well, thank you. I hear what you're saying," Mick said with prolonged eye contact. "And I agree."

Finishing the crust on her one large slice, Bianca stood up to go. "Daisy, do you have any diet cola?"

"Yeah, there's Diet Coke in the fridge. Help

yourself."

Returning with a can of Diet Coke, Bianca paused on the front-porch steps on her way to her car. "Do you guys remember Tab Cola? The original diet cola. I've been on a kick lately. Next time we have pizza, I'll bring some. The Tab's on me."

"I could go for some Big Red," said Daisy, "or Mellow Yellow."

"Green River," said Bianca.

19

In her lab in the Cascade foothills, Bianca played god. *How to make the people think?* she thought. Back in her grad student days at Berkeley, Bianca had developed drugs that made it more likely for a subject to interpret an arousal as anger or lust, one drug for each. Like Alice in Wonderland's eat me/drink me options, Bianca could choose the drug and make a mouse angry or sexy with the same stimulus. She had started with anger and lust because they were fairly easy to observe in mouse behavior and also because they were strong emotions critical for survival and therefore likely to have brain mechanisms more able to impose their will on the brain's interpretation. As interpretations bubble up in the brain and compete for hegemony, those seemed like chalk from the start.

Since those Cal days, she had refined the lust and anger interpretation molecules, but also engineered boosters for joy/happiness/contentment, angst/oppression/injustice, fear/worry/anxiety, and trust. Each of these could be coaxed from bubbling thought to take over the conscious interpretation; that is, from nonconscious signal to conscious experience.

A crucial advance over the last decade was that she could also pair a specific stimulus with the interpretation; the pairing allowed for a stronger emotional response. In the Cal days, the stimulus was limited to an electrical shock or a shot of adrenaline. But now, she could pair certain stimuli with certain interpretations, interpretations that normally wouldn't be produced by the stimuli, or not strongly. The stimuli she'd had success with were all fundamental human experiences. For example, she could pair the stimulus of hunger fairly strongly with the "negative" interpretations: angst/oppression/injustice and fear/worry/anxiety. It was much more difficult to pair with the "positive" emotions of lust, joy/happiness/contentment, or trust, but not impossible. She could introduce a relatively low probability boost to joy/happiness/contentment associated with a hunger stimulus. Of course, in all cases, the subject's primary interpretation was just "I'm hungry," but these other interpretations layered on: "I'm hungry and worried."

All of the stimuli she succeeded with seemed to relate to human social interactions. Hunger maybe the least so, but still for thousands of years humans had relied on social groups for food procurement and distribution. In addition to hunger, she'd effectively paired the stimuli of sight/smell of fire, laughter, rhythmic music, and social gatherings (groups of mice, monkeys, or humans). She had no success with many stimuli, including temperature—hot or cold, visual stimuli such as colors, auditory stimuli such as whistles or—sorry hungry dogs—bells; this wasn't Pavlovian associative learning.

None of the stimulus/interpretation pairings approached Manchurian Candidate precision, in which seeing the Queen of Diamonds triggered a man to turn into an assassin. That novel and movie embraced the promise of mind control in the 1950s and early 1960s, a promise that devolved into the CIA feeding massive doses of LSD to prostitutes and their johns in Project MK-Ultra. No, Bianca's effects were more on the order of a really hungry person feeling that the world had screwed them (oppression/injustice/angst) while they made a grilled-cheese sandwich or feeling anxiety while they prepared a cream-cheese bagel.

One problem, though, was that before the work at GFP, she'd only comprehensively tested the drugs on lab mice. This raised two issues. First, Bianca could measure activity by brain region and see correspondingly more activity in the target area; she could measure blood chemistry and hormone levels and identify elevated levels of targeted chemicals; she could measure heart rate, and she could observe the mouse's behavior. It was difficult, though, to define mouse behaviors that identify happiness, oppression, fear, and trust. The second issue was that the mouse brain is vastly different than the human brain. Cheese over chocolate. Monkey testing, while still not perfect, wasn't an option on the down low in her home lab. Safety and efficacy in humans were both potentially problematic.

Dedicated to the cause, Bianca had self-tested many of her compounds. After months of tests on mice to at least suggest safety, she would take one dose, then wait a week to assess any immediate negative reactions. She thought a single dose would likely not be sufficient to introduce the intended interpretation, but still she recorded emotional responses. The point of the first dose, though, was just to dip her toe in and test for obvious negative physical reactions. Next, she would dose for three days, then nothing for two weeks and assess for negative physical impacts. Finally, she would dose for a month and self-test her reactions to various stimuli. She would test that drug's target stimulus, but also all of the stimuli, along with any naturally occurring stimuli that stood out or caused an emotional interpretation in her that stood out in any way.

The initial self-testing was prone to bias. It wasn't double-blind; it wasn't even single blind, although some would claim it was short-sighted. Toward the end of her time at the pharmaceutical company, she had twelve drugs that seemed to her, based on mouse testing and self-testing, to produce the targeted interpretation for the targeted stimulus. There were five stimuli: hunger, fire, laughter, rhythm, and social groups; and there were six interpretations: lust, anger, happiness, oppression, fear, and trust.

Bianca's self-testing regimen became more sophisticated as she proceeded. The results were telling directionally at least. She would manufacture a month's supply of each of the twelve drugs, enclosed in identical capsules. She would also include four batches of placebo in identical capsules, and then put each drug in identical pill bottles with only a taped indicator on the bottom of the bottle identifying the drug. The identifying mark was covered with more tape. She would put all the bottles in a pillowcase, shake them up, pick one randomly, and transfer the pills from the chosen bottle to a new pill bottle, such that she couldn't accidentally see the drug indicator marking during the month of taking the pills.

She did this process eighteen times with her final molecules, with a month of no drugs in between each for a palette cleanser. She correctly identified the drug, based on her reactions to the target stimuli, thirteen times. Two of the five misses were placebo pills that she incorrectly interpreted to be stimulus/interpretation. Apparently, sex with a younger, hunky guy after a beach bonfire was of her own volition. One of the misses she guessed was a placebo when it was in fact trust stimulated by social gatherings. Trust had always demonstrated only borderline efficacy in her mouse testing, and she was only able to pair it with the social gathering stimulus. The drug's effect may have been weak or nonexistent.

On one of the other two misses, she had the emotional effect correct but the stimulus wrong. She thought laughter caused happiness with the candlestick in the conservatory, but it was really rhythmic music paired with happiness.

Finally, on the last miss, she had the stimulus correct but the emotional interpretation wrong. She guessed the drug was leading to anger based on social gatherings, when in fact it was angst/oppression/injustice caused by social gatherings. The anger and oppression interpretations were close emotionally. Originally in her research she was not going to consider them as separate interpretations. But it became clear as she progressed that different parts of the brain were at play in each. Certainly, there was a lot of overlap, but the injustice interpretation relied more on the cerebral cortex, a newer part of the human brain, whereas the anger interpretation relied more on the amygdala, a very old part of the mammalian brain.

Overall, Bianca considered her ability to identify thirteen of the eighteen samples an extraordinary success. That was a success rate of 72%, when random chance would have yielded 13%. The clearest cases in her estimation were the anger, lust, and fear interpretations. Given the primacy and potential strength of these emotions in humans, it seemed reasonable that these would most easily be boosted into conscious interpretation.

* * *

Bianca and Mina drank Starbucks coffee poured from a cardboard container, with whole milk awkwardly added from a paper cup. Neither were tempted by the muffin or bagel offerings in their familiar conference room. They talked of life in Tokyo. Mina had lived there for two years and spoke fluent Japanese; Bianca had visited and watched some anime.

Harry entered with three twentysomethings, two men and one woman.

"Good morning," said Harry. "How is everyone?"

"Let me start by apologizing," said one of the two men, with biceps bursting out of a plain black tee shirt. "I was out of line last week. I don't know what came over me. Maybe just frustration, I'm ready for action, tired of training."

"We're there with you, Joe," said the woman, toes curled, gripping her flip-flops. She wore an unbuttoned tactical shirt over a tank top. "We could extract Julia blindfolded. We're ready. We know the compound. We know the social structure. We know the routines. We don't need god-damned practice on the drum circle."

"Reject, accept, merge. Glory to the Glove of God. We got it. Three-day parties, nine-day parties, full moon parties. We got it. Daily work and worship. We got it. What we don't have is the plan," said the other man. His teenage hairstyle of longer hair on top with shaved sides and back perhaps disguised his age.

"Still," said black tee shirt, "I was out of line. I should not have shoved you, Harry, even if you are ex-Army." A joke to extend an olive branch.

"Forget about it. All part of the training," said Harry.

"You have to admit," said the woman, "practicing a drum circle is pretty fucking stupid. You hired ex-special forces operatives not camp counselors. Kumbaya mother fucker."

Mina laughed. "You have to admit, the scene was pretty comical. Joe accusing Harry of incompetence, wondering if he's getting screwed out of money, shoving Harry, 'I didn't sign up for this bullshit.' Amy and Sean charging off too. It was a drum circle. True it is hippie-dippie bullshit."

"I was just pissed off," said Joe. "It just came to a boil."

"Yeah. Long month," said Amy. "It came to a head. It's just frustrating—we need a plan, and we need to launch."

"We'll install the plan later today," said Harry. "The drum circle was the last test."

"Test?" asked Amy.

Bianca shifted in her chair.

"Let me introduce you all to Bianca Zanone. She's the reason you all hate drum circles. Bianca is a neuroscientist and chemist. Over the last year she has been refining a drug to instill a sense of angst and oppression in the cult members, a feeling of injustice and anger. But more than that, she has been able to tie it to a stimulus. Any guesses?"

"No fucking way," said a suddenly energized Joe. "Drums?"

"Drums, or rhythmic music in general," said Bianca. "The louder the better."

"You fed us this drug without our knowledge?" asked Sean, voice rising.

"It's all in your contract," said Harry. "The drugs have been tested for safety as much as possible. Efficacy tests have been more difficult to conduct."

"Think back," instructed Bianca. "Were you angry before the drum circle? Were you frustrated with Harry's leadership? Were you thinking this operation wasn't what you signed up for?"

"Holy smokes," said Joe.

"Yeah, no," said Amy. "We were fine, really. We were all fine."

"The drug boosts the likelihood of your mind interpreting the situation as oppressive and unjust. And also anger, it boosts the emotion of anger. We created a bit of a two-drug cocktail to achieve that."

"Great, a regular Harvey Wallbanger of experimental neuro-drugs," said Sean.

"I'll give you that," said Bianca. "If it's any comfort, I've taken the drugs myself for several years. Effects are transitory. The drug clears from your bloodstream in about two weeks after discontinuing use. We haven't observed any adverse consequences in any of the test ... subjects." Subjects being nicely more broad and encompassing than "monkeys" or "mice."

She went on, "The angst interpretation is boosted and takes over your consciousness. Once the interpretation is in place, you react to it. Then your brain sees you reacting a certain way, shoving Harry for example, and that reinforces the interpretation that you are angry over injustice. The key was to tie the reaction to a stimulus that many cult members would experience at the same time. Without a common trigger, the anger would likely just simmer and then dissipate. The cult instills strong social norms—making examples of those who attempt to leave through the gates, for example. We need a group of people of the same mind to push through that social conditioning, to identify with this new group of pissed-off people rather than with the conditioned teachings of the cult."

"An angry mob rushes the gates during the full moon party," surmised Joe.

"Sparked, fomented, fostered, and guided by three new members," said Mina, "to cars waiting just out of sight down the road."

"I'm feeling happy," said Joe. "Is that me or another drug?"

"That one's all you, Joe," answered Bianca.

"Okay, clever," said Sean, "but it seems a lot less certain than a simple helo extraction. Map Julia's movement patterns, target when she's regularly outside, plant one operative inside, drop in an injectable tranquilizer, the operative intercepts Julia as the helo approaches, tranquilizes her, and lifts out on a helo bucket rope. Almost no risk, given the description of the cult as not big on weapons."

"Two considerations led us away from that type of extraction," said Harry. "First, Julia would resent it and feel she was involuntarily forced to leave the compound. We need her to want to leave, to leave that chapter of her life behind. Second, Mr. Paulson wants to free as many members as possible, not just Julia. Julia is the impetus, true, but what about the others, the deluded souls who don't have a billionaire uncle."

"You mean everyone other than Huey, Dewey, Louie, and Juli—a?" deadpanned Bianca.

"So how do we administer the drug?" asked Joe, finishing off his chocolate-chip muffin.

"Yes, that was a problem," said Bianca. "We need a mechanism that will dose as many cult members as possible regularly for at least two weeks, but ideally for a month. There are really only three options. First, we could use some kind of airborne spraying."

Sean chortled at the idiocy of the option.

"You laugh, but the US government actually tested an airborne method specifically for the administration of mind-control drugs in the 1950s in San Francisco. They released a red powder into the air off the coast so that the wind would blow it to the city, and they could measure the dispersion. Part of Project Bluebird, a precursor to the better-known MK-Ultra mind-control experiments. Can you imagine? The famous blanket of fog rolling over the coastal hills into the city is red one day, 'Nothing going on here, continue about your business.'

But you are right, it is not feasible. It would take an enormous amount of the drug since the vast majority would not be ingested. Also, it would be ingested through the lungs which we have never tested.

"That left us with application through food or drink. The cult sources about a quarter of their food internally, vegetables, eggs, and cows/pigs/chickens. They purchase the rest from a variety of suppliers. We could potentially intercept the outside food and inject it with the drug, but they buy from many suppliers, and each introduces a risk of being detected. And without widespread application to all of the food, cult members may not get the drug if they don't eat the portion that has been doctored.

"We could administer the drug through their water supply. They get their water from a large spring-fed creek. It would be simple to administer the drug into the water before it reached the compound. But this runs into the same problem as the aerial approach, the volume of drug would need to be massive since such a small fraction of the creek's water would ultimately be consumed. Also, it would produce environmental damage; one can imagine the PR nightmare resulting from dumping tons of a mind-control drug into a mountain stream. And it would be readily detectable in the wastewater coming from the compound if anyone ever thought to look. On top of that, they filter and chemically treat the water, and we don't know their exact process; that could interfere with the drug."

"So what are we left with?" asked Sean, shifting in his seat.

"Fortunately for us, Kansha Kokoro likes their

alcohol," answered Harry. "The members are encouraged to have a glass of sake each evening and reflect upon the day."

"That's the one thing about this cult that I like," said Bianca.

"We think this is almost universally adhered to," Harry continued, "although some opt for beer. They also drink beer and sake at their three and nine-day festivals, and of course at the full-moon festival. They source their alcohol from a sleepy liquor store in Yamanakako, the closest town. The store delivers beer kegs and sake barrels to the compound every two weeks, in addition to bottles of liquor."

"If we can inject the drug into the beer and sake," Bianca said, "it will spread evenly throughout the liquid. Dosing will be erratic depending on each member's consumption, but over-dosing is not harmful, at least not on our monkey test subjects."

"How reassuring," said Sean.

"We let the cult ingest the drug for a month," continued Bianca, "and then break out at the full-moon festival. We tested to see if the drug could be detected by taste in the beer or sake, and none of us, the testers, could."

"And how do we get the drug into the alcohol?" asked Amy.

"Fortunately for us," said Harry, "we are the new owners of Happy Cat Liquor in Yamanakako."

20

Bianca sat at the bar in the Cloud Room in the Panorama Hotel, phone in front of her on the bar, drinking sangria early on a July afternoon. She wore a silky, silver camisole and slim, black skirt. The bar was largely empty at that time of day and Daisy, tending bar, also had a glass of sangria strategically hidden below the counter. Bianca picked up her phone, checked texts and her Twitter feed, and set it back down.

"Whatcha thinking about?" asked Daisy.

"Just work," said Bianca. Earlier in the week, Bianca had reached out to Hans Gerberding, professor of sociology at Humboldt University in Berlin and one of the world's leading experts on cults. Bianca had met Hans years earlier at an academic conference in Munich. They had spent an evening with a few other academics drinking huge jugs of Löwenbräu in a beer hall and listening to polka music. Bianca wanted information about Kansha Kokoro in general, and information on its leadership in particular. Hans knew of the group but had not studied it in detail. He did reach out to one of his contacts, though, in the Japanese government. The government monitored all active cults in the country.

The cult's leader, Masaki Kami, known as the Glove of God, had had a pedestrian early life. An average student, he graduated from Waseda University in Shinjuku, Tokyo, without distinction. He worked for an electronics manufacturer for a number of years. Never married. He quit his job in his early thirties and went to work on a dairy farm owned by his uncle. Not much was known about that period of his life. Five years later, he started Kansha Kokoro with his friend from university, Hamamura Niko.

Hamamura seemed to be the mastermind behind the cult. He graduated from university with near-perfect marks. Hard-driven and egotistical, he was arrested twice in his early twenties, once for rape and once for assault. The rape charge was eventually dropped when the woman refused to cooperate with prosecutors. Police suspected he paid her off. The assault charge was for a fight he had instigated outside a nightclub, leaving his victim blind in one eye. He paid a fine but avoided any jail time.

Hamamura bounced among management jobs following university, shunning the Japanese tradition of long-tenured employment; each bounce brought a bigger salary. He bought the cult's land, partly using an inheritance he received when his father passed away. Hamamura merely tolerated the spiritual aspects of the cult, leaving those primarily to Masaki. Hamamura embraced and ran the business side. The cult had two main revenue streams. First, many resident members donated all of their earthly possessions to the cult. Second, a larger membership base did not live in the compound but paid annual dues that gave them access to the Glove of God, the full-moon parties, and outreach events that Kansha Kokoro conducted in cities all across Japan.

Bianca sipped her sangria and checked her phone; nothing. She had texted Hamamura earlier in the day, having received his contact information from Professor Gerberding's contact in the Japanese government. She had introduced herself as Bianca Zanone from the University of California wanting to chat, the university reference to obscure her current work.

She and Daisy shot the breeze, sipped the wine, and ate the fruit. They discussed the intricacies of red versus white wine sangria. "Red feels more like Spain, white more California."

"Bzzz." Bianca's phone vibrated.

"Ms. Zanone, it is a pleasure to meet you. You apparently are well-connected. Neuroscientist?" Hamamura texted.

"Do you enjoy profiting by selling delusions to troubled minds?" - Bianca.

"I'm disappointed you feel that way. From what I hear you are a sharp intellect. You're sadly mistaken in this case. Good day." - Hamamura.

"Am I? Electrodes in blindfolds to produce a spiritual epiphany? You're a hack. We have one of the blindfolds." - Bianca.

Bianca waited for a reply, but none came. "*Uno mas, senorita,*" she said to Daisy who filled Bianca's glass. Bianca paced the bar like a caged animal, eager to fight, waiting for a reply. She sat back at the bar and fired a parting shot.

"I'm going to take you apart."

* * *

On the morning of the start of her PCT Section J backpack, a friend picked Daisy up and drove her to Steven's Pass. The trailhead was in the same parking lot as the ski resort. On the way, they stopped for breakfast at a diner in Monroe. The day before, the pair had dropped Daisy's car off at Snoqualmie Pass at the terminus of the trail.

Daisy slathered on sunblock and bug spray, hoisted her thirty-two-pound pack onto her back, set the length on her trekking poles, and was off. She wore a nylon-mesh baseball cap; white, long-sleeve, UV-blocking, micro-fiber shirt; camouflage tights (not selected for their camouflage property); wool Darn Tough high-ankle socks; and lightweight trail-running shoes (for the comfort—she wouldn't be running). She carried a pair of lightweight sandals for river crossings and wearing in camp. She brought one change of socks and panties, along with a lightweight down jacket for cold mornings or evenings.

It was 11:30 before she took her first step on the trail, a late start but not unexpectedly so. She had five days to go seventy-five miles, so a fifteen-mile-per-day pace. The first steps on the trail felt fraudulent, like a short walk in the woods, not a five-day hike, and certainly not a pilgrimage. That feeling quickly faded as sweat began to trickle down her back. The trail started with switchbacks up a steep slope through a colorful array of wildflowers. Occasionally she could see the Steven's Pass ski lifts patiently waiting for winter as she wound higher.

About half an hour in, the hike felt a little too real.

Her pack was heavy, the day was hot, and her legs were tired of the uphill. About an hour in, the trail crested the top of the slope, scooted beneath high-powered electrical lines, and bid farewell to modern life. The rest of the hike would be through unbroken wilderness. *Here we go*, thought Daisy, as she crested that first hill.

She had planned to just experience the trail and forest on the first day without directed thinking, to give herself time to shed normal existence, empty her head, and shred unchallenged beliefs. The trail wound among small ponds. Towering Douglas-fir and western red cedar provided shade. She got a second wind and her legs felt strong. She fell into rhythmic leg and arm strokes with her poles. This was only her second time using trekking poles; she initially thought she wouldn't want them, but a You Tube video had convinced her to give them a try. A shaded boulder field served as a stopping point for lunch. A marmot scampered for cover twenty yards away. Lunch was leftover pizza, her last non-dehydrated meal on her walk in the woods.

After lunch, she listened to music via ear buds and worked to clear her mind. She focused on the trail, on her footsteps, on coordinating her steps and her arm strokes, on her breathing. She adjusted her pack frequently to redistribute the load—thankful for her decision to splurge for the lightest-weight, reasonably priced gear. She focused on the music, on the forest, on the smell, and on the feel.

She stopped for the day in the late afternoon at a spot where the trail ran among shallow pools of water connected by a small stream. She'd only made it about eleven miles, but her Guthook app showed this as the last campsite with water for the next three miles. Despite her practice, she was not too confident in her ability to set up her tent and cook dinner, and she did not want to risk trying it after sundown. There was a lake closer ahead with campsites, but it would require hiking about a mile-long spur trail to get to it. *Screw that*, thought Daisy. She was far short of her fifteen-mile-per-day required pace but wasn't too worried since she'd gotten a late start, and what else did she have to do other than walk for the remaining days?

Daisy set up her tent as the mosquitos started to appear. When she looked for the best spot to collect water, she noticed frogs everywhere in the ponds, probably fifty or sixty frogs spread throughout the three ponds. *Ugh*, she thought, *this is gonna be frog piss*. There was no other water option, though, so she scooped up water from the least froggy place she could find and filtered it for dinner and for her bottles for the next day. She boiled water on her propane cook stove, rehydrated a package of red beans and rice for dinner, and ate it sitting on a rock that maddeningly would not present a comfortable sitting surface. Dragonflies chased mosquitos in the dusky sky.

Her sleep was fitful at best. She lost track of how many full three-sixty rotations she performed in search of sleep. The inflatable sleeping pad was fairly comfortable, but the inflatable pillow was not. More than anything probably, the novel situation was the main sleep deterrent. The wilderness seemed so much more ominous at night; she had her gun tucked in the corner of the tent for easy access.

The first light of the sun brought a small happiness

as she could officially wake up and start the day. She boiled water and made froggy coffee, with mist hanging over the small pools and surrounding meadow. She gazed through the mist at the forest beyond. Her body was stiff from the day before and the tent sleeping, but she was eager to get back on the trail, nonetheless.

The second day's hike started with a long climb. Eager to explore meaning and with her mind and body sufficiently reset from the day before, Daisy set off.

"I plunge into the abyss," Daisy spoke into her phone, recording a voice memo to capture her pilgrimage thoughts. "First off, the question itself: what is the meaning of life? A monumental question. The question. Maybe the most fundamental question. What could rival it? Maybe: why do I exist? The existential question. But this pilgrimage is for meaning, not existence. What is the meaning of life? A question that has spawned countless religions and belief systems."

She thought back to her decision to seek meaning shortly after dropping off Tom in Switzerland. Coop's advice to be rigorous about it still rang true. She'd outlined a list on her phone's notepad of topics to think through, to ensure proper rigor. The heading on the list was "The Meaning of Life."

The meaning of life, how grand! Daisy bounded along the rocky trail, energized, on her path.

Daisy had endured plenty of critical stares for bringing up the meaning of life question to customers. Maybe the setting was wrong, but what was the right setting? Receptivity had improved with the evening's cumulative alcohol level; maybe that suggested an underlying yearning to embrace meaning, but one that's soberly frowned upon in baseline society. Look at that foolish meaning-seeker.

The reason Daisy started the hike's thought regimen with the meaning-of-life question itself was to get to explicit belief that her goal was valid. She needed to get to the point where she could embrace her search for meaning without embarrassment. Perhaps modern America would claim that life had no meaning, and she was silly to ask the question, but it mattered to her. "I interpret it to matter and therefore it matters." She was ready.

The trail wound higher, with sweeping views of mountain peaks near and far.

Her next thought prompts were intended to review what she knew, or thought she knew, about meaning. She peeked at her phone notepad: "Continuous versus point-in-time."

"Continuous versus point-in-time. A way of life versus an achievement. So, this one seems obvious to me. The meaning of life has to be continuous. If it were an accomplishment that occurred at one point in time and then was over, where would that leave me? Just reminiscing about a past accomplishment. That's beyond hollow.

"That could be a purpose, to achieve something once, but not a meaning. What is the purpose of life—that's not my concern, on purpose. What I care about is value and meaning.

"True continuousness is probably not possible—a girl's gotta sleep after all—but at least something that occurs frequently. Helping others could qualify, because I could help others frequently—not continuously, but frequently enough that I would experience life's meaning regularly.

"The continuous requirement also jives with the idea that people change over time. If meaning occurred at a point in time, and then I changed, my meaning could be gone. Paths are personal—but meaning should be available all along the route.

"Most religions seem to fit the continuous mold, or at least what I know of the major religions. The Christian meaning is probably to love God, or to feel God's love, or to love one another, or something like that. In any case, a continuous feeling of love or grace. Buddhists try to achieve nirvana or existence beyond suffering induced by wants and needs—an ongoing state of being."

Daisy thought back to the ex-monk from the bar who had walked the Shikoku pilgrimage. *I'll bet he didn't walk any mountains like these,* she thought as she looked out upon towering granite peaks. She had reached the top of the ridge and started down the other side. Her app showed switchbacks ahead for the next two miles on the way down.

"There's really no empirical reason that life's meaning must be continuous rather than point-in-time. That's just a choice I'm making. I'd rather stay on an objective, empirical basis at this early stage of laying the foundation, but I don't think that's possible. I think I just need to define the continuous requirement as a choice I'm making. Another person might choose differently.

"I may need to abandon the hope of an empirical basis for a lot of this and just make choices. But I'll at least try to stay consistent with objective observations.

And, of course, require internal consistency among beliefs. Because I do value truth, after all."

It was late morning. She stopped at a creek that crossed the trail and refilled her two water bottles. Although she still had water from the night before, cold mountain-stream water filtered through sand, rock, and moss had more appeal than warm tadpole-slime water. She used a gravity filtration system, which had the added bonus of requiring a small rest while the water passed through the filter into her clean bottles. She drank a half liter of the fresh water and then resumed walking.

At midday, Daisy stopped at a creek that the trail crossed by means of a fallen tree with a horizontal cut that made a roughly flat surface on the makeshift bridge. The toes of her right foot had been hitting the end of her shoe on downhill steps. Her right heal also rubbed uncomfortably against her shoe. She'd only had a few practice hikes in her trail runners to break them in, now she might be paying the price. Her right foot was slightly larger than her left; that probably caused the issues.

She hopped off the trail down to the creek, took off her shoes and wool socks and soaked her feet in the icy creek. Initially, the water temperature was a shock and difficult to take, but she quickly became accustomed to it. She pulled out and ate her lunch: dehydrated cheese, pepperoni stick, dehydrated fruit bar, and Ritz crackers with peanut butter. A curious chipmunk approached and kept an eye out for any dropped crumbs. "Hello Chippy."

Her feet dried in the warm air while she ate. Before leaving, she doctored one of her water bottles with fruit-punch flavored powder that contained caffeine and electrolytes.

Back on the trail, Daisy's thoughts returned to her pilgrimage. *Alright, meaning is continuous. What else is known?* She checked her phone: "Physical versus mental." Dividing the world into physicality and consciousness, it seemed clear to Daisy that meaning is squarely in the realm of consciousness. Material accomplishments mean very little. Daisy thought back to Bianca's division of the universe into information and interpretation, physical and conscious. "The only thing that matters to me is the interpretation. How could anything have meaning other than through interpretation? Without interpretation, it would just be information, just data, valueless, meaningless. Information and interpretation, I & I.

"In a broad sense, interpretation itself could blanketly be considered meaning. Interpreting the meaning of the information. What does the information mean? That gets at a different definition of the word meaning, more implication/connotation than value, but still it speaks to the importance of consciousness to meaning.

"This one seems obvious. No physical rearranging of molecules (as long as they don't affect consciousness), no accumulation of riches can produce meaning.

"Now, physical actions could help. For example, if my meaning in life were to feel a sense of accomplishment, having physical accomplishments would logically help. However, if the accomplishments themselves were not meaningful, it's hard to see why the sense of accomplishment—for having achieved something meaningless—should be meaningful.

"Helping others might be considered a physical act that could reasonably be a life's meaning, but really it probably passes the feel test because it is helping other consciousnesses. It's not the physical act that passes, but rather the assistance to other consciousnesses."

The sun was high in the sky, and Daisy's feet were getting tired. It wasn't her legs or her back or her mind that bothered her, it was her feet and the extra thirty pounds she was carrying. Well, her mind did wander, but that was part of the point, to think things through from different angles and different feels. She sat down, rested her feet, had a chocolate chip Cliff bar, and drank flavored water. After about ten minutes, she was up again and off down the trail.

The trail cut across a field of granite boulders out in the open, then wound into a hemlock forest. Thousands of hemlock cones covered the trail about an inch deep. The small hemlock cones, measuring less than an inch each, were miniature trampolines, bouncing Daisy along. She appreciated the springy reprieve from the surface of roots and rocks. She grabbed at the soft, sprightly-needled hemlock branches as she went, letting them slip though her grip.

Daisy checked her phone for another of her known starting points: "Everything is transitory." *Yes! I love this one.* "Everything is transitory; everything is temporary." She could get odd emotions on the trail. "Life and consciousness will end. My time is limited. Striving for permanence is misguided. Existence is ephemeral."

These thoughts comforted Daisy, gave her a sense of freedom.

"I can exist and then be done." She smiled. "It's freedom. Nothing is permanent. This is obvious at the personal level, you die. But also probably true at the universal level—for the universe itself. Energy disperses over time on a one-way street. Now, who knows, science could have it all wrong at this point, but I think that current thinking with the second law of thermodynamics is that all energy in the universe will slowly disperse and become more diffuse. Energy will dissipate. That means all consciousness and all life will end. Even if that's wrong, and periodic big bangs are in the cards, that would still be an effective end, but with a recycling.

"And how lucky am I, having lived a life that's required very little renting out (or snatched by less moral means) of my mental or physical abilities (or snatch abilities). Throughout history, my situation is the clear exception. No slave labor, minimal rental of my thinking capacity. So while it is transitory, I've been in control of my life more so than most people throughout history.

"I'm not sure how the transitory nature of life and consciousness affects the meaning of life, but it feels relevant. Maybe it argues for the importance of experiencing meaning now, in the current moment. Since the future may be short or may not come at all."

Daisy rounded a bend in the trail and saw the river crossing ahead. There was only one potentially dangerous river crossing in Section J, and this was it. The river ran fast and cold through a boulder-strewn riverbed, falling down the slope from snow-covered peaks to the valley below. This river was no rock hopper. It required thigh-deep wading in fast-moving water. Daisy changed into her river sandals, secured with Velcro around her ankles and feet. Daisy had swum and played in Pacific Northwest rivers throughout her childhood, so she wasn't scared. But she was aware of the power of the water and how easily it could sweep her downstream. The risk wasn't of getting carried away, it wasn't deep enough for that, but the river could easily knock her off balance and tumble her downstream, banging into rocks. At a minimum that would get everything in her pack wet. At worst, it could cause bodily injury such as broken bones or concussion. In the middle of the wilderness, that's critically dangerous. *Maybe I should have carried a satellite communicator rather than a gun.*

She scouted for the best spot to cross, looking for shallower and slower-moving water as well as for larger rocks that she could grab onto. Having selected her spot, she used her trekking poles angled upstream for balance and resistance against the water's flow, the poles' carbide tips anchored into rocks in the riverbed. She crossed without incident, dried her feet on the small towel she had hooked onto her pack with a carabiner, and put her hiking shoes back on. After the river crossing, the trail gained elevation along the valley's sloping side in the downstream direction, aiming to exit over the valley's rim.

21

On the trail, Daisy checked her phone again. The last of her known starting points: "Unitary nature of consciousness."

"The unitary nature of consciousness. Forever alone. This also makes me happy—does that make me strange? An odd duck?" She had thought through this consideration well already. "The necessarily true conclusion: if I interpret something to be meaningful, then it is. It's the same logic that I applied to the meaning-of-life question itself; if I interpret it to be important to me, then it is.

"It's nice to be back on bedrock. This one isn't empirical; it's even stronger. It's definitional; it's logical. If meaning is based on interpretation, and if my interpretation is isolated and the only one I can ever access, then my meaning is only based on my interpretation. It's a truism. My consciousness is necessarily alone and sufficient, and my meaning will be too.

"Now, my interpretation could be that someone else's love is necessary for my meaning, but that would still be my interpretation. It isn't the other person's love that creates meaning, it is my interpretation of needing that love.

"The problem is, I don't have total control of my interpretation; I'll need to think that through. But I'm confident that my interpretation is all that matters to me.

"So only my interpretation matters, but I don't fully control my interpretation. That's a dilemma. Maybe that is the crux of this whole issue. I don't control my interpretations. Of course, only my interpretation matters, but what if I interpret myself to be lacking? The self-help shortcut would be to change my interpretation (easier said than done); although that feels a little fraudulent—like a death-bed opportunistic redefining of what a good life is. The long road would be to make my life conform with my interpretation of meaning (easier said than done); that feels like the honest route, but impossible without a well-defined definition of meaning.

"My own interpretation is all that matters, and I don't control it. What a fiendish world! Ha, this pilgrimage is really working—I had never thought of that before. And it does seem to be the crux of the human condition."

In need of a snack, Daisy stopped, took off her pack, and extracted a packet of peanut M&Ms. She'd realized over the first two days that her pack organization was suboptimal. She wasn't able to access her snacks without stopping and taking off her pack. Too much lost momentum. She repurposed a pouch on her hip belt to hold her daily snacks for the rest of the hike.

She had exhausted her phone note list of known considerations, but another consideration popped into her mind.

"One element of my interpretation of meaning,

right now, is that it must somehow be fundamental. It must tie into the universe, or to existence, or to consciousness itself. It can't be peripheral; it can't be a pastime. It must be foundational.

"That seems like a common element in people's interpretations. Religious meaning comes from the foundational god. Spiritual meaning comes from the foundational mystical fog. Fate as meaning, to be forever buffeted by forces beyond your grasp, comes from the fundamental nature of existence, not a triviality.

"The problem with all of those, though, is that the why is undefined! People feel the foundational importance of the belief system, but they don't know why it's true (or not true). The interpretations are faith based. Have faith that this mystical voodoo is true. Or maybe, in the case of fate, it's more like, well, this is the best interpretation I have so I'm going with it. How do faith-based belief systems still hold sway in the world today? They're so antithetical to truth. Having faith is the same as not caring about truth. Why would that resonate with someone? Maybe fear.

"People, you don't just gotta have faith. That's the exact wrong approach. Embrace the feel—the what. Search for the truth—the why."

Daisy reviewed her known starting-point list once again, and edited it slightly based on her trail thoughts:

- My meaning is continuous.
- Meaning is in the realm of consciousness.
- Everything is transitory.
- Consciousness is unitary – meaning is interpreted by each consciousness alone.
- Meaning is foundational.

She was pleased with her day so far, both the hiking experience and the thinking. She had gotten to the point in the hike where she could transcend modern American life. Just drinking in nature, walking miles as the trail unfurled, existence feeling more valuable, flavor dialed up, colors over-saturated.

Two hairy young men passed Daisy heading northbound. One wore short running shorts and a tank top, the other an unbuttoned shirt. A cloud of BO emanated from them. *Glad I brought my deodorant*, thought Daisy.

Daisy explored a tangent that had popped into her mind during the day. "One of my starting considerations is that everything is transitory. But the interconnectedness of all physical items in the universe does have some appeal. Not really for meaning, maybe, but that my physical actions will continue to reverberate until the end of time, in some small way. So, in a way, refuting my starting consideration of everything being transitory. The physical state of the universe will always be different based on my presence and actions—that rock I threw in the river will affect the state of the universe for billions of years. Just like every Bitcoin transaction will forever affect the output of the hash function.

"Could all consciousness be connected, like all physical matter is connected? We can't rule it out, given how little we know about consciousness. And it does seem that the universe has a structure that facilitates consciousness, so maybe—maybe that structure links consciousnesses somehow, like all physical matter is linked. Although I experience a solitary consciousness, perhaps the linkages are just too small to be perceived.

"Alternatively, my consciousness could reverberate until the end of time through a cascading influence on other beings' consciousnesses across time. The love I give gets paid forward. That could be meaningful—it resonates. In that way, my consciousness will reverberate far into the future, in at least a small way, just like my physical presence.

"Lots of maybes, lots of potential for people to choose their own interpretations. I think I'll stick with things being transitory and consciousness being solitary for now. Those interpretations seem more relevant to me."

The sun was starting to set over the forest. Bugs were starting to swarm; birds called. Daisy was pounding miles, propelled by her legs and trekking poles, trip hop in her ear buds, meaning on her mind.

Daisy checked her app and saw that there were a few nice-looking campsites alongside a rocky stream about one mile ahead. She resolved to camp there for the night.

Her day's thinking had led her to a critical question: "Is the meaning of life exogenous or endogenous? External or internal? Does it exist external to me for me to find, or do I create meaning from within? The question itself, 'What is the meaning of life?' asks for *the* meaning, suggesting one meaning for everyone, suggesting its source is external and each individual only has to find it. But that doesn't seem right.

"First of all, if there were one meaning of life, surely someone would have found it and told everyone else by now. And plenty of people are willing to tell you the meaning of life, love is all you need, for example. But their claims always ring hollow.

"If meaning's source is external, where would it come from? God? The universe? Western culture ignores meaning because it isn't inherent in the physical universe (or not obviously inherent, at least). How can a search for meaning be successful in a physical world with no meaning? But I've already established that meaning is mental, and my mental state is isolated from anything else. So I, my mental self, am the only source of my own meaning. Searching for meaning is incorrect. I can't find meaning in a meaningless physical world. I create meaning.

"But it doesn't seem that meaning's source is entirely internal, either. Consciousness interprets meaning, but consciousness has both internal and external influences. So, I think meaning is a bit of both. I create and discover meaning. Probably with more weight on the create part.

"There is no right answer to 'What is the meaning of life?' There is only each person's answer, each consciousness's answer. Consciousness creates and discovers meaning. Consciousness interprets meaning." The thought resonated with Daisy like the right answer popping into her head, neurons synchronizing. "Don't search for the meaning of life, search for my meaning of life."

* * *

Bianca turned the glossy, letter-size, two-sided sheet of photos over in her hands. Harry logged into the network in the nameless South Lake Union office. He opened a video file and he, Bianca, and Mina watched drone footage of one thousand of the sheets dropped throughout the cult compound, fluttering down in the still air. The footage showed cult members picking up the picture sheets and passing them around.

"You should have gotten a shot with the fliers raining down with Mt. Fuji in the background," said Bianca.

There were four color photos on each side. The first showed Masaki, the Glove of God, at a casino table with a stack of chips in his hand, bigger stacks in front of him on the felt, smoking a cigar with an Asian woman in a sleeveless red satin dress that barely reached her upper thighs draped over him. Another showed Hamamura making it rain cash in a strip club, a naked pole dancer in the background. Another showed Masaki in a luxury garage next to a Rolls Royce, with a Bentley, an Aston Martin, and other expensive cars receding into the background. One showed a bank account statement under Hamamura's name with a balance of over a billion yen (equivalent to over ten million US dollars).

Printed at the bottom on each side in both Japanese and English was the statement: "The Glove & Hamamura do not reject money and the modern world, they swindle you out of your money. Kansha Kokoro is fraudulent."

"This is a good seed planted. Our drug will cause it to grow," said Bianca.

Later, the project team found out that the cult had ramped up discipline following the picture drop. Throughout the compound, silence was required of the members for two weeks, other than essential communication. Any rules infractions were met with harsher than normal punishment. Every resident, without exception, was required to attend the daily worship, which stretched to one-and-a-half to two hours. The tone of the sessions was aggressive, not defensive. The Glove blamed the fliers on members who had lied about their resources and continued to hoard earthly wealth, saying they had brought evil into the community. The evil reverberated, he preached, and attacked the Glove himself as the shepherd of the flock, manifesting itself in the fake photos. Faith was being tested. Anyone with external resources must relinquish them for the good of the community, in order to purge the evil and restore harmony.

"We are in a battle with the demons of the material world," the Glove preached. "Do not condemn your fellow enlightenment seekers to failure, to live in an environment beset with lies and material striving."

About a week later, Bianca got a text from Hamamura. "Amateur hour. You're a joke. Nice photoshop work, though."

When the text came in, Bianca was in the middle of dinner at El Gaucho with Brian Stevenson, her long-time friend and shorter-time coworker. Brian's curls had been shorn and he was clean-shaven, but for some reason Bianca still thought he looked like a goat.

Bianca cut a piece of medium New York steak and bit down on it, savoring the flavor.

"What's your favorite insult, Brian?"

"Just in general?"

"Yeah, think back to your school yard recess days. Let your inner punky kid out. Someone stole your candy bar; how do you taunt him?"

"Your mama wears combat boots?" offered Brian tentatively.

"Really? Hmmm. Not sure that would translate. Not sure it's even very effective in America. You probably didn't get in many fights, did you?"

"Yeah, no," said Brian.

"Okay, I'm going vulgar and gender-bender," said Bianca.

"Suck my dick," Bianca texted back to Hamamura, chomping on the olive in her Grey Goose martini.

"Who are you trading insults with?" asked Brian.

"Just an evil worm. No one I can't handle," said Bianca.

"We're making money off of your little stunt. I should give you a commission." - Hamamura.

"Why target us anyway? Is a friend or relative here? Maybe I should show them a little special attention." Eggplant emoji - Hamamura.

"You're a disgusting con-man who preys on vulnerable souls. You steal their ability to think. You're pathetic. Like Moses said, you better let my people go go go." - Bianca.

"You harbor much resentment. You should join our group, experience enlightenment." - Hamamura.

"Like the girl you raped? You're vile. Go to hell. I'm coming for you." - Bianca.

22

Early sunlight had already filled the tent when Daisy first opened her eyes. She had slept much better than yesterday, thanks to two days of exertion and a sleep deficit from the night before. The sound of water splashing down the rocky creek by which she camped didn't hurt either, a natural noise machine set to gurgling mountain brook. She lay under her sleeping bag like a quilt since the night was warm, although her inflatable sleeping pad stuck lightly to her skin. In the warmth of her bed, she checked her phone for her first thinking cue: "What does consciousness feel like?"

The stream beside her campsite had run flush with water the night before but only trickled along in the morning. Daisy was amazed at the volume change overnight, wondering if yesterday's volume was just from snowmelt that day.

She boiled water and rehydrated Starbucks Via powdered coffee, extra strong, double strength. She focused on the taste of the coffee. Bitter. Perky. Pure. *Maybe I should stop putting milk in my coffee back in the real world, er, the modern world.*

After a breakfast of rehydrated Spanish scramble, Daisy broke down camp into her pack, swung her pack onto her back, and got back on track. *What does consciousness feel like? That might be a tough nut to crack*, she thought. Her morning muscles were stiff from another night of tent sleep, but once on the trail such trivialities faded away with the morning mist. She relished the miles ahead.

"What does consciousness feel like? Human consciousness, of course. And really, all I can truly address is my consciousness, actually.

"Well, let's start with the main elements: sensory inputs like sight and hearing, sensations like pleasure and pain, abstract thought, language. Anything else? Emotions, but those are probably part of sensations. Memories, those are probably a mix of the more basic components. Imagination? No, that's probably also a mix of the others.

"Should language even be its own category or is it just a part of abstract thought? Maybe it's more a tool of abstract thought, rather than a part of consciousness. Okay, let's kill it. So three basic components: sensory inputs, sensations, and abstract thought."

The trail sloped gently downhill in a wide valley, following the valley down for many miles. The trail was overgrown with leafy plants, and Daisy often could not see the trail surface. Her toes, which continued to hurt from hitting the end of her shoe, occasionally absorbed a stubbing from a kicked rock or root. She was fairly sure she had a blister forming on one of her right toes.

The day was heating up and the vegetation became stifling. Devil's club's spiky stems attacked her arms and legs as she forced her way through the overgrowth. Despite a river running not too far away at the bottom of the valley, she hadn't crossed an accessible stream in hours.

Daisy considered and excluded as redundant several candidates for elements of her consciousness: body movement control, math and logic, considering the future and past, considering others' motives, empathy, self-awareness. All seemed like a mix of sensory input, sensation, and abstract thought.

"Maybe just awareness itself deserves a spot. Awareness is at the heart of consciousness. But, on the other hand, maybe it's just a synonym for consciousness, and not really an element of it? Awareness is implied in my three core elements."

Daisy had been walking without focusing on the trail, just walking and thinking. The trail cut across the valley midslope, with viewpoint vistas every few hundred yards. Looking around, she realized the entire micro ecosystem had changed. She was in a huge swath of vine maples. Swarms of thin trunks and petite green leaves danced in the light breeze. Small blue butterflies chased each other, looking for a little love perhaps. Daisy plucked one of the leaves and smelled it, tore it down the seams of its lobes, and scattered the remnants.

Sensory input, sensation, and abstract thought. That was what Daisy came up with in her attempt to classify her conscious experience.

"Sensory input is bugging me a little. It isn't really the input that matters, it's the sensory interpretation that is in consciousness. So let's revise the wording: sensory interpretation, sensation, and abstract thought.

"Of those, sensory interpretation seems mainly like a means to an end. Sensory interpretation lets me interact effectively with the world. It doesn't seem important in my search for meaning. Assume that beauty were my chosen meaning. It seems like the meaning would not be in the sensory interpretation of a beautiful sunset, for example, but instead in the emotional feel of the beauty, the sensation. It is a bit of an odd question, how does beauty feel, but most people might grant that you can feel beauty, rather than just see it.

"If we set aside sensory interpretation, that leaves sensation (including emotion) and abstract thought as the potential homes for meaning. Sensation is the chalk, the heavy betting favorite; love is all you need. But sensation isn't the whole story. Every religion combines emotion with an abstract-thought-based story to explain the emotion. And the problem is, the religious stories are silly given modern knowledge.

"Meaning is the combination of sensation and the abstract thought explaining why. You need to feel it, and you need to understand it. The what and the why, the feeling and the understanding.

"That really is the problem of religion; the sensation is generally fine, but the understanding is silly.

"Maybe a lot of people are content to just recognize that good sensations are meaningful and don't care about the why. That rang true with a lot of customers' answers.

"But I'm getting ahead of myself; I was supposed to just be exploring what consciousness feels like. Or maybe behind myself; I've seemed to have looped back to my what-and-why thinking from yesterday—but nice to see how it ties to consciousness. Ah, screw it. I should have a good feel for consciousness by now at forty-five years old. Let's move on."

She turned off her music and focused on the trail, how her legs felt, bounding down the trail, eating miles. She had reached a large, narrow lake with a rocky outcropping. She took a rest and snacked, sitting on the rocks. No one was around, so she stripped down and eased herself off the rock into the cold water. She swam a few breaststrokes, becoming acclimated to the frigid water. She dunked her head under the water and ran her fingers through her hair.

Drying herself back on the rock, she doctored her blistered toe, popping the (somewhat cleaned by the lake) blister with a sanitized safety pin, and covering it with a blister bandage.

Back on the trail, she sequentially thought about everyone who had played a big role in her life: childhood friends, parents, high school friends, boyfriends, college friends, lovers, Tommy. She kept the snacks flowing, random songs shuffling, and memories flooding.

That night, Daisy camped high on a mountainside, overlooking a large lake far below. The day had been hot with a cloudless sky. At her elevation, the evening turned cold. She slept in her zipped-up sleeping bag, not blanket style. She slept fitfully. At one point in the middle of the night, she slipped out of the tent to pee and was astounded by the night sky's brilliance. Isolated by the wilderness from ambient-light pollution, the stars were incredible. Millions of stars were visible, it seemed. Everywhere, there were pinpricks of light of varying intensity. She could see lighter swaths of sky in some areas.

Are those spiral arms of the Milky Way? she wondered. She stood in awe.

* * *

Bianca paced the elevator lobby of the SLU office building like a caged tiger, complete with tiger-stripe-variant silk blouse. Joe Wasserman, one of the operatives who had been in the compound for the rescue, exited an elevator dressed in jeans and a gray polo shirt. Bianca pounced.

"Joe!" Bianca greeted him with a high-five. A handshake just didn't feel like enough.

"It was pretty incredible," said Joe.

"471 out of 513, not bad," said Bianca.

"Yeah, that caused some logistics issues with the buses," Joe said, laughing.

They left the building and headed east three blocks to a rooftop bar. "Thanks for meeting me," Bianca said. "All I got was a phone call that said the rescue had been successful; Julia and 470 others were extracted, and the three of you were safe. Well, that and a note that said only 'Thank You' along with a bottle of Krug Clos d'Ambonnay."

"I got Dom Perignon White Gold. I wonder how they chose."

They walked past a sidewalk closed for the construction of a building on the way to the bar. "So, I am under a strict non-disclosure agreement," Joe said. "I assume you are too? I'm not sure whether this conversation would technically be allowed, but I doubt anyone would care. But just to be sure, this is just between us, right?"

"Yes, just between us. And yes, I'm also under an NDA."

They reached the bar. It was not crowded at midafternoon. They sat outdoors at an umbrella-shaded table overlooking Lake Union. Joe ordered a Coors Light and Bianca an Aperol spritz.

"I wish I could've been inside with you guys and seen it all go down," said Bianca.

"Yeah, you had them champing at the bit for a fight, all right," Joe said.

"So tell me what happened! I'm dying to hear."

"Okay. It was, of course, at the full-moon party. Sean and I were rotating among the rooms; Amy was keeping eyes on Julia in the drum room. You could feel the tension rising in the dance room and the drum room. People openly complaining about the conditions, limitations on interactions, imposed silence from the photo drop, even the quality of the beds. We could tell that pot was ready to boil.

"The funny thing is even Hamamura and Masaki were agitated. At the start of the night, they were in the drum room arguing with each other loudly. I couldn't understand the Japanese, but Sean said they were arguing over the compound's operations and scheduling. Hamamura reached out with both hands, as if emphasizing a point, and Masaki flung Hamamura's arms away. Hamamura stormed off. I had to stop myself from laughing. 'Score one for Bianca,' I thought."

"I love it," said Bianca.

"Small skirmishes were breaking out as the night progressed. There's a private room for non-resident members, those who pay the annual fee for access. The room is a short distance down a hallway from the dance room. I think it has couches, quality food and drink, and private sleeping rooms for the night. Quite a few paying members had come for the full-moon celebration. Well, a group of residents took offense that they were not allowed into the room. They started harassing a group of paying members as the group walked from the VIP room to the dance room. A shoving match ensued, and security guards came to break it up. The paying members were bewildered because the night's mood was so different than the normal celebrations. A powder keg ready to blow.

"The trigger that started the exodus was in the dance room. There was a buffet spread of food and drink in the back of the room: crackers, fruit, breads, cheese, but they had run out of meat. There had been a tray of turkey, ham, and roast beef. There had been grumbling about the food earlier. Well, then a security guard was eating a big sandwich stuffed with meat—like a big hoagie. I'm not sure where he got it, maybe they had a separate source. Anyway, two men started to harass the guard and then actually try to take his sandwich. The guard was swatting them away with one hand, playing sandwich keep away with the other. It was comical.

"Sean saw the opportunity and lit the fuse. He joined in, shoved the security guard. The guard shoved him back and Sean punched the guard in the jaw, dropping him. A cheer went up from the crowd that had gathered around. Another man who had been dancing charged the only other security guard in the room, but that guard took off his hat, which served as the indicator of his security duty. He took it off, threw it on the ground, and kicked it.

"It turned into a mob scene at that point. The dance room spilled into the drum and meditation rooms, looking for security guards or who knows what, overturning chairs and tables. Well, Masaki was in the meditation room, and quickly a circle formed around him, everyone yelling, people starting to shove him. Masaki pushed through the crowd, covering his head, and made it through a doorway to the leadership's private rooms. That must have been a well-reinforced door because the crowd pounded and kicked at it, but the door didn't budge.

"The problem then was we needed to redirect this mob to want to leave the compound. We really needed an oppression/anger-and-then-escape drug. Work on that for next time, will you?" Bianca laughed. "By then the music had stopped. I yelled 'Guard posts!' wanting to get the momentum headed to the exit. Sean repeated the yell in Japanese, and it became a chant. People massed toward the guard posts at the main exit. The guards must have been hearing what was happening on their radios, because they abandoned their posts and ran off when they saw the crowd coming. The crowd dismantled the guard houses.

"It was an avalanche; once the exodus started there was nothing going to stop it. We had arranged for two cars to be on standby essentially, and to drive by on the public road as people were evacuating. We had buses ready in the closest town, with the ruse that the first car driver would call for support, the request would get elevated to the equivalent of a mayor, and he would offer up the buses. We couldn't very well have buses waiting outside the compound; that would have looked fishy. Sean and Amy started spreading information that a hotel in the nearest city was putting members up free of charge.

"So it worked well, the first two cars were there, and one called in for support, supposedly, and shortly thereafter three buses arrived. But we hadn't expected almost five hundred people. The buses could only hold about sixty people each, so they had to make three trips, with some people waiting in the night for close to an hour. We're lucky we didn't have any issues from that.

"The cult's leaders never reemerged; probably happy to escape unharmed.

"Sean was in one of the first cars in order to coordinate a place for everyone to stay. We had an agreement with a hotel to use one of their ballrooms for the night. Amy stayed close to Julia, to make sure we always had tabs on her and that she was extracted, but that wasn't a problem, she was raring to go. I was left to try to maintain order outside of the compound.

"471 people extracted, out of 513, that's almost incomprehensible," said Joe.

"I understand Mr. Paulson will give everyone temporary housing, job training, and job placement. That's very generous. He's one of the good guys. I'll bet you guys were well-paid?" Bianca asked.

"As were you, I'm sure," Joe answered.

Joe checked his watch. "I need to run. I need to catch a flight tonight. Well, cheers to a job well done," Joe said raising his beer. Bianca tapped it with her glass and Joe downed what remained in the Silver Bullet can.

"You know I'm calling you from here on out anytime

I need a commando," Bianca said.

"Coming from you, that's not an idle threat," Joe winked. "It's too bad you missed the action; I'm sure you would have loved it." He got up to go, offering to walk her to her car but she declined.

She sat back watching kayaks and sailboats putter around Lake Union, sipping the remnants of her spritz. *There may still be some action for me.*

23

The next day was Daisy's fourth, out of a planned five, on the trail. Her thinking prompt for the morning was the classic "Who am I?" The media was saturated with answers in coming-of-age stories. The media stories were all focused on entering stage two, though, not stage three. Perhaps one's thinking could change over the thirty or so years in stage two.

The start of Daisy's answer was clear. "I'm a mom, I'm a woman." But then she wondered, which should be first? "Not important, but always a mother first. I'm a person; I'm an American; I'm an animal on spinning Earth, rotating around the sun, lollygagging in a lesser spiral arm of the Milky Way, generally receding from other galaxies, in a universe that's fourteen billion years old. I'm a sentient being. I'm a sexual being. I'm part of a line of evolving life that has been going for a long time." She wasn't sure how long. "At least a billion years.

"I breathe. I interpret. I think. I feel." Daisy reflected again on thoughts of her own life cycle, powered by yesterday's walk down memory lane.

A couple hours into the day's hike, a light sprinkle

began to fall. The wind had picked up and dark clouds were fast approaching. Daisy had brought a rain poncho, so she took her pack off and began to extract the poncho from the depths of the pack. The rain fell harder, and Daisy scurried beneath a towering western red cedar for protection, still trying to find the poncho. With a crack of thunder, the squall unloaded with driving rain. Daisy sat dry leaning against the cedar's trunk, the tree shedding water off its scaly foliage, leaving a large dry circle ringing the trunk. She found her poncho but didn't need it under the tree. She just sat under the cedar, rain pelting the ground outside her arboreal shelter. Rivulets formed and ran down the trail. Daisy felt the dry dust beside her; she felt the tree's layered, leathery bark. She soaked in the situation.

She remembered being told about one of her great grandfathers who had been orphaned as an infant, dropped off at a church in Germany. She imagined him left under an entrance archway, rain falling beyond its shelter. The child was taken in by the pastor's family, eventually coming to America, becoming a grocer, marrying, and having five children. *That's my direct ancestry line; that was me orphaned, wailing, hungry.*

She thought of the thousands or millions of sexual encounters that led directly to her and of the hopefully millions more in the future (*C'mon Tommy, you can do it*). She thought of all the rapes and mother childbirth deaths that it took to get her here, now. Also the perfect loves, the youthful loves, the surreptitious affairs (*no DNA tests or Ashley Madison hacks back then guys, you're safe*). And that was just in the human stage, think of all the prehuman evolutionary hook-ups required.

After about twenty minutes, the rain slowed then stopped, and patches of blue sky appeared as the clouds blew away. Weather changes quickly in the mountains. Daisy thanked the cedar with a fist bump and returned to the trail, poncho back in the pack but now easily accessible.

Daisy had taken a consumer-ancestry DNA test at one point, and it confirmed her expectations for the most part, but also had some small-slice surprises. She was mainly northern European, primarily German and Scandinavian, but with slices of southern European, Southeast Asian, and Native American. She was a high outlier for Neanderthal DNA. She thought of the teenage trysts that bore fruit, *Viking boy meets Germanic girl.*

She thought of the ancestors who almost died in childhood before continuing her chain of life. Very recently, in the scale of time she was contemplating, Daisy's paternal grandmother had almost died from the Spanish Flu in 1918. The grandmother was an infant and three of her siblings died, but somehow she pulled through.

"It's a cliché, but we're all the longest of longshots. Think of all the couplings that were required, all the close calls that cheated death, multiply that by the number of potential egg and sperm combinations."

She thought of all the roles her ancestors filled. "Man and woman, of course. But also, ruler, slave, warrior, laborer, farmer, sailor, housewife, cook, schemer, priest, princess, wretch, runt, jester, athlete, bookworm, human, Neanderthal, homo erectus, shopkeeper, swindler, gambler, grocer, judge, criminal, bartender, drinker. I am all of these things. Can I push it to trees, too? I think there was a common ancestor."

The trail wound endlessly through heavy spruce forest. Emotion ebbed and flowed for Daisy throughout the day. Sometimes her thoughts would bounce along, shooting down tangents, patterns popping up new thoughts, punctuated by bird song or music through her phone and ear buds. She would take in the view of the forest, the mountains, the rocks, the leaves, the ferns, the flowers, the bugs. At other times, the day would drag, her feet hurt, her left shoulder hurt from the backpack's strap, and all she saw was the trail directly in front of her.

At one point, she had been zoning out, focused only on the trail. She looked up and realized she was in the midst of hundreds of ferns in various states of unfurling. All around her, frond patterns repeating.

Hydration helped her mental mood; food did too. Attitude helped, but that was circular. Altitude hurt. Scenery change helped. Too much of the same view and, no matter what it was, it became baseline. She needed to transcend the baseline. Music would work for a while, then it was baseline. A new category of thoughts would work for a while, then that line of thinking became baseline. *That's a lot like life*, she thought, *stuck on the baseline.*

She felt her thinking was haphazard that day and not making much progress toward her goal. She was hashing through thoughts she already knew well, slightly new flavors maybe, but nothing life changing. It would be a failure to just come out of this hike vaguely affirming her prior hunch that experience was the point. Hadn't she thought that a year ago, and explored that, and was still searching?

So many conifers. So much shade. So much trail. The trail crossed a lazy, shallow river that required wading across. Daisy changed to her river sandals, rolled up her tights and crossed, then changed back into her hiking shoes and socks on the other side. She ate a protein bar flavored like a maple bar.

She fully believed the conclusion she had come to earlier in the hike, that a person mainly chooses meaning, rather than finds it. "But the trick is choosing something that resonates, something that I can really believe in." So, she was searching for her choice.

"I still care too much about what others think." It wasn't unusual for her to consider how she thought others would react to something. "God damn it Daisy, millions of years of ridiculously long odds didn't hit so you could worry about what others think." She thought back to Mick's comment that a mind-control scientist, a Netflix programmer, and an advertising executive could be a dangerous combination. "In a sense the media, culture, and religion are all weak forms of mind control. They frame what questions are asked and what society's default answers are. Okay, tossing off societal baseline thoughts. Tossing off media expectations, and media expectations reflected in other people, and youth and love culture reflected in the media in the first place." Four days in the wilderness helped, but a lifetime of expectations in the modern world were not easily transcended. She knew that no one else's opinion really mattered, other than Tom's. She knew she needed to choose for herself, an isolated consciousness.

The trail burst out of the shady forest into Delate

Meadow, a sea of leafy-green vegetation. The earlier squall had completely blown over and the sun shined brilliantly down. The late-afternoon breeze set leaves dancing. Purple, white, and yellow wildflowers dotted the green. *Everything's gone green.* The air turned heavier, warmer, oxygen infused, vegetative. Daisy stopped at the border between the forest and the meadow, stunned by the abrupt change. Shady forest wonderland, fern-dotted, forest green and dirt brown into buzzy, bright, warm, flower-dotted meadow. She stood facing the meadow and a joy rose inside of her. She turned to the forest and the joy rose more. She followed the trail into the meadow, excited for the new ecosystem but missing the cool protective forest. She turned and looked at the forest, and the joy rose. She followed the trail, and the joy rose.

This felt like the moment of choice, the moment of discovery; only one day remained on her pilgrimage. The meadow swept her mind upward. "I must choose. I create and discover meaning."

It felt like a mixture of reflecting on discoveries from her life's lessons and unfettered personal conscious choice, a blend of Daisy and the universal, a blend of discovering meaning and creating meaning. A huge Doug-fir had fallen across the trail and had been cut to allow the trail through. The cut was about five feet in diameter. The hulking log continued over one hundred feet into the heart of the meadow. Daisy felt the wood, the grain of the cut worn smooth over many years, examined the growth rings, smelled the wood. She climbed the log and walked on it into the meadow, trekking poles providing balance when it eventually narrowed. Far from the trail, she took her pack off and lay on her back on the log, looking at the meadow away from the sun. The smooth log, long since stripped of bark, fit the curvature of her back. Bugs buzzed; butterflies fluttered; leaves turned carbon dioxide into oxygen and energy and carbon biomass. She could see the forest on the meadow's perimeter, cool and unconcerned.

She closed her eyes and focused on the sounds. Bird calls in the foreground, backed up by a choir of smaller contributors, an occasional buzz, leaves rubbing in the breeze, but mainly bird song. She focused on the smell, leaf-and-wildflower perfume, blended with wood, dirt, mud, and mountain air.

She layered on the visual, opening her eyes. Deep breaths. She rolled onto her stomach and grabbed the log with her hands. She rubbed the smooth wood and focused on her sensations: joy, happiness, tiredness, soreness. She completed the gestalt with abstract thought: "I am here in the meadow on a fallen log. I am *here* in the meadow on a fallen log." She focused on each word's meaning. Deep breaths. She imagined what she would look like to an onlooker, and then she dismissed the thought.

She thought of the lifespan of the tree she was on, hundreds of years at least. The massive amount of wood that had accumulated at its base, narrowing with growth toward the top. She thought of the bright-green new growth each year, taking its turn, propelling life further in time, then fading back into the core.

"Life. Wow. So fucking incredible." She closed her eyes, covered her ears, and emptied her thoughts. Then simultaneously turned all senses and thought on with a deep breath. "I exist. Unbelievable. And yet—real. And amazing." She was overcome with a sensation of appreciation.

She chose her meaning: appreciating consciousness. "The point isn't experience itself. It is appreciating experience. Appreciating conscious experience."

"Appreciation is hard when I'm bumping along a baseline. How much of my life has been small and isolated attempts to transcend that baseline plain, every alcoholic drink a hammer strike at the oppressive baseline, the norm, the nothing. Attempts to gain elevation and perspective; attempts at appreciation."

She travelled the log back to the trail, committing those enlightened log-walking steps to permanent memory. She reached the trail and continued on. Before too long, she crossed Delate Creek on a wooden bridge as the creek tumbled down the hillside in an impressive waterfall. Delate Creek drained Spectacle Lake, which was where she would camp for the night, another mile or so on the trail.

The day had been fully redeemed, she thought. "Appreciation resonates as my goal. It fits the criteria, and it fits my life. It is continuous, a state of mind that can be ever-present. It is solitary, not dependent on anyone's love, approval, or interaction. It's not only part of consciousness, being a sensation itself, it also has consciousness as its object, appreciating consciousness. It is foundational; it recognizes consciousness as paramount, an amazing gift. It doesn't strive for permanence, appreciate each moment now, while it happens, while I'm living. It accommodates that people will change, everything will always change, appreciate it. It is consistent with consciousness as interpretation, appreciate it.

"It's also consistent with choosing meaning. Nothing argues that appreciation of conscious experience has to be the meaning of life, only that I choose it as the meaning of my life. It's also consistent with discovering meaning; it's the answer that resonates for me, the answer that seems true.

"The what and the why.

"How did I choose appreciation? Yes, I did ultimately choose it, but it also just popped into my mind, propagated itself throughout my brain to enter consciousness, and suggested itself. And, really, has done so repeatedly over time. I hadn't put in the thought work to choose it prior to this hike, but there was always an element of appreciation in my earlier goal of experience. So there is a very real sense in which I found my meaning. But even if it is some combination of discovery and choice, I have created the meaning. After all, even if it popped into my head, that's still my head and consciousness. And without my assigning it meaning, it wouldn't have meaning. A bit of discovering, a bit of critical thinking, a bit of learning about myself, a bit of interpreting, a bit of choosing."

She reached the spur trail to Spectacle Lake and descended to the lake. She found an isolated campsite next to a creek that fed into the lake and set up her tent. She boiled water on the propane stove, ate dinner, and prepped her water for the morning. Then she climbed into her tent and relaxed. The blister bandage had worked wonders on her toe. She stretched out on her sleeping bag on her air mattress and relaxed, taking in the moment. She tried to release the tension and aches from each of her muscles, starting from her feet and working her way up to her shoulders. And then she emptied her head. She would finish up the hike tomorrow, a long day of seventeen miles plus the spur trail to reach Snoqualmie Pass.

Twilight slipped by into warm night; moonlight lit the campsite. A series of small boulders lined the creek next to Daisy's tent site. She grabbed her flask that held a few remaining shots of bourbon and scrambled atop the largest rock, sitting with her knees pulled into her chest, arms around her legs.

This is a private rite of passage, she thought. *This marks my creation of meaning*. She took in the moon, the forest, the lake, the creek. She took a swig of whiskey, concentrating on the flavor. She breathed deeply. She appreciated the experience.

Feeling the need to push to extremes, needing to mark the moment, she stripped down and waded into the creek. The icy water shocked her feet. The creek was wide but shallow with water splashing over and around rocks. She found a deeper pool with a relatively smooth rocky bottom and sat facing downstream toward the lake, easing into the chill. She stretched out her legs into the water. Even in July, the water was very cold snow melt, having hidden in the dark recesses of the ground since melting, avoiding the summer sun's warmth. She leaned her torso back into the stream, her head propped up on a smooth rock. The water streamed around the rock and her head, flowing over her body. So cold, her nipples hard, she thought of her twenty-degree-rated sleeping bag. Then she let the thought go and appreciated the moment and her rite of passage. She listened to the nighttime forest. She breathed. She embraced the cold. She drank the last two swallows of bourbon. *I appreciate*, she thought. She repeated it to herself like a mantra, not trying to convince herself, but instead trying to infuse appreciation into her core. She repositioned herself and laid her head back into the stream. She was in the water cycle of the Earth, in the physical cycle of the universe, in her own mind. *This is good*, she thought, as water streamed over and around her. *I appreciate.*

She felt the stream bottom with her hands, rocks worn smooth by millennia of tumbling and scraping, at least the last several decades in that creek. Her left hand found a flat rock, roughly oval shape that fit in her palm. She took it with her as a marker.

Later, she would have the rock polished and inscribed with words on one side spiraling toward the center: “Information & interpretation. I create meaning. I appreciate.”

24

Daisy awoke the next morning with the sun's first light, as she normally did when tent sleeping. Mist hung over the water of Spectacle Lake, soon to be burned off. She broke camp for the last time, her pack much lighter than at the start of the hike due to the food she'd consumed. She started down the trail.

She would end at Snoqualmie Pass that day, where her car was waiting to transport her back to the modern world. Even five days in the wilderness, and a wilderness with occasional hikers at that, had shifted her mindset. She'd lost track of the day of the week. She was less concerned with clock time and more concerned with sunrise and sunset. Nature made it easier to transcend the baseline, to be sure, to escape the default cultural assumptions that community instilled in its denizens.

But her decision wasn't to appreciate nature. It was to appreciate consciousness, to appreciate being able to interpret, to appreciate being an interpretation. It might be easier to reach that state of mind in nature, apart from society, but it wasn't dependent on nature. The trick would be to actualize her decision at every moment. It would be easier to appreciate in some situations more than others. Negative events wouldn't produce happiness but could still be appreciated.

She would work on techniques. Still, she would always find it easier to appreciate while outside of buildings. In particular, the first time she stepped outside each morning was a natural moment of appreciation and a daily reminder that she could always count on. Back at home in Wallingford, the morning newspaper was tossed up on her front porch each morning. She greeted each morning with appreciation as she retrieved the paper; appreciation flowed in every season, every type of weather, every world news environment, every personal news environment. Often, she would be outside before the paper delivery, sitting in the overstuffed easy chair on the porch, drinking coffee, ostensibly waiting for the newspaper but actually intensely appreciating her consciousness, her existence.

She thought of the distinction between appreciation and joy or happiness. "People will think I'm espousing a joy of existence, or those who scorn me, a joy of nature. But my aim isn't to always feel joy, only to appreciate. Likewise with happiness—that's not my aim, only appreciation. And don't get me started on love."

She followed the trail over the crest of a ridge into an expansive alpine valley. For several miles, the trail cut across the face of the granite mountain at the head of the drainage, providing sweeping views of the valley below. The surface of the trail was loose scree.

There had been a loose end rattling around in her head for a while. "Am I something doing the interpretation or am I the interpretation itself. The physicality side of the information/interpretation yin/yang is clear; my body is the physical information; anything that science currently measures is the information. But the mental side is less clear. English language suggests I'm separate from the interpretation. For example, 'I interpret.' The 'I' is separate from what it does, 'interpret.' But clearly, we know there's no homunculus driving the mental train, just the mental train itself. There is no third person. Maybe there is no real difference whether I interpret or I am the interpretation, just a vestige of English syntax, but being the interpretation strikes me as more accurately describing reality, so that's what I'll go with. And maybe it kind of skirts the Hard Problem, being the interpretation, rather than being something else experiencing an interpretation.

"Really, this only affects the verb 'to interpret' as other mental verbs can reasonably be performed either by 'I' or by 'the interpretation' as in 'I appreciate.' I, being the interpretation, appreciate. That is, the interpretation appreciates.

"I thought yesterday about who I am. Maybe the better question is what I am. Am I really just an interpretation? Information and interpretation in an abstract void. Answering what I am, the natural reaction is to point to my physical body. But perhaps the right answer is that I'm an interpretation. That's all I really experience. I'm an interpretation.

"What exactly had decided that appreciation was meaning. It was me, of course, but what exactly? The interpretation changed and defined appreciation as meaning. What changed the interpretation? The decision came to me, like any other decision throughout life. It popped into my head and resonated. I can weigh the pros and cons; I can logically think through constraints and consistency with other beliefs and opinions (which, dear listener, you know only too well that I have), but at the end of the day, it just happened."

For Daisy, the short answer was she would appreciate conscious experience. But conscious experience is expansive. Daisy thought back to the bar customer who, when asked the meaning of life, had replied with a long list of items, some generally considered positive, some negative: romance, love, hurt, heartbreak, flavor, deep breaths, friends, etc. The bar patron had ended with: "You know, just everything, just all of it." That had stuck in Daisy's mind and seemed like the true object of appreciation. *You know, just all of it.*

She thought through the consequences of her meaning, and there were surprisingly few. "Really, it is a thing in and of itself. There are no actions that I'm compelled to take, nothing I have to accomplish. As long as I can appreciate every moment, I could be doing anything under the sun. No need to help people, no need to do good deeds, no need to strive, no need to succeed. It will be easier to appreciate in certain situations or with certain actions, for sure. Uplifting others makes appreciation easier. Physical pain is a real bitch and would be hard to appreciate. Chronic pain can wear a person down. Drug addiction could easily rob someone of appreciation and meaning. Could less obvious culprits do the same? What about love? How easy is it to fall in love and slip into dependency on another's approval? Eh, maybe for youngsters, not for me."

Daisy walked the Kendall Katwalk, where the trail had been blasted out of the face of a granite mountainside, precipitous drop to the left and cliff wall to the right. Following the Katwalk, the trail crossed a rocky saddle into another drainage. The hike's last six miles descended gradually from the Cascade crest to where Interstate-90 cuts through the mountains at Snoqualmie Pass. Daisy walked the path, bordered by Doug-fir, western hemlock, broad-leaf flowering plants claiming any dirt-enabled open space not dominated by conifers, and granite boulder fields housing whistling marmots. Finally, the parking lot appeared. Daisy tossed her pack in the backseat, cranked the engine, cranked the AC, and was home in Seattle in an hour.

* * *

The August night was hot. Daisy did not have air conditioning in her 1920s-era Wallingford house, something she regretted two or three days per year. The lack of southern exposure usually kept the house reasonably cool, but this night the temperature would stay in the upper seventies, hot for Cascadia. She stripped her bed down to only a sheet. She sipped a small glass of ice water and watched an uninspired late-night comedy/talk show.

Her phone buzzed. "How was the hike?" It was a text from Mick.

"Hard but good. Sleeping was tough. I never got to fire the gun." - Daisy.

"Overall fulfilling experience." - Daisy.

"Glad you didn't need to fire. That's the best kind of

security." - Mick.

"Whatcha doing?" - Daisy.

"Thinking about you." - Mick.

"Horror show?" - Daisy.

"I have some time off from security. Join me for fishing in Bozeman?" - Mick.

God damn it, thought Daisy, *I just wanted to let this float undefined.* She was torn on how to respond. She didn't want a relationship; she knew that much. She wanted to embrace aloneness and grow her appreciation, but she did enjoy Mick and would welcome an occasional dinner and hook-up. The time gap was growing for her response. Mick had to know something negative was coming.

"Look, I'm not looking for a relationship right now." - Daisy.

"Although I'm a looker." Winking emoji, Daisy added after rereading her prior text, deflecting with humor. *Ugh, that's terrible*, Daisy thought of her text.

"It's not you, it's me." Three tilted laughter tears emojis - Daisy.

"I was worried I'd never get to use that one in life—something to check off my list." - Daisy.

"We could just fish and drink and not talk to each other. No relationship." Winking emoji - Mick.

"One day we'll do that Mick, if you're still on the market." - Daisy.

"Ciao" - Daisy.

"Gnite" - Mick.

* * *

The Fremont was buzzing with activity on a Thursday night just prior to the Labor Day weekend. Daisy was alone behind the bar; Sandy, the other bartender, had called in sick. When Sandy's call came in, Daisy thought of the old Steven Jesse Bernstein Sub Pop spoken-word piece that went something like "I feel too good to go to work. When I'm sick, I will go to work." It was easy duty at least, pulling beers and making some occasional well drinks.

Bianca came in, wearing jeans and a tee shirt, and greeted Daisy at the bar. "Busy tonight, huh?" The bar had Pilsner Urquell on tap and Bianca ordered one. "You're still doing this for fun, right?" Bianca settled in at the end of the bar and tickled her phone.

Between pouring drinks, Daisy told Bianca about her backpacking hike.

"You did that voluntarily for fun, too?" Bianca shook her head. "Were you god almighty bored?"

"Not too much," answered Daisy, "sometimes. I can take a little boredom if it's coupled with physical activity—not unlike tending bar."

It was too busy to talk much, so Bianca finished her pilsner and got up to go. "Hey," she called out to Daisy, who came over, "I might not see you for a few weeks. I'm headed to Tokyo. I'm presenting at a conference there."

"You are an in-demand conference speaker. What a badass."

"This one should be fun; lots going on ..." Bianca's thought seemed to trail off. "You know that five-way, or however-many-way, intersection where everyone crosses at once? Shibuya crossing? The hotel is right near there." Bianca headed toward the door. "See you, sis."

"See ya," answered Daisy, pulling a beer.

At home that night, Daisy poured herself a Woodford Reserve on the rocks with a healthy dose of pure vanilla, two maraschino cherries, and two spoonfuls of the syrup from the cherry jar. She took her drink and sat on the overstuffed porch chair to unwind toward sleep.

"Wanna hang out in Tokyo?" she texted Coop.

"When? I'm in Hong Kong right now for a week." - Coop.

"Serendipity, synchronicity–now we gotta do this. I'll get details." - Daisy.

"It's morning here, shouldn't you be asleep?" - Coop.

"No sleep till ... Brooklyn. Strike that ... Tokyo" - Daisy.

"You been drinking?" - Coop.

"Ya you know me" - Daisy.

Daisy sipped her bourbon and watched the night sky. She thought back to the billions of stars she had seen at her mountainside camp and compared that to the few hundred she could see from her porch. *Tradeoffs*, she thought. A sliver of a new moon hung in the western sky. Daisy tracked it over time across the sky. Another summer was about to end, another quarter turn of the celestial clock.

25

Daisy exited her train at the Shibuya station completely disoriented at 11:00 a.m. Tokyo was already steaming. The buzz of the city tried to offset the jet lag and time difference—being 3:00 a.m. in Seattle. Stepping out of the station, Daisy walked by the statue of Hachiko, the faithful pup that had returned to Shibuya Station every day for years to check if his deceased owner would come home from work. The patter of Japanese, which she didn't understand, provided background music. Daisy stumbled upon the gonzo crosswalk of Shibuya Crossing, waited for the walk sign, and participated. Midrise buildings with retail stretching up to the top floor dominated the view down every street in every direction, each hung with lighted signs and video screens. Japanese kanji and kana shared the sign landscape with English.

Daisy ducked into the Starbucks bordering the crosswalk for a little Americana and Americano, got her bearings, and pulled up directions to her hotel on her phone. She chose an intentionally circuitous path to the hotel in order to stretch her legs after the interminable plane ride but unintentionally got lost several times on the non-gridded streets and alleys. She wandered into a pachinko parlor and was astounded by the thunderous roar of the steel balls pounding down the nail boards. *I've got to give that a try,* she thought, although the game's goal and process eluded her. *Beats the hell out of slot machines.*

Eventually, Daisy made it to the hotel. The Cerulean Tower Tokyu was a large business hotel, located only a short walk from the Shibuya station if one were to take a direct route, and was the location of the conference at which Bianca was speaking. The cold air conditioning was a welcome reprieve as Daisy walked a long hallway toward the front desk. Signs announced the Tokyo University Neuroscience Conference.

An Asian man looked out of place in a Hawaiian shirt drinking perhaps an Arnold Palmer. "Coop!" Daisy called out when not too far away so as not to offend the culture.

"There she is," said Coop. "Good flight?"

"Ugh, no, too long. How do you deal with so many flights? How long have you been here?"

"I got in yesterday. Flew in from Hong Kong. Nice hotel, two steps up from where I was in Hong Kong."

Daisy checked in and deposited her bag in her room, rejoined Coop in the lobby, and the two went sightseeing in the sprawling metropolis.

* * *

Tokyo University Neuroscience Conference attendees streamed out of the hotel's main ballroom, grabbed light snacks and drinks that were provided for them in the foyer, and formed eddies of conversations in the stream of people. Attendees were on their own for dinner, and many first filtered into the three lobby bars in the Cerulean Tower Tokyu hotel.

One of the bars overlooked the other two, one floor higher, connected by a sweeping staircase. Daisy and Coop were perched in the top bar, drinking Long Island iced teas, ordered primarily to see what the Japanese bartender would create. He came through admirably. "Better than you would make," Coop poked at Daisy. They waited for Bianca to appear, wanting to surprise her with their presence. "So I guess we're becoming groupies at Bianca conferences," Coop said.

Bianca emerged from the hallway leading from the ballroom to the lower-level lobby bars, walking with an older gentleman. They stopped, shook hands, and then the man walked to the elevator banks while Bianca surveyed the lobby area. Two Japanese men approached her, one a short man dressed in a cream-colored linen suit, the other a hulking young man in jeans and a tucked-in polo shirt. The larger man put his hand on Bianca's shoulder and the three walked to a table at the back edge of the bar area, where another large man was already seated.

"There she is," said Daisy, pointing Bianca out to Coop. "Let's go say hi." The two started toward the staircase to the lower level. Before they reached the top step, a man came out of nowhere and intercepted them, arms outstretched to corral them back toward their original table. It was Mick.

"Mick! What the hell are you doing here?" asked

Daisy.

"I'll explain, but let's sit first," as they returned to their table.

"Are you stalking me?" asked Daisy.

Mick put his hands on the table, controlling the situation. "I need you to be quiet, stay calm, and listen," he said in a hushed voice. "I'm a US federal agent. I've been assigned to keep tabs on Ms. Zanone for a couple years. We're watching her because of the mind-altering, or some might say mind-controlling, drugs she's been working on developing. The Arizona conference was the first time I had actually made contact with her, which was probably a mistake, as she seemed to quickly identify me as a government agent. In any case, it did net me a friend or two." He looked in Daisy's eyes, then Coop's.

"Under false pretenses," countered Daisy.

"Occupational hazard," said Mick. "Here's the deal though. Bianca's not here to just present at this conference. You need to stay out of sight.

"Do you remember when we were eating pizza at your house, and Bianca thought I should have artichokes on the pizza, and then she saw a bluebird project? Well, Project Artichoke and Project Bluebird were CIA mind-control operations in the 1950s, precursors to the more famous MK-Ultra work. She was telling me she knew I was a government agent keeping tabs on her mind-control work."

The henchman's hand was heavy on Bianca's shoulder, directing her to a seat. His fingers dug into her muscle. The two thugs sat close on both sides of Bianca, with the short, suited man seated across the small bar table.

"Hamamura Niko, I presume?" asked Bianca.

"Nice to welcome you to Tokyo, Ms. Zanone," said Hamamura in reasonably clear English. "What can I get you to drink?"

"I'm not thirsty, thanks."

"I insist," Hamamura said, and motioned with his hand to one of the muscle men who then went to the bar and ordered a glass of white wine and a glass of water.

"Hey!" Daisy called out, pointing at the thug at the bar. Daisy instinctively grabbed her empty glass in her right hand as a potential projectile and started to stand. Mick grabbed her forearm hard and yanked her back down.

"Sit down and be quiet," he commanded.

Her yell had caused a minor shift of attention toward their table, but with no follow-through the room quickly returned to the din of drinks and appetizers.

"That big man slipped mickeys into the two drinks he's carrying," Daisy whispered.

"It's under control," Mick answered. "Bianca knows the situation. She reached out to me last week to let me know what was happening."

Daisy reluctantly loosened her grasp on the lowball glass.

"What kind of wine is it?" Bianca asked her tablemate.

"White. It's white wine." Said the muscle man who had gone to the bar.

The thug set the drinks on the table in front of Bianca and resumed his flanking position. Bianca raised the wine glass to her nose, smelled it, and returned it to the table. She did the same with the water. "These smell a little off," she said. "Maybe your two friends could taste them to make sure the drinks have not gone bad."

"You've fucked with the wrong person, Zanone," said Hamamura.

"Someone has fucked with the wrong person; I'll give you that. Maybe your mother when she conceived you, you evil little soul-sucker."

"How'd you do it? How'd you get everyone to riot?"

"Maybe they just woke up to reality, you little slug."

Hamamura nodded to the thug on Bianca's left, the one who had not gotten the drinks. Bianca felt a sharp poke in her thigh. Soon she felt lightheaded, then heavy-headed, trance-like and starting to disassociate from reality. *Ketamine?* she thought. *Amateurs.*

The muscle men helped Bianca to her feet, propped her arm around the shoulder of the one who'd injected her, and walked her out as if she'd had too much to drink.

Bianca regained reasonably full clearheadedness in what seemed like the back of a van. Countless club nights with bumps of ketamine had helped prepare her. No K-hole could hold her. Her hands were bound behind her back, and her feet were also bound. Her mouth was gagged, and a blindfold covered her eyes. After a short ride, the van rumbled to a stop, and the men carried her into a warehouse. The air had the briny smell of being near the harbor. Once inside, the men removed her blindfold and gag and sat her down on a wooden chair.

"You fucking bitch," Hamamura screamed. He slapped her across the cheek. "Was it worth it now? However you did it, you're going to pay now." Another slap. He grabbed her throat, choking her for a moment, and then pushing her back. The chair fell backward, and Bianca tumbled to the floor. One of the men resituated her on the chair. Bianca looked around. Only the three men from the hotel were there.

"Where's your master, Masaki Kami, The Glove?" Bianca asked. "You know where I come from, there's only one glove and it's Gary Payton." Bianca spit at Hamamura.

"Masaki-san is a bad joke. Who the fuck knows or cares where he is. Probably herding elephants in Sri Lanka. I'm the one you need to worry about."

"What are you going to do with me?"

"First, tell me how you did it. How did you cause the riot?"

"I don't know what the fuck you're talking about."

"We have time, Zanone. We have remote property no one knows about. We'll hold you until you talk. We'll break you. It won't be pleasant." Hamamura circled the chair in satisfaction, circling his prey. "You know, I was tired of all that consensual bullshit anyway—reject, accept, merge. Who the fuck would buy into that? It was like living with moronic sheep. Baa baa bullshit. This might be a little more fun, having you as a plaything. I'll have you begging for the smallest luxuries: a drink of water, a blanket. Yes, this will be fun. Breaking the bitch."

"A drink of water wouldn't count as a luxury, you fucking moron."

"Maybe I'll just kill you, or maybe keep you

prisoner. I'm not sure. Either way, I'll enjoy it. The world has seen the last of you Zanone. Kaito, bring the new car to the loading dock. Daichi, knock the impudence out of her, then let's get out of Tokyo."

"The what, Hamamura-san?" asked one of the henchmen, looking at the other.

"What you don't know, Hamamura, is that I have friends in high places," Bianca said. "They'll find me."

"They won't find you."

"God, your plan is so idiotic. If I go missing, they'll look at hotel-camera footage. It will show you shooting me up and abducting me. You're the mastermind? No wonder your summer camp went bust."

"I can disappear, pop up somewhere else as someone else," Hamamura answered. "No one cares when you have money, and I have money. You see, we have tradition of honor and of revenge. You need to suffer for your deeds. I will make you suffer, and I will make you hurt."

"So no more preying on yoga girls?" Bianca flexed her shoulders back to reposition her bound arms. "Athleisure chic finito?"

"Could you be any more annoying? Fucking bitch!" he screamed.

"You scream like a bitch," said Bianca. "Like a weak little bitch."

"Okay, let's go boys. We need to teach Zanone respect. Let's get out of here."

"My people will find me, Hamamura, and then they'll hang you."

"Well, they better find you fast, Miss Bitch, unless you like pain."

"Like the tentacles of a sea creature, arms turning over every stone, they'll find me. You'll hang." Bianca glared in his eyes. "Like a giant eight-legged cephalopod ..."

"Fucking shit you are intolerable. Why don't you just say octopus? It's a fucking octopus!" Hamamura screamed.

Explosive blasts rang out all around them. Doors crashed down and windows shattered. Police in commando gear flooded into the warehouse from multiple doors and windows, laser-sighted rifles trained on the three captors.

"Oh, yeah, octopus. I probably didn't mention that was my safe word—that ketamine must have made me forget." The police handcuffed Hamamura and the henchmen, and were untying Bianca. "Do you know that many scientists think cephalopods, you know, octopi, developed consciousness independently of other animals? Meaning consciousness evolved multiple times. Ponder the implications of that as you rot in jail, mother fucker."

26

"What bar are you in? We're never going to find you in here. Text me the name of the place so I can get directions," Bianca texted Daisy. Bianca and Harry, the project manager for the Kansha Kokoro liberation and subsequent leadership sting, wandered through the maze of tiny bars in Shinjuku's Golden Gai, seemingly thousands of bars piled on top of each other, jumbled together in a low-rise throwback to old Tokyo. Many of the bars seated only five or six patrons. Sketchy, rickety stairways led to second-story bars and additional seating. Pedestrian-only alleyways, and even narrower shortcuts, wound through the ramshackle district.

"It has an *Our Star Blazers* theme," Daisy texted. "Well, among many other themes. It's not clear if there is a name." Tear laughter emoji.

"I know," she said to Coop and Mick, "I'll text them GPS coordinates."

"Here ya go: 35.6939° N, 139.7046° E." - Daisy.

"That's never going to work in this maze," said Mick.

About fifteen minutes later Bianca and Harry

walked in. "We took a few wrong turns," laughed Bianca.

"Hey!" Daisy hopped off her stool to hug Bianca who squeezed between the wall and the bar stools to reach Daisy. "You are one badass bitch."

"I couldn't let Harry's crew have all the fun." Introductions were made. The group filled five of the available six seats, and it was cramped at that.

"I saw them doctor your drinks back in the lobby bar. I started to make a scene, but Mick stopped me," Daisy said.

"I know you've got my back, sis. Thanks for keeping the peanut gallery in check, Mick." Mick nodded.

"So," said Bianca, "do we get your real name now? Having passed our patriotism test." The bartender poured five shots of Suntory whiskey. "Cheers!" Glasses clinked and shots drained.

"Why Americans only drink Suntory?" the bartender asked.

"*Lost in Translation*," said Coop. "A movie; an aging Bill Murray was a Suntory pitchman, hanging out with Scarlett Johansson. Best advertisement you could hope for. Cult classic with staying power."

"I want a name," Bianca persisted.

"C'mon Bianca, his name's Mick," Daisy said.

"Well," said Mick, "Bianca's right. Mick is not my real name. But it's just easier if that's what you call me. What's in a name anyway."

"Bullshit," said Bianca. "I'm surprised you guys didn't screw this up."

"We didn't even have people here," said Mick. "US intervention in Japan would not go over well. Plus, with the private army of commandos that were backing up the Japanese police, I'm not sure there would have been room for anyone else. How many people did Paulson send, anyway?"

"Enough to keep my ass safe," said Bianca. "God damn, what a bar," she said, directing to Coop and Daisy, nodding at the *Our Star Blazers* mural over the bar. "Where are we in the countdown to school being out? Use the wave motion gun!"

"I missed out on this apparently classic cartoon as a kid," Coop said.

"Were you afraid that the cops, and the private commandos, would lose you?" asked Daisy.

"I had four trackers, one of which was ingested and one implanted under my skin. They weren't going to lose me. I also had three mics and two cameras, both cameras in my boots. Plus, you won't believe this, I had a knockout gas I could trigger in my boot. My blouse would have functioned as a weak gas mask if I could have gotten it over my nose or mouth, supposedly enough to let me retain consciousness while everyone else in the room would be out."

"Just to take out the cult's leadership, huh?" Coop asked.

"Yeah, we didn't want them to just reopen with another batch of brainwashed lost souls. Hamamura, it turns out, was the brains behind the operation. The guru, the one they call the Glove of God, is in la la land. Not surprising maybe."

"But why you?" asked Daisy. "It seems like risky work for a scientist?"

"It was my choice," answered Bianca. "I thought it would be fun. I'd tried to create a personal feud with

Hamamura; I wanted to take him down. He is not a good person."

Bianca entertained the group with the play-by-play of the takedown.

"I don't get it," said Daisy. "What does the idea that octopi evolved consciousness independently from other animals imply?"

"Well, I think it could imply a lot of things—good for long hours of pondering in prison. It could imply that the evolution of consciousness is fairly easy in this universe," said Bianca. "It isn't a one-in-a-trillion anomaly if it has happened independently in multiple evolutionary lines. It might suggest that consciousness is an important component of information processing in living things; no zombies thrive in this universe. But most importantly, it might imply there is something special about this universe that enables consciousness. Something beyond physics. Think of flying—multiple animals evolved the ability to fly independently: birds, insects, bats. That was possible because the universe's physics produce an environment in which flight is feasible: lift, drag, air resistance and all that. Maybe it's the same with consciousness; something in the universe's physics enables it—or maybe we need a word that is broader than physics (other than metaphysics); something in the universe's totality enables it."

"The Zanone field," said Daisy.

The group rambled from bar to bar, struggling to stay together as a group. In one slightly larger bar, seemingly dedicated to Christmas lights of every era, Daisy had a corner seat with Mick. Bubble lights, small twinklers, modern icicles. Daisy preferred the larger colored bulbs from her childhood.

"You okay, Mick? You're quiet."

"Yeah, I'm okay. Not sure I'm really part of this group though. I feel like an interloper."

"Come here," Daisy stood up and hugged Mick, sliding into a seated position on the bench next to him, keeping the embrace. "You're a good guy, Mick. Or whatever your name is ..." She gave him a peck of a kiss on the lips.

"You're not mad about my deception? Hiding my true role?"

"You did what you had to do. You're walking your path, all for the greater good. You're a good man, Micky."

"But not good enough for a fishing trip?"

"Plenty good enough. That's just on me right now. I want to be alone—not attached."

They wandered to more bars. Some charged a small cover charge. Daisy and Coop had a conversation about the economic wisdom of a cover charge in the Golden Gai with so many alternatives at hand. No definitive conclusion was reached. Mick defected back to the hotel.

The group entered a punk-rock-themed bar with a Misfits skull on the sign. Only four stools were open, out of six total, in groups of two. Daisy and Bianca took the back two, and Coop and Harry took the two near the entrance. The dulcet tones of Jello Biafra singing "California Über Alles" filled the bar.

"So, I get that there are things you can't tell me, but why were you involved in this at all?" Daisy asked.

"Yeah, I can't really get into that. I'll just say Kansha Kokoro recruited someone who they shouldn't have, someone well-connected."

"That was the cult? Kansha Kokoro?"

"Yeah, it means thankful mind."

"Ha! Really? That's funny. That's what I chose as my meaning: appreciation. Appreciation of consciousness."

"Oh yeah? I like that, big sis. That fits you. On your hike?"

"Yep."

"Well, trust me, maybe the semantic meanings are similar, but you would have hated this group. Their mantra was 'reject, accept, merge.' Reject the material world, accept the natural world, merge with the spirit. Such bullshit. It just goes to show, when you isolate people and control all the information flow, people will follow like sheep."

"Well, I do think the media and modern culture are hugely influential, so you could say in a way I reject the material world," said Daisy. "But really, I just object to the limited perspective we get clobbered with, how they set the agenda and control the narrative; I rather like the rest of the material world. And I do find it easier to appreciate outside—in the natural world so to speak. So you could say I accept the natural world. And, oh my god, this is ridiculous, one of my core tenets is that meaning comes only from consciousness, not from the physical world, in other words—the spirit. Ha. I feel like you're going to start hunting me."

"Alright, I'm assuming you don't steal life savings from weak-mined people?"

"Right, I'm in the clear there. Plus, what do they mean by the spirit? I'm guessing it is very different than my interpretation."

"Well, their other leader claimed to be the brother of Jesus and the Buddha, so ..."

"Yeah, a little bit different."

Eventually, Bianca and Harry peeled off back to the hotel. Daisy and Coop migrated to a new setting and sat in a second story bar at a window overlooking one of the alleyways. A cat prowled the room. "So, this is a pretty classic drinking environment, right?" asked Daisy. "This should qualify for your fetish."

"Yeah, it definitely is. I hadn't heard of this place before coming to Tokyo, but it seems like I should have. No historic or pop-culture tie in, at least that I'm aware of, but it seems to deserve a place in the world's pantheon of drinking locales."

"Ya know, Coop, our friendship is pretty rare. Pretty odd." Daisy sipped her whiskey on the rocks. "I mean, I really don't have any friends. I know people; I have acquaintances; I have lovers, but not really any friends recently." She watched drinkers stumble down the alleyway. "That's pretty cool. My bartending paid off with a friend."

"Yeah, suffering through your bartending netted me a friend, too," Coop laughed.

Coop went back to the hotel, after protesting that Daisy shouldn't remain alone and shouldn't train back to the hotel alone, but Daisy insisted. She walked the alleyways and took a seat at a new bar. It had a lighted Japanese lantern in front and two people sitting at a five-stool bar. She took the far barstool and ordered a shot of Suntory, which she had been drinking all night.

The bartender set it in front of her on a coaster advertising something that Daisy could not interpret.

She leaned against the back wall and took in the scene: bar, bartender, patrons, alley. Her mind was not sharp at the end of the night, but her emotions were dialed up. Her feel was on. She looked at the whiskey, at the shot glass, at the coaster. In life, she'd never really gotten over the desire to keep drinking once she had started. *I am who I am,* she thought. She raised the shot glass as if honoring it for a moment, then drank the shot in a slow, smooth motion, head tilted back, and placed the empty shot glass upside down on the coaster.

* * *

The next day, Daisy, Bianca, Coop, and Harry sat in a sub-street-level restaurant near Shibuya Station eating udon. The counterperson showed a confused Harry how to self-serve the broth; the rest of the party learned and were glad they were not first in line.

They hopped the JR train to Harajuku Station and wandered Takeshita Street. Their presence increased the average age on the street materially. Teen and preteen Japanese youth jammed the pedestrian-only street lined with cat cafes, owl cafes, cotton-candy cafes, sugar cafes, and any other type of cafe that pop-culture obsessed kids would frequent. A group of cosplayers passed them; no one in Daisy's group could identify who any of the characters were. "Why do you dress so boringly?" Daisy asked Coop.

"Karaoke!" Coop exclaimed, rounding a corner. "C'mon, who's game? The quintessential Japanese experience."

"Really Coop?" asked Daisy. "That is the quintessential Japanese experience in your mind? Geisha? Samurai? Pachinko? Sushi?"

"Let's do it," said Harry, "I'm tired of walking around with all these kids," as a trio of Hello Kitty–clad early teens drinking bubble teas barreled through the group.

"I'm not a fan of karaoke, never done it," said Daisy. "I don't really like the spotlight, you know. I'm more of a backup singer."

"C'mon, it'll be fun. What do you say, Daisy? *Lost in Translation*. We were drinking Suntory last night, now the karaoke scene," said Coop.

"I've never seen it," said Daisy. The group waffled, waiting for direction.

Daisy thought about choices. Choices usually weren't option A versus option B, karaoke versus owl cafe, for example. Instead, they were option A versus a default, karaoke versus not karaoke. Choosing the default too often, or just not choosing and defaulting to the default, left one stuck on the baseline. She knew she had to transcend the baseline, continuously. She had to appreciate existence. *Avoid the default option*, she thought.

"Okay," Daisy conceded. "But I'm gonna need a drink or two before I listen to you sing, Coop."

The group purchased a private room and a round of Sapporos. Padded bench seating lined the walls in the small room, with two small drink tables in the middle.

"So, does this count, Coop, as recreating a pop culture scene?" asked Daisy, taking her first sip.

"Not really, with the location being different."

"What's this?" asked Harry, "You like to recreate scenes?"

"Not just pop culture," said Coop. "Really just anything historical. This here doesn't count though, for me. It needs to be in the same physical location. So, for example having a drink at the bar in the Ritz in Paris, a dry martini, like Hemingway did when he liberated the Ritz from the Nazis. Or at least celebrated the liberation.

"Or at a battlefield, for example. Omaha and Utah beaches and the D-Day landing. I went there with one of my daughters a few years ago. It's a weighty place. You feel the magnitude of the battle, of the lives lost. It makes history more real, but more importantly it makes you feel more real, or more dialed-up. It's like the weight of the place's history carries on through time, but only if you know the history. I'm sure there are centuries of momentous events here in Tokyo, but I just don't know of them."

"Not just be there," interjected Daisy, "that would be tourism. Coop has a drink in the location."

"True. True. In general, yes, I have a drink in the historic local. At the D-Day beaches I had a flask of Jack Daniel's, gin, and maple syrup to honor the American, British, and Canadian soldiers. It was actually pretty tasty. I had a Berliner beer at Hitler's bunker, in Berlin, where he committed suicide. It's a parking lot now, not far from the Brandenburg Gate. I sat on a parking curb in the lot and enjoyed a brew, thinking about Hitler swallowing a cyanide capsule and shooting himself in the head sixty or so years earlier, right below me.

"These locations just feel different too me, more

resonant. A hotel room where a celebrity overdosed or got in a fight with their lover. If you stay in that room, the feeling still ripples through time—if you're aware of it."

"We never did any of the Seattle scenes we talked about," said Daisy.

"Not yet," said Coop.

"What do you have your eye on in Tokyo?" asked Harry.

"Nothing really. I don't know."

"Godzilla battles King Kong?" asked Bianca. "Wasn't that in Tokyo?"

"For me, it's just a different way to experience a place. Rather than getting routed on a tourist trail, it gives you a destination. It is still often touristy, but at least there is some authenticity to it. And it connects you with things across time."

Bianca lowered the lighting, settling on a fuchsia mood accented with white light shooting at the spinning mirror ball in the middle of the room. "Kick us off, Daisy," said Bianca.

A waitress brought another round of Sapporos. Daisy grabbed hers, "Cheers," took a few large swigs, and punched in a song. *No defaults*, she thought as she grabbed the mic and slid into a rendition of Amy Winehouse's "Rehab."

Coop followed with "The Rainbow Connection" in his best Kermit the Frog voice.

Bianca and Harry paired up for a duet on Zeppelin's "Rock and Roll."

The beer and music flowed. Three hours later the group ambled back up Takeshita Street toward the train station. Coop walked beside Daisy.

"So I haven't heard the outcome of your pilgrimage, yet. Did you find the meaning of life?" Coop asked.

"I did, Cooper."

"And?"

Daisy took in the youth culture scene, anime come to life.

"Which song is real?" asked Daisy.

"Huh?"

"Exactly," said Daisy. "Huh. Asking someone the meaning of life is a bit like asking which song is real. It's meaningless; all songs are real. You just like some and dislike some. Some resonate for you and some don't. Each person creates meaning, or doesn't. For me, it's appreciating conscious experience."

27

Familiar clouds blanketed Seattle in November. Enough to produce an occasional sprinkle and nothing more. Daisy and Coop sat at the bar in Murphy's on 45th, drinking Harp. Coop was again in Seattle on business. Daisy had made Murphy's her local. It had a homey Irish feel and was within walking distance of her house. It had a normally pleasant mix of regulars and new faces, although lately the regulars had been regularly boring to Daisy.

"Coop, if you could go back and live the last twenty years again, would you?" Daisy asked.

"Not a chance. No way. Too hard. I barely cleared many hurdles the first time through; I'm not running that course again." Coop took a drink. "I assume you mean without keeping my current knowledge?"

"Right," said Daisy, "just able to do it all again, without voodoo powers. No one I've asked has said they would take the opportunity. That's fucked up. Really, truly, fucked up. Life is hard, yeah, but also what an experience. What a gift."

"I just think of all the work, all the hard times, all

the challenges, all the fights and heartache."

"I didn't realize you'd had a lot of heartache."

"Maybe not heartache, but strained relationship certainly."

"But you wouldn't give up any of your future life, right?" asked Daisy.

"Right."

"That seems inconsistent."

"Yeah, I guess so, but I think it's how most people feel."

"We mourn suicides but wouldn't relive life if we could. I'd take the offer to relive my last twenty years," Daisy continued. "Maybe that means I've had an easy time of it compared to everyone else I talk with. Time is fleeting; I'd take an extra twenty."

"If it meant Tommy had to renavigate childhood and might not turn out as great? If it meant you might not have had such investing luck and had to slog through a nine-to-five job for forty years? If it meant you wouldn't find appreciation?"

"True, maybe not. But I'd do it again if I could live it exactly the same. Same result. Same events. Same feelings. Not you, with those rules?" Daisy asked.

"No, too much work. I survived it once. That's enough. I don't want to do it again."

The bartender brought another round of Harp.

Next to Daisy was an empty stool and beyond that were two men whom Daisy had not seen before; they weren't regulars. They were in their late twenties or early thirties, and soft. Probably software engineers, IT project managers, or the like. Daisy had been eavesdropping on their conversation. The one closest to her was consoling the other who had apparently been dumped by his fiancée shortly before their wedding date. The gloomy non-groomy shed an occasional tear. He wasn't bad looking—and if Daisy were right about his employment, he should make a reasonable salary. Daisy wondered what his prior fiancée looked like and what her motivation was.

"This could be a break for you," the consoler said. "What if you'd had kids, and then she left? What if you were miserable together for twenty years before breaking up?" *Reasonable advice*, Daisy thought. But the man was not consoled.

"Everything happens for a reason," the friend said. "Everything happens for a reason."

"Excuse me," Daisy interrupted, "if I may. I heard a little of your conversation. That's terrible advice. Everything happens for a reason is exactly wrong. Things don't happen for reasons."

"Who are you?" the friend asked without wanting an answer. "Mind your own business."

"C'mon, you wouldn't get so defensive if it were good advice. Things don't happen for reasons, they just happen. Physical reasons, yes. Moral or fateful reasons, no. You just have to roll with the punches. Endure."

"Seriously, lady, no one asked you," the friend said.

"Look, there's no reason to make up vague universal spiritual mumbo jumbo. That doesn't help. Shit happens."

"C'mon, Josh," the friend said patting his friend's shoulder, "let's move to a table far away from this person."

"Hold on," Josh said, "let's hear her out. I kind of

like what she's preaching."

"I'm not sure I have anything more to say," said Daisy. "It's just that phrase 'Everything happens for a reason'—pet peeve maybe, but not helpful."

"How do you know there aren't moral reasons?" the friend said, grasping at straws.

"You don't even believe in moralistic fate, so why go there when your friend needs comfort? The truth is far more comforting," said Daisy, dismissing him. "Your earlier advice was on point; this change might be for the better. An opportunity for your friend. Maybe he avoided disaster. No need to go to things happening for reasons."

Josh laughed and tried to lower the steam pressure rising in his friend. "Any advice to replace it?" he asked Daisy.

"Time heals everything," Daisy answered. "Something like this—from what I overheard, a premarriage break-up? Time will wash it away before you know it."

"Oh, deep," said the friend.

"At least it's true, you dipshit." Daisy even surprised herself with the dipshit epithet. *Better dial it back,* she thought. "Time heals everything. Verifiably true. Something like this is relatively minor."

"Verifiable?" the friend sneered.

"You'll die. You'll feel nothing. Verified. But no need to push to extremes over something like this. A few months will wash away a break-up."

"Great solution, you'll die someday. Very reassuring." With that, the friend moved across the bar to a corner table. Josh got up to join him, but first walked to Daisy and Coop. "He'll be fine; just doesn't like getting called out like that. I understand what you're saying, though. Any other advice?"

"Nah, the rest you have to learn for yourself."

With that, Josh joined his friend. Daisy asked the bartender to put their bar bill on her tab.

"Do you want to eat?" Coop asked, perusing a menu. "All this beer's making me hungry."

"You go ahead, I don't like their non-meat options here."

"Are you vegetarian?"

"Trying to be. As of a few months ago."

"Really, why?"

"Well, Coop, if my meaning is to appreciate conscious experience, it seems like a bad choice to kill consciousnesses to eat them."

"Okay," Coop laughed, "can't argue with that. Good thing alcohol isn't conscious." He ordered some Irish nachos, without meat. "What the hell are Irish nachos?" he wondered.

28

A little over two years later, on the morning of the winter solstice, Daisy was up early, as she always was, made coffee and headed to her front porch. She opened the front door and smelled the cold, wet world. She appreciated. In sweatpants and a parka, she slurped her coffee sitting in the overstuffed porch chair watching the dark world spin. A single string of Christmas lights decorated the porch. At about 6:30 a.m., the Seattle Times and Wall Street Journal were tossed onto the porch by a vehicular paper deliverer. She retreated inside to read the papers, refilled her coffee, and returned to the porch to watch the sunrise just before 8:00.

She had defined the two solstices as personal holidays. On these days, she focused on appreciating conscious experience. Practically, this involved a lot of sitting on the porch.

The sky started to brighten to a heavy cloud cover and light sprinkle. Daisy thought of the Earth spinning, her longitude starting to face the sun, the northern pole tilted away to its maximum, about to start back on the flip side. She thought of seasons and life stages. She thought of time, and limited time. She thought of things that were interesting and that she cared about. She reminded herself to not spend time on things or people that didn't make the cut.

After sunrise, she went for a jog and showered. Then she resumed porch sitting, having swapped the sweatpants for jeans. She turned on a restaurant-style portable heater for warmth. She listened to the pitter-patter of the rain, the traffic noise in the distance, the occasional wind. She took in the neighborhood and its Christmas decorations.

She rubbed the inscribed rock in her pocket and thought of her rite of passage. She thought of creating meaning. She thought hers was the latest in a long line of belief systems to appropriate the solstice for a holiday, for a day of focus.

Tom rode up on his bike. He was in his sophomore year at the University of Washington, living in a large house near campus with four other guys. "Hi Mom, solstice sitting?"

"Yep," Daisy smiled and laughed, "solstice sitting." He popped up to the bedroom of his youth.

Daisy walked down the hill to Gasworks Park and walked to the top of the sundial hill. She looked out over the Lake Union houseboats with Christmas lights reflected in the water. She looked across the lake at South Lake Union where Paulson's Brain Institute was housed. She looked at the downtown skyscrapers, including the one in which Tom was conceived. Walking back to her house, she smelled marijuana coming from the park's covered area, an area filled with now sanitized and painted pipes from the old gas works.

Instead of returning home, she walked past her house further up the hill to Dick's on 45th for fries and a chocolate shake. She did miss Dick's Deluxe hamburgers. *You're welcome, cow*, she thought. *You better appreciate it*. Back at home, she toasted a garden burger to pair with the fries and ate on her porch.

She pulled her rite-of-passage rock from her pocket and read the inscription: "Information & interpretation. I create meaning. I appreciate." She listened to the audio recordings she'd made on the trail. She thought about her hike, her pilgrimage, and why appreciation was her meaning. The what and the why.

Somewhat chilled, she went inside and lit a wood fire in the fireplace. She'd considered replacing it with a gas fireplace years ago but didn't want to lose the feel of a wood fire with its glowing embers on those few occasions that she actually used it.

She turned on a classic country and Americana deep cuts music mix. *Loud music works better*, she thought, and cranked it up. She lay down on the couch, listened to the music, and just thought, just appreciated.

Tom bounced down the stairs. "The neighbors might need to call the cops to shut this rager down." Heading to the door, "See ya, Mom."

"See ya, Tommy. I love you."

Sunset at 4:20 p.m. was approaching. Daisy went to her liquor cabinet to concoct a celebratory sundown drink. The bar was still well stocked from her training days. She muddled a Hennessy old fashioned and took a sip. She laughed thinking back on the looks of people's faces taking the first sips of her drinks. *Good that I don't have to make a living at it*, she thought.

She sat on the porch, drinking her brandy old fashioned and watching the sky darken as the sun set. The streetlights clicked on. The rain started to come down harder. A rivulet formed against the far curb until a storm drain interrupted its flow.

I appreciate conscious experience, ace up *my sleeve*, thought Daisy. *Keep interpreting. Keep participating. Keep appreciating. Just keep pounding, you know the way.*

About the Author

August Delp

Thanks for reading my debut novel, *Hotel Bars*. I sincerely hope you enjoyed it. Follow me on Twitter @AugustDelp for information on any additional writing I might do.

I live in the foothills east of Seattle. If you see colored light spilling out of my home office at night, you'll know some writing project is in the works.

CPSIA information can be obtained
at www.ICGtesting.com
Printed in the USA
BVHW072122030222
628054BV00012B/133